Saved by a Handsome Stranger . . .

A strong hand lifted her to her feet, and she looked up and found herself staring into the bluest pair of eyes she had ever seen. They were like the blue of the sky in April, clear and warm, and they quite took her breath away. She was vaguely aware of a fine strong face, a firm yet sensuous mouth, and a week's growth of beard that glinted like old gold in the morning light. But it was those eyes, warm and overpowering, that held her rooted to the spot by their magic. She felt a jolt in the very core of her being, a distinct physical sensation that made her tingle all over. She caught her breath and blushed, wondering if her rescuer had felt the same shock, then forced herself to lower her eyes and turn away. She shook her head impatiently as if to break the spell.

Marielle

Ena Halliday

A TAPESTRY BOOK
PUBLISHED BY POCKET BOOKS NEW YORK

An *Original* publication of TAPESTRY BOOKS

A Tapestry Book published by
POCKET BOOKS, a Simon & Schuster division of
GULF & WESTERN CORPORATION
1230 Avenue of the Americas, New York, N.Y. 10020

ISBN: 0-671-45962-7

First Tapestry Books printing October, 1982

10 9 8 7 6 5 4 3 2 1

PART I

THE DREAM

Chapter One

THE HUGE PRISON DOOR SLAMMED SHUT BEHIND MARIELLE with awful finality. She shivered in the chill morning air and wrapped her woolen cloak more tightly around her slim body. Through the barred opening she saw the look of concern on the jailer's face, and was suddenly filled with fear and doubt. What if her brother Gervais were not here? Dead? Her heart sank at the thought and she shook her head. No! Gervais could not be dead! Not Gervais. Not her sweet and gentle brother, her childhood's companion. He must be here, a prisoner in this terrible place!

"Mademoiselle," said Jacques, the old jailer, "if there be anything you need, remember that I shall be here until the noon meal."

"I pray *le Bon Dieu* that Gervais is here. I have been near to madness since the battle—and my brother missing. May the Holy Mother bless you for your goodness to me," said Marielle with a wan smile.

3

"It was the least I could do to honor your father's memory!" he said fervently. "He was a fine doctor. But for his ministrations . . . my dearest daughter. . . ." He stumbled over the words and his voice trailed off. His good simple peasant face radiated the gratitude his tongue could not express. "Remember, noon. And then I shall not return until nightfall to stand my watch. Trust no one! Since this struggle began, there are too many strangers on guard here—brought by the Huguenot nobles. And who knows how many townspeople are loyal to my lord Bonfleur?"

"You are loyal to Bonfleur and the Huguenots, Jacques. And my family and I are Royalists. Yet you help me!"

He cleared his throat gruffly. "It is a small matter—to smuggle you in and out of prison—that you may find your brother. May *le Bon Dieu* keep you safe!"

With a sigh, Marielle turned back to the cell. Until the latest Huguenot uprising against Louis XIII, early in 1629, it had been one of the stables of La Forêt, a huge stone room with a packed dirt floor. Massive pillars and arches broke up this space into dark nooks and hidden corners that, here and there, still held large piles of straw, so recent had been its conversion. Even as a stable it had been dark and gloomy, with the smallest of windows, for the town and fortress of La Forêt had been built in the ancient times, when raiders with crossbows and catapults would come swarming out of the forests to assault the castle. Now the windows let in even less light, owing to the hastily thrown up ironworks that barred the prisoners' escape. When it had seemed that the small dungeon of the fortress could hold few more prisoners than its usual complement of pickpockets, thieves and whores, the Duc de

Bonfleur, the Lord of La Forêt, had sent for Livot the ironmaker to fortify the stable on the east wall for use as a prison. It was this same Livot the ironmaker who, spying Marielle by the river the next day, had told her the news which had brought her to this dismal place.

"Mademoiselle Saint-Juste!" he whispered hurriedly. "I think I have seen your brother! As I was leaving through the east gate the Duke's soldiers were moving some of the prisoners from the small dungeon. A sorry lot! If that's the best that Richelieu can do, there will be a new king on the throne of France by summer!"

"Alas, Livot!" she said. "If France has a new king by summer, we will have civil war before the leaves turn. But tell me about Gervais!" She held her breath. It had been four days since the battle, when the King's troops had appeared outside the walls, and Gervais had gone out to join them. A grisly battle, an uneven contest. The King's troops had been slaughtered, and the remnants of the army had been dragged to the prison in La Forêt. Marielle shuddered, remembering the corpse-strewn field, as the awful task of burying the dead went on. In vain she had sought Gervais among those tortured bodies, glad not to find him, yet agonized because the doubt and fear continued. After that, she had hardly let herself think of him or wonder at his whereabouts, so strong was her dread.

Livot's heart melted at the look of pain on her lovely face. He passed a work-worn hand across his eyes, suddenly reluctant to tell her his unpromising news.

"I cannot be sure, of course. You must not hope too much . . . but it might have been Gervais. Very bad off he was, with two of the prisoners dragging him along. His head was down . . . I cannot be sure . . . mayhap it was your brother!"

Marielle clenched her fists and closed her eyes tightly, as if she would hold back her pain as well as her tears. It was the first news she had heard, but such dismaying news. And how could she be sure it was Gervais?

"Listen," said Livot. "Doesn't Jacques still guard the Duke's *donjon*? Mayhap he has seen Gervais or can get close enough to the stable to seek for him there. He owes his Berthe's life to your father . . . surely he will not refuse this small measure of help."

Remembering, Marielle turned back to the gloom of the prison. Jacques had tried to help her, but he had not seen Gervais. He had found it almost impossible to search through the stable without arousing the suspicions of the other guards.

"They watch us so carefully, Mademoiselle Marielle," he had said with a shake of his head. "Bonfleur still trusts the men of La Forêt who serve him, but that blackhearted Marquis de Gravillac cannot forget the townspeople who went out to help the King's men. That devil has his men watching everywhere. Forgive me, *ma petite*, I wish I could have done more."

Then it was that Marielle determined to search the prison herself. She knew that Bonfleur, in his haste, had allowed the King's men to be thrown in at random with the rest of the prisoners. There were enough women, streetwalkers and the like, that she might pass unnoticed through the stable.

The sight now before her gave her a chill that had nothing to do with the April morning. She was used to sickness and even death; had she not accompanied her father many times to the hovels of the poorest, the meanest peasants of La Forêt? But those poor serfs had suffered the trials of living, the sicknesses, the accidents, the grief that was part of man's lot on earth. They bore their suffering with dignity and nobility, no matter how lowly their station, trusting in the will of God.

The degradation and despair that now met her eyes had been caused by man's inhumanity; there was nothing ennobling about it. The stench and corruption of the wounded and dying, the gaping sores and mangled limbs, the crowding and the filth had produced an air of utter hopelessness which reduced the inmates to animals. She picked her way carefully through the gloom, her eyes ever searching, searching for a familiar face. A soldier in a torn leather jerkin sat cradling a young man in his arms, rocking and crooning low like a mother with her babe. The young man's face was the color of the gray stone walls, and he breathed heavily with a terrible rasping in his throat that made Marielle bite her lip and turn her face aside in pity. A man with a horrible oozing wound on his thigh sat staring at it as one who is drugged, and as Marielle passed he clutched at her skirts with bloodstained hands. The eyes he turned to her were blank and unseeing, as though pain and suffering had numbed his brain, and he gasped out, "Please. Please. Please. Please," as though the word alone might ease his agony.

She cursed silently to herself. If only she had bandages, medicines. Perhaps, when she had found Gervais, she might beg Bonfleur to let her return to the prison and nurse the wounded. Filled with helpless pity, she turned away from the tormented soldier and nearly collided with a ragged and filthy creature who had been furtively gnawing on a dirty crust of bread. His eyes flew wide in fear and distrust, like an animal at bay. With a snarl, he clutched the bread to his bosom and slunk away to a dark corner, glancing suspiciously behind him as he went.

There were some who moaned and whimpered, and others who, lost in despair, sat numbly as if awaiting something they could not even name. Here and there, in the darker corners, were the streetwomen, brazenly plying their trade for an extra crust of bread, a ring, a coin that Bonfleur's guards had managed to overlook. Marielle shrank away in loathing and averted her gaze. For the first time in her life, she was painfully aware of her vulnerability as a woman. She pulled the hood of her cloak far down over her forehead to shield her face and wrapped its folds around herself to hide the soft curves of her young body. She! Marielle Saint-Juste! She who had walked the streets of La Forêt with her head held high, fearing no man's abuse! Who would dare to insult the daughter of Doctor Saint-Juste? There was hardly a family that did not owe a life to the kindly physician.

The Duc de Bonfleur himself! Had he not returned painfully from that long-ago battle, his arm hanging limp and well-nigh useless? Those other physicians and healers—what did they know? Glorified barbers, that's all they were! They would cut off the arm, or render it scarred and crippled, cauterizing it with hot steel and pitch! But her father, who had studied in Paris with the great surgeon Paré, would have none of it.

"There are ways to heal," he had said, "that do not do more damage than the affliction. This is the seventeenth century! In the name of all that is good, let us relegate the hot irons and hacking knives to the torture chambers of the past where they belong." He had carefully cleaned the wound, eschewing the pastes and foul-smelling salves proffered by the others, and loosely bound the arm in clean linen, freshly washed and dried in the sunlight. Every day he would come to the chateau to change the dressings, sometimes bringing the child Marielle or her brother with him. When at last the limb was healed and restored to its full use, Bonfleur's gratitude was boundless.

"You are a wizard, a magician!" he exulted, slapping Saint-Juste on the back to show the strength of his arm. "You have healed my wound!"

Her father laughed gently. "Ah, no," he said, shaking his head. "Paré used to say 'I treated him, but God cured him.' I think we forget in our pride and arrogance how much God can help us if we do not spurn His natural laws."

After that the two became fast friends. Marielle and Gervais would play happily in the Great Hall of La Forêt while the two men argued and discussed Love and War and Death for hours on end. It was Bonfleur who comforted the good doctor when Madame Saint-Juste, sweet and gentle and always frail, sighed softly, turned her face to the wall and died. It was the Duke who watched Marielle bloom into radiant womanhood, and delighted in seeing her blush scarlet when he threatened to bring half the gay blades of Paris to La Forêt to fall at her feet. And when Gervais wanted to go to Lyon to study law, it was Bonfleur who sponsored him at the university.

Gradually, however, a strain began to develop between the two men, a deep ideological rift that could not be healed. They quarreled violently about the King, the autonomy of the nobles, the future of France. The more Cardinal Richelieu's star rose in the court, the more the petty princes and dukes saw their feudal prerogatives slipping away. The Huguenot nobles feared the erosion of the Edict of Nantes which granted them religious freedom, but many more lords used the religious issue as an excuse to reaffirm the absolutism of their power over their lands, and against the rights of the monarch. Small pockets of resistance began to build up throughout France, as alliances were formed, dissolved and formed anew. Rumor and intrigue hung like a serpent over Paris and Versailles, and the poison touched La Forêt and indeed the whole of the Languedoc region in the south of France. There were whispers of plots hatched by King Philip of Spain, of cabals formed by the followers of the Queen Mother of France, Marie de Medici, who chafed to regain her dominance over her son the King.

The Duc de Bonfleur began to take small trips away from La Forêt, and Doctor Saint-Juste knew he was meeting with the other great lords of the region. In vain he argued against a course of action to which Bonfleur already seemed committed.

Their last meeting was a stormy one. Marielle had been present as they paced the room angrily, each heatedly refuting the arguments of the other. At last, with an air of cold finality, Bonfleur turned to the doctor.

"Do not pursue this further," he said grimly. "You have been my friend, my physician, but you know nothing of politics."

The doctor shook his head impatiently. "I know enough to know that your way leads to chaos. And if you depose Louis? What then? Who would you put in his place? His Spanish wife? Would you bow to the will of Spain and Philip? Or perhaps 'Monsieur,' the King's brother?"

Bonfleur grunted angrily. "That one, at least, would be easier to control."

"Bah! That fat fool!" spat the doctor. "He spends his days plotting against his own brother! He has inherited the Queen Mother's ambition, but it would seem, alas, her stupidity also. I sometimes think he must rail even against Heaven itself for putting him second in line to the throne!"

Bonfleur shrugged. "What matter?" he said. "What concerns us most is that Richelieu should fall. Without him . . . who knows? . . . Even Louis might soften his attitude." He paced the floor angrily, sunk in black thoughts. Suddenly he burst out, "Richelieu! That one! He sees his life as a Holy Mission to break the backs of every prince or duke who would threaten the King's supremacy! Sanctimonious villain! I would see him dead!"

Saint-Juste stepped back in alarm, shaken by the venom in the duke's voice. "Bonfleur," he said gently. "My old friend. You risk much with such treasonous words. Richelieu is powerful . . . remember how he crushed La Rochelle . . . remember the suffering of that terrible siege . . . be guided by my counsel and give up this mad plot."

"La Forêt is not La Rochelle," said Bonfleur through clenched teeth. "We cannot be besieged here. Richelieu will have to fight in the open, and we will have the advantage." He turned to Marielle with a tired sigh. "Marielle," he said, "take your father home and bid him hold his tongue. The Languedoc region, with his willing it or no, will be united in this affair. Gravillac . . . Vautier . . . Barrault . . . all of the nobles. La Forêt is my domain. My serfs will stay with me out of

11

loyalty or need. My mill grinds their grain. My hayfields feed their sheep. Loyalty is kept by a full belly and lost by an empty one." He looked pointedly at Saint-Juste. "Those who cannot willingly join us had best be silent. I beg of you . . . for the sake of the friendship we once shared. . . ." His voice trailed off. Suddenly he whirled on the doctor. "Confound it, man! I cannot protect you from every lord in the district if you will not be silent!"

So Marielle had taken her father home to the comfortable cottage near the marketplace, and she and Gervais had tried to keep him occupied with his work and his books. Gervais would challenge him with some fine point of the law, hoping for a rousing argument as in the old days, but the old man debated his points in a lackluster way, or wandered to the window to stare out at the busy street.

Barrault arrived with his men from Clerbonnet, then de Gravillac from Quiot. The town bustled with activity. Against the east wall, fronting the river Allier, breastworks were hastily thrown up. On the west, where the ancient walls of the old town crowded up against the forest, scores of men were set to work clearing a wide swath of trees and setting up high wooden scaffolding behind the parapet. If the King's men should cross the river to the north, and descend on the fortress through the woods, the musketeers could easily sight them from their vantage point.

Most of the townspeople accepted the changes with resignation, and went about their business as before. The castle was filled to the rafters with soldiers . . . pikemen, archers, musketeers and the like. Every house and cottage within the walls of the town provided billet for the nobles' retinue. The farms which lay beyond the walls were stripped of their winter stores and livestock, until the granaries of the castle were overflowing, and the sheep, escaping from their crowded pens, wandered crying through the narrow streets.

Those peasants who objected to the mobilization, or proclaimed too loudly their allegiance to King Louis, were driven outside the walls to scrape out whatever existence they could in the mean hovels that crowded and huddled against the old stone battlements like beggars in the winter sun.

It was inevitable that Saint-Juste, going about his rounds among the sick, should try to persuade those he met of the folly of their course. And equally inevitable that news of this should reach the lords sitting in the Great Hall. A man of such prestige could exert a dangerous influence on the peasants and shopkeepers, if he were not taught a lesson. And so in due course the soldiers came and turned the Saint-Justes out of their home with scarcely aught but the clothes they wore. While they looked on in horror, the torch was put to their cottage filled with all the things they loved. Marielle's mementos of her dear mother, her father's instruments and medicines and most of all his books, books that had refreshed his mind and spirit time and again. By the flickering flames she watched the life go out of his eyes. They managed to find a hut that kept out a portion of the raw wind, and the townspeople, dismayed at their fate, kept them supplied with enough food and warm clothing, but they could not compensate for the emptiness of their existence. Without his law books, Gervais turned surly and bitter, quarreling with Marielle for the first time in their lives. Saint-Juste seemed to have aged overnight. He was not allowed to practice his art and, without his patients, without his beloved books, he took to wandering the streets like a sleepwalker. Once he tried to see Bonfleur, and Marielle had not the heart to dissuade him. When he returned, his face ashen, eyes filled with pain and humiliation, she dared not question him, but held him tightly in her arms, feeling his frail body trembling. He died soon after. Marielle persuaded Lamarc the goldsmith to go to the castle to beg Bonfleur that the old man be allowed to lie in the churchyard next to his wife.

Now Marielle was in this terrible place, searching for Gervais. If he were dead, would his body ever lie in the churchyard? She steeled herself against the wave of panic that suddenly gripped her. Her eyes swept the room desperately, almost willing him to be there, to still the suspense and dread that threatened to choke her. There! In the far corner! Ah, *Dieu!* Could that be Gervais? She stumbled over a sleeping peasant and threaded her way past a couple locked in an obscene embrace, straining to see more clearly in the thin morning light. With a cry, she fell to her knees before him, laughing and crying with relief and happiness. He turned his pale face toward her. His eyes, dark and hollow in their sockets, burned into hers. She caught her breath as a cold dread seeped through her body. At her father's side, she had seen Death often enough to read it now on the face of Gervais.

Her eyes quickly scanned his body. Where his left leg had been was now a mangled stump, barely recognizable as a human foot. She remembered that, before the battle, one of the farmers had told her the troops were hauling large boulders atop the parapet for those soldiers who might come too close to the wall. Gervais would have been one of the bold ones in the front line, ready to storm La Forêt, to avenge his father's death.

Gervais smiled wanly at her and groped for her hand.

14

She tried to manage a cheerful look as she bent to kiss him, but he shook his head.

"We are not fools, Marielle, you and I. I have been lying in this place of death long enough to have made my peace with God, so do not grieve on my account. It is you I worry about. I should have liked to know there was someone to look after you." He clenched his teeth as a wave of pain swept over him. After a moment, he recovered his breath and laughed softly. "You know, I probably would have made a terrible lawyer!"

The exertion of talking had left him white-faced and shaking. He closed his eyes. Marielle saw great beads of perspiration on his forehead. Lifting the edge of her skirt, she tore a large piece of cloth from her linen petticoat and dabbed gently at his brow. Too late she realized that her action had left her dainty feet and slim ankles uncovered. A heavy hand fell on her shoulders as she struggled to her feet and found herself in the grip of a foul-smelling man who leered at her like an animal with his prey.

"And what have we here?" said he, grinning, as he revealed broken and rotting teeth. "Where have you been hiding, pretty one?" He snatched at the folds of her cloak, trying with anxious fingers to reach her bosom. She wrenched herself away, sobbing with disgust and loathing, and as she did so the hood of her cloak fell back, releasing the luxuriant tresses beneath. The sight of that radiant chestnut glory seemed to fuel his desire, and he lunged toward her, grasping her hair in a cruel grip that drove her to her knees. As he forced her down, she saw Gervais gasping, vainly trying to rise, to help, and she cried out, as much for her brother as for her own pain and fear.

She heard a low, angry growl, and saw her attacker

flying across the width of the stable, where he fell in a heap, winded and defeated. A strong hand lifted her to her feet, and she looked up and found herself staring into the bluest pair of eyes she had ever seen. They were like the blue of the sky in April, clear and warm, and they quite took her breath away. She was vaguely aware of a fine strong face, a firm yet sensuous mouth and a week's growth of beard that glinted like old gold in the morning light. But it was those eyes, warm and overpowering, that held her rooted to the spot by their magic. She felt a jolt in the very core of her being, a distinct physical sensation that made her tingle all over. Gervais, ever the wise older brother, had once spoken of the spark that could pass between a man and a woman . . . some alchemy that not even their father could explain away, with all his knowledge of the human body and soul. She caught her breath and blushed, wondering if her rescuer had felt the same shock, then forced herself to lower her eyes and turn away. She shook her head impatiently as if to break the spell. It seemed suddenly so foolish, so incongruous a thought in this place of misery and death.

But when he spoke, his voice low and vibrant, she knew with certainty that the thrill of their encounter had not escaped his notice, despite his seeming nonchalance.

"Ah, Mademoiselle," he said mockingly, "do you have that effect on every man you meet?" And he laughed softly at her discomfiture.

Chapter Two

ANDRÉ HAD AWAKENED AT DAWN, AS THE FIRST THIN RAYS of April sunlight crept through the iron bars high above him. He had been dreaming of Vilmorin. It was a recurring dream from his childhood, one that he had almost forgotten. Strange that it should suddenly come back to him after so many years, and in this desolate place.

He was in the garden of Vilmorin on a lovely summer's day. He could feel the warmth of the sun, see its rays glancing off the pond. His mother was walking in the garden, in a lavender dress with skirts so wide she seemed almost to be floating, moving through the rosebushes without touching the ground. There seemed to be birds surrounding her, what kind he could never discern, but he knew they were beautiful. He started to walk toward them, but the more he advanced the more they receded, and however much he called out to his mother to wait, he could not seem to lessen the distance between them. Suddenly, one of the birds took flight.

He saw now that he had a small bow and arrow in his hands and, aiming carefully, he let fly the arrow. It traveled very slowly through the sky, following a path that almost seemed visible, and leading directly to the bird. But somehow it was no longer a bird, it was his mother. In vain he would recall the arrow, cry out to her, warn her, but it was too late. As the arrow pierced her breast, he perceived that it was once again only a bird, who did not fall, but turned on him a look of infinite sweetness. He tried to stretch out his arms, to reach her, but he saw that where his arms should be, there was nothing, only flapping empty sleeves.

He awoke, as always, with a sense of ineffable sadness.

From where he lay on the dirt floor, cushioned by a small mound of hay, he could just catch a brief glimpse of blue sky through the high window. It was a sky that seemed to presage spring, and he thought with longing of his chateau on the Loire. In a few weeks the fruit trees would be a riot of blossoms, filling the air with scented drifts of pink and white. In all his years of travel, of wars in the service of his King, he had never felt such a yearning for home and peace. He was tired of war, tired of the waste of good men, resentful of all the Vilmorin springtimes he had missed. He laughed ruefully to himself and wondered if he were growing old. What nonsense! As though a man of thirty-one were ready to sit back in slippers and pantaloons and watch spring drift past his door! Still . . . and he gazed up at the spot of blue and let his thoughts wander once more.

There had been spring in the air three weeks ago, when he and the Chevalier du Trémont led their men out of Paris. At first, he was aware only of gentle, almost indefinable changes—the smell of the earth thawing after the winter, the reddish, almost imperceptible haze that seemed to hang in the trees. But as they moved further south, the rosy haze became a misty green and then the first tentative leaves appeared. André led his men slowly, deliberately; despite the Chevalier's impatience (young fool!), there was no great hurry. The secret dispatches he had received in Paris told him that the King and Richelieu were just concluding their Italian campaign, and would be moving their forces westward toward La Forêt. André had to admire the tactics of Bonfleur and the rest. La Forêt was the largest and best-fortified stronghold in the district; by combining their forces in the one spot, they presented the King with a unified and formidable opponent. But Richelieu was no fool either. He knew that Bonfleur and the others would expect the Royal forces to come from Italy, but they might not count on a separate force from the west. Nor could Bonfleur know that the Royal army intended to strike from the river side, with the cannon they had confiscated in Italy. Thus, with André's forces attacking from the woods, La Forêt would be caught between the jaws of the two armies.

So they rode into spring, André and the Chevalier du Trémont. The Chevalier was the darling of Paris and the salons, having recently married the King's second cousin. At the King's urging, Richelieu had grudgingly included the Chevalier's forces in the plans for the battle, trusting André's cooler head and wisdom to keep the headstrong young man in check. This decision produced unexpected and somewhat disquieting results that Richelieu could not have anticipated. The Chevalier proved to be like a magnet, for every young blade in Paris was anxious to show his mettle by fighting under the banner of the reigning court favorite. As a result, André found himself in the peculiar position of commanding an army the larger portion of which owed its loyalty to his second-in-command.

André had watched them with some uneasiness as the march progressed. They were all so young, so untried, so green in the ways of war. They laughed and joked as though they were off to Versailles for a picnic, and when they spoke of the battle at all, it was to brag about the honors they would win, the glory of returning to Paris as heroes. They chafed with impatience at,the slow pace of the march; they were restless and anxious to attack. As they approached La Forêt, they were met by some four score townsmen, loyalists to the King, ready to fight on his behalf. Armed with little more than pikes, pitchforks and eagerness, and bound only by their hatred of Bonfleur, they had seemed to André to be a rather meager addition to his forces. But to the Chevalier and his friends, already buoyed by their own enthusiasm, the arrival of the townsmen had seemed to be a sign from God that whipped their fervor into a state of almost uncontrollable excitement.

"Damn fools!" muttered André to himself, then started as the clang of the cell door woke him from his reverie. What poor devil had got himself locked up now? Or were the guards just removing another corpse? He looked around at the sick and wounded; they seemed to fill every corner of this foul place. Burdened by guilt and remorse, he pressed his hands tightly against his eyes, blocking out the sight, wishing he could still the sounds of pain and misery.

Damn the Chevalier! "For France and glory!" And before André could give the order, could bid them wait for a sign that Richelieu was near, the Chevalier had led his men to the attack and André, knowing that his force alone would be too small, had been compelled to give the signal to his own troops.

Now he groaned and held his head. He did not like to think of the carnage that followed, nor of all the good and true men he had lost because of the Chevalier's stupidity. He knew only that had he not seen the Chevalier with a musketball in his breast, he himself would have run him through. Even now, five days later (and Richelieu still not in sight!), André was filled with an anger, a rage at the waste of good men that made him feel murderous.

Lost in his fury, he was suddenly aware of the sounds of struggle nearby. Glancing up, he saw a filthy oaf attacking one of the women. A harlot, probably. Still, there was something in the way he clutched at her, twisted her hair, wringing a cry of pain from her lips, that pierced even his black mood, and touched some chord of chivalry deep within him. In two strides he reached them, picked the man up by the shoulders and hurled him against the nearest wall, feeling a satisfaction that drained all the bitterness and anger from his soul.

Stooping, he helped the woman to her feet. Surely he had been mistaken. This was no streetwalker. His gaze took in the proud set of her chin (though her lovely lips still trembled), the honest intelligence of her hazy green eyes, the blush of shame that stained her porcelain cheeks. *Mon Dieu!* What was this exquisite creature doing in a place like this? He felt foolish, flustered at her presence, at a loss for something to say. Well, he'd be damned if he'd let the wench know she had so shaken his composure!

He smiled mockingly, made a frivolous remark and watched the blush color her face again.

André regretted his flippancy almost at once. Marielle, her eyes filled with concern, had already knelt again at her brother's side and was tenderly stroking his forehead.

"Mademoiselle," he said sincerely, kneeling to face her across Gervais' body, "is there anything I can do to help?"

She glanced at her erstwhile attacker and shuddered, then looked up at André and smiled gently.

"It would seem that you already have, Monsieur, and I thank you for that." She looked down at Gervais, who had fallen into a fitful sleep. When she looked again at André, she held her brave smile by the strength of will alone, but her lovely eyes misted with pain and tears.

"And then, if you are a religious man, Monsieur, you might say a prayer for my brother," she said softly.

Looking more carefully at Gervais, André recognized one of the Royalists who had come out from La Forêt to join his forces. Poor devils! How their hearts must have swelled to see him approaching with the banners of the King. They had come to join him in glorious battle; he had led them to slaughter and destruction.

"I'm sorry," he said, and felt the inadequacy of the words. "But surely *le Bon Dieu* will see your brother through this crisis."

"Pray do not mock me," she said impatiently. "You are a soldier, Monsieur? You have eyes? You have a nose? Then do not speak to me as though I were a fool!"

It was true, of course. The sickly stench alone

indicated the extent of the gangrene, and the lad's deathly pallor told the rest of the tale.

"Forgive me," André murmured. "I meant only to spare you. A gentle maiden such as yourself should not have to see these things."

"Ah, my fine soldier," laughed Marielle sadly, "I have probably seen more 'things' in my lifetime than you have in all your years of soldiering. My father was the finest doctor that La Forêt has ever seen. I'll wager that Bonfleur and his men miss his services now—may their wounds rot and fester!" she concluded bitterly.

"Your father is dead?" he questioned.

"They killed him," she replied simply, "if you can kill a man by breaking his heart."

He looked at her with sympathy. He was struck by her honesty, her directness, the innocence of a child who speaks truth because it would not occur to her to dissemble. He thought of the ladies of the court who painted their faces, but covered their hearts and souls with far more than rouge. Useless, tiresome women in artificial settings! It seemed as though spring had come into the gloomy cell with this lovely creature.

"What is your name?" he asked suddenly.

"Marielle Saint-Juste," she answered.

"A fitting name," he laughed. "I have no doubt you are just. As for the sainted part . . . if God will allow a chestnut brown halo . . . well . . ." He gently fingered a shining curl that lay on her shoulder.

She blushed and turned back to Gervais. If only the man did not look at her with those eyes that made her head spin! He watched her now as she tenderly placed Gervais' head on her lap, trying to make him more comfortable, to soothe him back into sleep.

He smiled gently at her bent head. "Well, Mademoiselle Marielle, the doctor's daughter, tell me about your father."

She looked at him gratefully, glad for the distraction. It was easier, somehow, to watch the life draining out of Gervais if a part of her brain could be elsewhere, reliving again the good times at La Forêt. She told him of her father, proud and strong, stubborn and arrogant with fools, gentle and warm with the little people who needed him. She spoke of her mother's sweetness, of her brother's zest for living, of her own happy days at La Forêt. It was so easy to talk to him, and as she spoke she felt the pain and grief of the last few months, that had sat like a block of ice in her heart, melt away under his warm and sympathetic gaze. She had almost forgotten where she was, when Gervais began to tremble violently.

"Ah, *Dieu!* Marielle!" he cried. "It is so cold in here, so cold!" He stretched out his arms to her, shivering. She untied her warm cloak and, with André's help, wrapped it around the shaking body of her brother and held him as tightly as she could, trying to still his quivering.

He smiled up at her. "Ah, Marielle," he murmured, "next time I come for vacation, I will bring my friend Claude to meet you. What say you to that?" His dark eyes, as she stared into them, were like two glassy pools, deep and far-away and lost. She stifled a sob.

"That will be fine, Gervais," she said, trying to control her voice.

"Do you remember the butterfly we caught?" He smiled at her and, with a look of childish wonder on his face, gave up his life.

Marielle looked up at André, her eyes blank and

uncomprehending. She gently laid her brother's head onto the ground, then rose unsteadily, her face working to keep its composure.

"It was a yellow butterfly," she said shakily. "Gervais said we were catching a sunbeam."

Her brave smile collapsed at the same time her knees gave way. But for André's strong arms, she would have fallen.

Chapter Three

FOR A MOMENT, WAKING, MARIELLE COULD NOT REMEM-
ber where she was. She felt strangely drained, empty,
neither happy nor sad, only peaceful. Then the remembrance of the morning flooded back upon her, and she
closed her eyes, wishing she could sleep again and blot
out what had happened.

Reluctantly, she opened her eyes again to find the
handsome stranger peering down upon her, his blue
eyes filled with concern. Strange! He was the only
friend she had in this desolate place, and she did not
even know his name! But for him, she could not have
survived the morning; she would have gone mad with
grief. She had clung to him, sobbing out her pain and
misery, shedding tears she had not let herself shed
before, not even for her father. He had pressed her
tightly in his arms, trying to give her his own strength,
and stroked her hair, murmuring what words of comfort he could. When at last her tears had abated, he had
gently urged her to rest, to sleep. She vaguely remem-

bered him covering her with her cloak as she drifted gratefully into oblivious sleep. The cloak reminded her now of Gervais. Gervais! She sat up suddenly, wildly looking around. Gervais! Where was he?

As if divining her thoughts, the stranger placed a comforting hand upon her shoulder.

"Be at peace, Mademoiselle," he said reassuringly. "The soldiers took his body out for burial. There is a priest who will say the words over him, you may be assured of that."

"But I would bury him myself!" she cried, pushing aside his restraining hand.

"In this prison?" he said. "Think, Mademoiselle. How long might it be until we are released or rescued?"

"Ah!" she cried, and jumped to her feet impatiently. "I am not a prisoner here! Jacques the old jailer let me come in to search for Gervais!" Her eyes flew suddenly to the windows. How long the shadows seemed!

"Ah, *Dieu!*" she cried. "What time is it?"

"'Tis well into the afternoon," he answered, mystified by her behavior.

"Oh!" she cried in dismay. "Are you sure? Then I must wait until nightfall when Jacques returns to release me! Only he knows that I am here." She cast her eyes wildly about, filled with apprehension and dread. "What shall I do?"

"There is nothing to do but wait," he said, trying to ease her fears. He took her gently by the hand and, leading her to a quiet corner, urged her to seat herself. His calm concern stilled her uneasiness, and she sat down. After all, she could endure this place until dark.

"You have eaten nothing all day," he said, producing a small piece of bread. "It is not much," he admitted ruefully, "but my lord Bonfleur's hospitality is not noted for its generosity. Nor is his wine the best vintage," he laughed, indicating the small water trough that served the prisoners' needs. "But what do they know about grapes in the Languedoc?" he said with contempt.

Finding herself surprisingly hungry, Marielle had been busily eating the bread as he spoke, but now, hearing an odd note in his voice, she stopped and looked up quickly. His face was wistful, with a faraway sadness in those blue eyes. Without quite realizing what prompted her words, she spoke.

"And where are your vineyards, Monsieur?" she asked gently.

André looked at her in surprise. Again that direct-ness, that honesty which seemed to cut through his defenses, to see into the depths of his heart, to hear the longing in his voice.

"The Loire valley," he said. "The greenest paradise in all of France."

"And the land is owned by . . . who?" she prompted.

"Forgive me, Mademoiselle Marielle. I have quite forgotten my manners!" He bowed his head to her in courtly fashion. "The land is owned by myself, André, Comte du Crillon, master of Vilmorin, and your obedi-ent servant."

"Ah! I should oblige you with a curtsy, my lord," said Marielle with a wicked gleam in her eyes, "but at the moment this crust of bread seems to have more nobility than you do!"

"As to that, Mademoiselle," said André with a pained expression, as he attempted to smooth his stained and ragged doublet, "I fear I have misplaced my manservant!"

Marielle laughed at that, her voice a silvery bell. André looked at her lovely face, hungrily drinking in her delicate beauty. She grew uncomfortable under his steady gaze, and turned away shyly.

"Tell me about Vilmorin," she said simply.

They sat side by side on the rude earth floor, while André told her of the gentle hills, the verdant valleys, the grapes that hung heavy on the vine, filling the air with their rich, sweet scent. As he spoke, he kept his eyes fixed on the patch of blue that gleamed beyond the window, as though the sight of that bright sky brought him closer to Vilmorin. Marielle was grateful for the chance to watch him unobserved. She noted the tawny gold of his hair that fell almost to his shoulders in the current fashion, the burnished copper of his skin that bespoke the soldier's life he led. When they had stood together, she had seen that he was tall—taller even than her father. Now she noticed the breadth of his shoulders, so strong and wide that they might fairly burst from his doublet. His hands looked powerful, sinewy, long-fingered—the hands of a soldier with the soul of a poet. It was clear from his manner that he was well-bred and educated, yet when he spoke of his vineyards it was with the earthy delight in the land that one might expect from a farmer. Watching him, she smiled, grateful for these few hours they had to share. To touch someone's soul, to weld a bond with another heart, however brief the time . . . these things would feed her spirit, no matter how lonely the years ahead, the grief at her loss.

He had stopped speaking, and was watching her in his turn. He held her for a long moment with his eyes, those blue pools that might drown the unwary.

"Did Gervais ever bring his friend home?" he asked suddenly.

She smiled softly, remembering. "Yes, he brought Claude, and a few of the other law students."

"Students!" he scoffed. "He should have brought kings and princes to pay court to you!"

"That is all very well for you, Monsieur le Comte," she said ruefully. "Perhaps someday when you have daughters you will bring royalty to meet them, but a doctor's daughter comes with a meager dowry, and a lawyer is a good catch."

"The man who would win you would have dowry enough," he said earnestly. "He would be a fool to ask for more."

She turned crimson at his words.

"You are lovely when you blush. No, do not turn away," he said, cupping his hand under her chin and turning her face back to him. "You should not feel ashamed. The women of Paris have forgotten how to blush . . . it is their loss."

"I must seem a country fool, after the women of the court you have known," she said.

"They suffer from the comparison, I assure you, my sweet Marielle," he said, and launched into a description of the more eccentric court ladies and their foibles that had Marielle laughing gaily. He seemed determined to keep their conversation light, trusting in the healing power of laughter to ease her sorrows. Marielle was grateful for his concern, although, for a brief moment, she wondered if he were using humor to hold her at arm's length, to deny the bond she felt.

Only once in the long afternoon did a cloud pass over his face. He had been speaking of Vilmorin, when she suddenly interrupted him.

"Are you alone there? No wife, brothers, sisters? Do your parents yet live?" she asked.

"My sister is married and lives in Strasbourg. My parents are dead." He bit off the words with such finality, his brow darkening, that she dared not question further, but quickly changed the subject.

Evening came quickly. They seemed lost on an island in time, preoccupied with one another, oblivious to their surroundings. The men who recognized André as their commander respected his privacy and left them in peace. When the guards brought in the evening meal, André fetched two portions, bread, a few meager turnips, and they ate in silence, filled with a sense of loss at the coming of the night.

"What will happen to you?" asked Marielle suddenly.

"Richelieu will arrive and we shall be saved," he replied.

"And if he does not?" she persisted.

"Why then, I fear me I shall die of a surfeit of turnips!" he laughed. "And you," he said, suddenly serious. "What will you do when you leave here?"

"*Le Bon Dieu* only knows," she replied wearily. "These last few weeks have been like a nightmare. I have no home, no family, no place to go but a rude hut by the river."

"You have a friend in me, Marielle," he said warmly. "When this is all over I shall seek you out in your hut. Surely I will be able to be of some service to you." He stood up, and helped her to her feet. Suddenly, he put both his hands on her dainty waist and whirled her around until her feet barely touched the floor.

"I shall take you to Paris," he whooped, "and dance you through the Louvre Palace to the delight of the men and the envy of the women!" Abruptly, he stopped turning and put her down, his face darkening. "Come," he said gruffly, "Jacques must be here by now."

"Wait . . . André," she said haltingly. It was the first time she had used his name. "May I . . . kiss my friend good-bye?"

His eyes, clouded now like a stormy sea, were unreadable as they searched her face, but he inclined his head slightly to her kiss. She reached up gently with her hand, lightly touching his bearded cheek, and, standing on tiptoe, she softly pressed her lips to his. *"Adieu, mon ami,"* she whispered, and turned to go.

She felt herself caught, swept into the circle of those strong arms, pressed against his lean, hard body. He bent his head and covered her mouth hungrily with his own, pressing, insistent, until she felt she would surely swoon. No one had ever kissed her like that before, and she pushed him gently away from her, unsteady on her feet and a little frightened at her own reaction. He was smiling down at her, and his eyes were clear and untroubled now, as though the kiss had answered some unasked question.

"Not *adieu,* Marielle," he corrected gently. *"Au revoir, ma chère."*

He took her tenderly by the hand and led her back through the prison to the barred door. Although the guards had lit a few torches high up on the walls, it was darker here away from the windows, and they had to walk carefully to avoid the other prisoners. When they reached the heavy oaken door, André peered through the barred opening to the gloom beyond.

"You there," he called.

A grizzled face appeared out of the darkness. "What do you want?" said the guard. "Things not fancy enough for you in there?"

"Where is Jacques, the old man who was here this morning?"

"What do you want him for?" asked the guard suspiciously. "Come on, speak up! Or should I call the Captain of the Guard?" he added, as André said nothing.

André looked apologetically at Marielle. "He . . . promised to get me another woman, and I grow impatient!" he said with a swagger. "Mayhap the other cell has better pickings!"

"Well, now," said grizzle-face craftily. "Perhaps it can be managed without him!" And he rubbed his hands together greedily.

"Ah, alas, my good man! I have given my last two *sous* to Jacques on account, and unless he appears tonight, I fear I must resign myself to this ugly wench!" Saying this, André quickly tugged at the hood of Marielle's cloak, pulling it well down over her face.

"So be it!" said the guard. "For Jacques will not be here tonight."

Marielle uttered a cry of dismay which André quickly smothered, pulling her toward him and clapping his hand over her mouth.

"And wherefore not?" he said with a nonchalance he did not feel.

"They have set him to watch the small dungeon tonight. The regular guard took sick."

"And when does he return here?" asked André, trying not to see the terror in Marielle's eyes.

"Tomorrow at noon," came the reply. "But if you're

looking for someone to relieve you of the wench for tonight . . ." He peered in through the bars, interested suddenly in the cloaked figure André held.

"You wouldn't like her. She bites," said André, moving away as quickly as he could, and leading Marielle back to their sheltered spot at the far corner of the cell.

She turned to him, her eyes wide with fear.

"André!" she cried, and her voice was shaking. "I am afraid! What if Jacques does not come back? Shall I be trapped here? Ah, it's too much, too much!" she sobbed, sinking to her knees.

He knelt beside her and took her roughly by the shoulders.

"Listen to me, Marielle Saint-Juste!" he said firmly. "It took courage for you to come to this prison! I cannot believe you have suddenly lost your courage because of a few hours' delay! Jacques will return, and if not? What harm? We shall spend a few days together and be rescued when the King's army arrives."

Reassured by his words, Marielle gulped and smiled up at him. He gently wiped away her tears and kissed her tenderly on the cheek.

"And will we dine together on turnips, Monsieur le Comte?" she asked, her good spirits returning.

"Elegantly, Mademoiselle!" he replied with a laugh. "Come, sleep," he encouraged, suddenly serious. "The day has been so long and terrible for you. There is healing in sleep." He sat down with his back against a stone pillar, and put his arms around her, drawing her to him. She leaned her head against his chest and felt herself encircled by his comforting arms. She could hear the muffled beat of his heart with its soothing rhythm, feel the warmth of his body next to hers. And so, with a small sigh of contentment, she closed her eyes and slept.

She awoke with the moon shining in her face. She was still in André's arms, but had shifted her body as she slept, and now lay cradled in his arms, her face looking up into his. His face was in shadow, and she could not at first tell if he were asleep, and so she lay very still, hearing the soft sound of his breathing. Around her were the small noises of the other prisoners —a soft moan, one who cried aloud in his sleep, restless stirrings here and there. The moon was very bright, and it silvered the sleeping bodies it touched, but otherwise the cell was in darkness, the torches having burnt out hours since.

Suddenly, he spoke, his voice low and thrilling, and she felt her heart leap.

"I have been watching you sleep," he said, his voice husky with tenderness, "and wondering how a man can lose his heart so quickly."

She caught her breath, feeling giddy with happiness. She had known almost from the first moment that she loved him, though she had tried to deny it to herself. Once Gervais had tried to describe it, what it was like to be in love, and had contented himself finally by saying that she would simply know it when it happened. He had been right; she loved, and it was foolish to deny it. And now this man, this man that she hardly knew and yet had somehow known all her life, was giving her his heart in return! She felt as though her own heart would burst with the joy and wonder of it.

"And did my face give you answers?" she asked softly.

"Your face gave me pleasure," he said. "Why should I need answers?"

He bent low and gently kissed her eyelids, her delicate chin, her earlobes. His soft lips tenderly explored every inch of her face, sending waves of feeling rippling through her body. She felt herself tremble with sensations that were new to her, thrilling, yet frightening too, because they filled her with emotions she could hardly control. Fiercely she threw her arms around his neck and pulled his mouth down to hers, abandoning herself to his kisses. With an effort he reached up, pulled her arms away from his neck and held her at a distance.

"*Nom de Dieu,* my girl," he said hoarsely. "Do you know what you do to a man? Do they not teach you country girls not to throw yourself at a man?"

She drew back, hurt. "Don't you want to kiss me?" she asked softly. She moved out of his arms and turned away.

He laughed unsteadily. "As to that," he said, "I think I can cope with kissing you; it's when you decide to kiss me back that I begin to feel uneasy!" And he laughed again.

She looked at him, a puzzled frown upon her face.

"*Ma chère!*" he cried, sweeping her suddenly back into his arms. "You don't know what I'm talking about, do you? Love is so innocent for you. I kiss you, you kiss me back. It is as simple as that to you, *n'est-ce pas?* It would not occur to you to be coy or difficult. *Mon Dieu!* I did not think women like you existed anymore."

"Are you sorry?" she asked softly.

"Sorry? Ha! When we get out of here, *ma chère,* I will stand with you on the highest hill above La Forêt and shout till they hear me in Toulouse that I love the most adorable woman in the world. What do you think of that?"

"I think," she said timidly, "that I should very much like you to kiss me now, if you could manage it."

He kissed her then, gently, tenderly, a kiss of such sweetness that she thought her heart must surely burst with the love she felt for him.

Then, like a father putting his beloved child to bed, he smoothed the straw on the floor and put her gently down, draping her with her cloak and tucking it around her chin. He knelt and kissed her softly on the forehead, then lay down beside her, covering her protectively with his arm. She nestled close to him, feeling safe, shielded from the world outside.

"Good night, my love," he murmured softly.

When she woke again, the moon had set, and the large cell was very dark and still. André had turned away as he slept, and now lay with his back toward her. Dear André! She thought of his kisses in the moonlight, reliving every tender word and gesture, pondering the things he had said.

It had been so bewildering, knowing there was something she had been expected to understand, and being treated like a child because she didn't. *Mon Dieu!* She almost said the words aloud as a sudden thought struck her. Could that have been what he meant? She felt her face flush with embarrassment. No wonder he had laughed and called her innocent! In her sheltered world, there was love and there was the desire of the flesh, and until this moment it had not occurred to her that one had anything to do with the other. Love was a pure and noble emotion that filled the heart with rapture; it was courtly and kind. She had read about it often enough, and watched her parents' gentleness toward one another. Sleeping with a man—that was for marriage, for babies, even for the traffic of the streets, but not for a maiden—and surely not for pleasure! The fact that André loved her she found quite natural and acceptable. But that her kisses could excite his desire, that he could want her body in a lustful way—she scarcely could believe that was part of the same love. What a naive innocent she was indeed! How little she knew or understood of men! The young students who had come to call, who had courted her and kissed her, had treated her with awe and respect. She knew from Gervais that they sometimes visited certain sections of town—and certain women—but it was not her concern. They were responding to uncontrollable urges, to something base in their natures—it was natural and understandable, if unseemly, but it had nothing to do with her relationships with the young men. As for herself, although she had found their kisses pleasant enough, they certainly had not excited her. Now, remembering how she had thrilled to André's kisses, she suddenly wondered if a woman were capable of feeling the same desires as a man. She had never had such thoughts before—she found them strange and disquieting, yet oddly exciting. She sighed deeply. How much she had to learn!

There was a movement beside her. André had turned and was leaning on one elbow, looking down at her. In the gloom she could just make out the outline of his face.

"Are you awake, Marielle?" he whispered.

"Yes," she murmured, reaching up her hand to stroke his cheek. "Did I wake you?"

"No," he said hoarsely, and there was a ragged edge in his voice. "I have been lying here thinking." He laughed harshly. "The dark of night is not a good time to think—there are too many goblins in the shadows!"

"André! My love!" she said, alarmed. "What is it?"

For answer, he held her tightly in his arms, and when he spoke, there was despair in his voice.

"Too many days! Too many days have passed! Richelieu will not come, something has happened, we are abandoned here!"

"Ah, no, André, it is not so," she soothed. "The King's army will come. As you said, it is just the goblins of the night."

Now it was she who was the strong parent, comforting and reassuring. She pulled his head down to her bosom, stroking his forehead, murmuring soft words to still his fears. In a while, he raised his head to her face and kissed her gently on the lips. Her mantle had fallen back, and now he kissed the softness of her neck, his lips moving lightly over her naked skin like the wings of a butterfly. She felt the warmth of his breath as his lips traveled from her neck down to her bodice, and thence upward again to find her mouth. This time he kissed her fiercely, hungrily, his mouth forcing her lips apart. She felt her senses reeling, her heart pounding as if it would leap from her breast.

"Marielle!" he breathed, pressing her back against the straw, his hand moving insistently along the length of her body.

"Ah, no!" she cried, pushing him away and scrambling to her feet. He jumped up and turned her roughly to him, one hand going around her waist, the other behind her head, tangled in her curls. He bent her back across his arm and kissed her passionately, his mouth now hot and determined. Her head was spinning, her breath coming fast and hard. Despite her will, she felt herself softening, melting in his ardent embrace. She could feel his desire, the hardness of him pressing against her body, and she trembled all over.

"Marielle," he pleaded hoarsely. "What if the sun should never rise? And we are trapped here—frozen in this moment of time? I would know your sweetness, the beauty of your surrender. I ache to love you beyond mere kisses!"

His hand caressed her body, sending exquisite shivers through her whole being, as he tried to urge her down onto the straw.

"Come, my love," he whispered, "it is dark. Come. Only we two exist in this corner of time."

With supreme effort of will, panting with her own suppressed desire, Marielle pushed him away.

"André!" she sobbed piteously, shrinking back from him. *"Nom de Dieu!* I cannot! I am not one of your Parisian ladies who can give herself to a man and not fear the wrath of God. As Damnation awaits the sinner, I have sworn to God to keep my purity for the man who is my husband. I beg you, do not ask me to go against my vows! Help me to be strong, André," she finished miserably.

She peered at him through the gloom, sensing in his silence the despair and turmoil he must feel. She knew that he wrestled with his conscience against his baser nature, cooling his desire with the greatest effort of will. After a long moment, he turned away, his shoulders sagging in resignation and disappointment. She lifted her hand and tenderly touched his arm.

"Ah, André," she whispered softly. "The sun will rise, the dawn will come and with it will come the forces of the King. You'll see," she said with simple faith. "I know God could not be so cruel as to give us this wondrous love and then snatch it away."

He turned then, and smiled tenderly at the beauty and innocence of her faith. It set her apart from all the women he had known, this sweet crystal purity that shone in her eyes, shaped her every word and action, permeated her very being. He knew, with a certainty that suddenly lifted the weight from his shoulders, that he could never be the one to shatter that crystalline sweetness, no matter his desire. He felt suddenly lighthearted, like a stripling lad smitten by a country shepherdess. He laughed softly, swooped an imaginary hat from his head and bowed low.

"Mademoiselle, when we are released from these unsavory surroundings, I trust you will allow me to call upon you and press my suit."

Marielle smiled and curtsied prettily to him.

"To what purpose, Monsieur? May a humble country maid inquire as to your intentions and plans?"

"Certainly!" he said decisively. "I shall marry you, spirit you away to my chateau and make love to you in every room of Vilmorin!"

She giggled. "In front of the servants?"

He nodded confidently. "It will be better recompense than the *sous* and *livres* I usually pay them!"

She threw her arms about his neck, laughing, glad to forget the terrible moments that had passed. He held her tightly and shared her joy.

Suddenly her laughter caught in her throat and became a sob.

"Oh, André," she whispered against his ear, and clung more tightly to his neck. "If this is all we have . . . if something should happen . . . will you forgive me? Will you know that I am yours alone, before God, for all eternity?"

"Hush, hush," he comforted, stroking her hair gently. "Whatever the day brings, whatever our future is to be, know that I love you beyond measure. As for the rest, I can wait."

Chapter Four

RENARD, MARQUIS DE GRAVILLAC, PACED THE GREAT
Hall of La Forêt. His spurs clanged on the stone floor
with every impatient step he took. The early morning
sun glinted on the hard steel of the breastplate around
his neck and on the fine sword that hung from the
buckled harness at his waist. One hand, still gloved,
clenched his other leather gauntlet, which he slapped
irritably in the palm of his bare hand as he paced. Tall
and lean, he moved with the grace of a tiger, each step
charged with pent-up power, ready to strike at any
moment. More than one woman had found him
attractive—dark hair graying at the temples, small
pointed beard and trim mustache—but the black eyes
that peered out from beneath his heavy lids could
glitter cruelly when he was crossed. They flashed now
as he turned to Barrault, who sat lolling in a large
velvet armchair, seeming indifferent to the other man's
agitated state.

"I tell you, Barrault," said Gravillac with a frown, "I care not what the others say. There is no cause for rejoicing at this early date. Richelieu is not a fool! Why would he have sent such a small force against us? There is no sense to it. Surely he knows our strength! If he meant to defeat us he would have sent a larger army. If he wanted to negotiate, why send a force at all? I do not care for it one whit! And there is our ally Vautier already drawing up terms of agreement, conditions for peace. A fat pension for himself, the governorship of a province. . . . Bah! With whom will he negotiate? A King who does not come?"

"Why disquiet yourself, *mon ami?*" responded Barrault. "There is time for whatever will be. You rode this morning through the hills. What did you see?"

"I saw nothing, neither to west nor east, from where I was. But the river bends away to the north, before Digne, where the best crossing would be. If the King should decide to ford the river at that point, we could not see it from here. Devil take Bonfleur! Why will he not send out a small patrol to Digne? I think the man is losing his reason."

Barrault rose easily from his chair and poured himself a glass of wine from a carved and gilded pitcher.

"I begin to wonder the same," he said thoughtfully. "Ever since the battle, when the musketeers fired on his own townspeople, he has been distant and distracted. Vautier had to see to the burials . . . Bonfleur found things to do that kept him far from the west wall!"

"It was a stupid attack," said de Gravillac contemptuously. "I could not believe my eyes when I saw André du Crillon's banners above the smoke."

"Perhaps the man's reputation as a great general was

unmerited. I'll warrant the best campaigns he has waged have been in the bedchambers of Fontainebleau! Or so my dear sister would lead me to believe!"

"Nay," said de Gravillac, shaking his head. "He was at Pluvinel's Academy for a time while I was there. I remember his horsemanship did not match mine, but his tactics were brilliant." He fell silent, stroking his beard thoughtfully. "However," he mused, "I saw the banners that day of the Chevalier du Trémont. I wonder. . . ."

"That prancing peacock!" scoffed Barrault. "The last time I was at Court, I had to listen to the King go on at length about his skills and attributes, although the only skill I imagine he would need was the one he brought to his marriage bed with a princess of the blood!"

"That's just it!" exclaimed Gravillac. "Why would the King abandon the husband of his cousin? His forces must be on the way to La Forêt!"

"Perhaps the Italian campaign went badly," suggested Barrault, "and the King has been delayed. We have had no word from our spies in the Piedmont. Who knows? Maybe Louis has decided to return to Paris!"

"Nevertheless," said Gravillac with certainty, "there must have been a plan."

"Then ask the man himself," said Barrault with a shrug. "From what I have been led to believe, du Crillon was taken prisoner and resides at the moment in Bonfleur's malodorous stable!"

De Gravillac's eyes glittered with malice. Motioning to a guard by the door, he whispered his instructions. The guard nodded, and vanished into the corridor, where they could hear him passing on his orders. In a moment, a sweaty laborer in a leather apron appeared, carrying a small brazier on a tripod. Crossing to the large stone fireplace, he scooped up a small spadeful of hot coals, which he placed in the brazier and proceeded to fan with a small bellows. Reaching into his apron, he pulled out a long steel bar with a wooden handle, which he set into the center of the glowing coals.

"Very soon," said de Gravillac with determination, "we shall have all the answers we need!"

Marielle and André were standing quietly at the far wall in the corner of the prison when the huge oak door banged open. They had been uneasily silent all morning. For her part, Marielle found it hard to look at André, reluctant to see into his eyes, fearful of reading reproach written there. She knew that no power on earth could have made her behave any differently last night, but in the light of day she was assailed by doubts that shook her faith. Ah *Dieu!* Was it more sinful to deny love to someone who loved you with a pure and holy love? All her life, she had toiled by her father's side, succoring the sick, comforting the needy, feeling God's approval for the work they did. Was not André's need as great? Were his wounds not wounds of the soul that needed the healing balm she alone could give? Filled with remorse, she averted her gaze from his eyes.

As for André, his thoughts had been on the women he had known. There had been one or two who stirred his heart as well as the juices in his body, but they had been brief passions that seared his soul yet left him feeling strangely untouched, with no regrets and no memories. Far too many had been other men's wives, and he wondered whether he had found them attractive because there had been no real danger in such liaisons. Well, perhaps a small danger! But he had managed to survive the few unavoidable duels with the obligatory drawing of blood (his own or his adversary's), and the scars that they left were only skin-deep. He had not really believed in his heart that a woman could be faithful—to one man, to her own virtue, to her beliefs. It mattered little. It left him free to live his life, to seek his pleasures where he might, to come and go as he chose. And now this chestnut-haired siren beside him had turned his world upside down. He thought again of the night. *Mon Dieu,* but he had wanted her! He could have taken her, with or without her consent! More likely with it. He had seduced enough women to know how to soften their resistance. But he had been afraid. Yes, afraid! Frightened of this lovely, vulnerable creature who opened her soul to him, who gave him her heart, without guile, without pretense, and begged him to protect it. He had said he wanted to marry her. A mad, moon-struck thought. Still . . .

"André, Comte du Crillon!" He looked up suddenly at the sound of his name. The Captain of the Guard stood before them. "You are to come with me!"

"No!!" shrieked Marielle, clutching his arm tightly. "You cannot!"

He wrenched her hand free, swung her around, and shook her by the shoulders roughly, urgently.

"Listen to me, Marielle!" he said hoarsely, riveting her with his eyes. "Guard yourself well in this place. Do not wait for me! Go when Jacques arrives! Do you understand?"

She nodded dumbly. He took both her hands in his and pressed them fervently to his lips.

"Go with God, my love," he murmured. He turned and strode away with the guards. She raised her hands

47

up to her lips, as if to taste the kiss he had put there, and sank to the floor, wrapping her mantle tightly around her, trying to hold back her tears.

Renard de Gravillac looked up from the map he had been studying as André was ushered into the Great Hall.

"Ah! Monsieur le Comte!" he said, bowing with elaborate ceremony. "How good of you to come!"

André's eyes were wary as they swept the room, but he nodded gravely to Barrault and Gravillac, and returned their courtesy with the same mocking sincerity.

"Gentlemen," he said, "such distinguished company! I fear me I have neglected to dress." He fingered the tattered edge of his shirt. *"Dommage!* My best lace cuffs, sitting at home at Vilmorin!" He shrugged his shoulders helplessly.

"But then I have heard, my dear Crillon," said Renard with a smile, "that the laces of Italy are as fine as any from France. Perhaps you should arrange to have some delivered whilst you are here." And his dark eyes flickered dangerously.

"An excellent suggestion, Renard. But alas, there is no one in Italy to whom I can send at the moment." André plucked daintily at a thread on his sleeve. "Besides, who goes to Italy in this damp season? It simply isn't fashionable, my dear fellow."

Gravillac whirled on André with barely controlled fury, his eyes flashing. "The King goes to Italy!" he said through clenched teeth.

"Ah, then," said André. His voice was low and seeming at ease, but a cold, hard light shone in his icy eyes. "Shall I have the King fetch you a pair of Italian cuffs as well? But then I've heard that you prefer to buy and sell among your Spanish friends!"

"Enough!!" roared de Gravillac. "I would know when Richelieu and the King arrive, and by what route!"

"What makes you think they come at all?" laughed André.

"Come, come, man," said Barrault nervously. "Do not make things more difficult than they must be! My friend Renard is a gentle man but"—and here he eyed the brazier apprehensively—"he does not like to be thwarted."

"Your friend Renard is as gentle as a rattlesnake!" retorted André. "Tell me, de Gravillac, do you still whip your horses and thrash your grooms? You were ever the talk of the Academy!"

Furious, de Gravillac signaled to the guards, who seized André roughly by his arms and dragged him into a chair, tying his hands behind him with a long cord. His linen shirt had fallen open as they did so, uncovering a portion of his chest. It was to that patch of vulnerable flesh that the man in the leather apron now directed his iron bar, glowing red from the hot coals.

"The King's plans!" insisted Renard. "I would know them!"

André said nothing, but laughed contemptuously. His eyes, cold and filled with hatred, stared unwaveringly at Gravillac. Even when the signal was given and the stench of burning flesh filled the room, his eyes did not flicker, but beads of perspiration broke out on his upper lip. An ugly welt glowed red and charred upon his breastbone.

He turned slightly to Barrault, his voice still strong and steady.

"It would seem our friend Renard has not learned manners since our school days," he said mockingly. "Did you know, Barrault, that they would have thrown him out but for his father's intervention?"

Something seemed to explode behind de Gravillac's eyes. His face contorted with rage, suffused with purple, and he clenched his fists. With a sound that was like the howl of a feral beast he seized the handle of the hot poker and pressed it hard against André's chest. This time they could hear the flesh sizzle under the brutal assault. André turned his head away and gritted his teeth, his face ashen, trying desperately not to cry out. Barrault, shocked at Renard's almost uncontrollable frenzy, snatched his arm away with a sudden wrench that sent the hot iron clattering across the stone floor.

"The plans!" said Gravillac in a strangled voice.

"Go to the Devil!" said André hoarsely, and fainted.

"If you kill the man," burst out Barrault, "we shall have no answers!"

Gravillac took a deep breath, making a conscious effort to recover his self-control. He poured himself a large goblet of wine, and drank it slowly and steadily as if to ease his nerves. He did not like to be beaten, and it seemed as though he and du Crillon were engaged in a deadly struggle of wills in which André's cool steadiness would prove the victor. If he killed the man, still he would not break, and suddenly Gravillac knew he wanted to put fear in those icy blue eyes almost more than he wanted the King's plans. There must be another way!

One of the guards whispered to Gravillac. He laughed softly, an ugly, gutteral sound, and nodded at the guard, who left the room.

Gravillac glanced at André, who was shaking his head, trying to clear the mists from his eyes.

"Barrault, we have been ungracious hosts," said Renard softly, and evil glittered behind his hooded eyes. He turned to the soldiers guarding André. "Untie our guest. Give him a cup of wine. The poor fellow looks haggard. But see that he does not get up from his chair!"

André drained the wine cup gratefully, feeling the strength return to his body. He looked uneasily at de Gravillac. Damn the fellow! What was he up to now? Watching Renard sauntering around the room, chatting casually with Barrault, that unfathomable smile upon his face, André wondered if perhaps he did not prefer the raging Gravillac, even with a hot poker in his hands. It might be painful, but he knew at least what to expect of his enemy, and could gauge his own strengths and weaknesses accordingly. He did not like this wondering and waiting.

There was a noise outside the Great Hall. The door burst open and a guard dragged in a struggling Marielle. At sight of her, André started from his chair, his wine cup crashing to the floor, then sank back quickly, feigning unconcern. The movement had not been lost on de Gravillac, however, and his eyes, like the tongue of a snake, flicked hungrily back and forth from André to the girl.

She stood tall and proud, shaking off the guard's restraining hand, but her eyes cast nervously around the room as though looking for a familiar face, and came to rest with a worried frown upon André.

"Mademoiselle," said de Gravillac pleasantly, "welcome!" A slow smile spread itself across his handsome features. "You do us honor!"

Marielle viewed him warily. His words were innocent, his manner almost charming, and André seemed at his ease, but she had heard enough about this Marquis de Gravillac in the last weeks to be on her guard.

"Come, Mademoiselle, let me take your cloak." With deft fingers he untied her mantle and swept it from her shoulders, dropping it gently to the floor. He stepped back, his eyes raking her trim form. She was wearing a snugly fitted jacket that revealed the rounded swell of her breasts, and his eyes rested appreciatively on her young curves. She stirred uneasily under his gaze; there was something so nakedly hungry in his look it gave her a chill, yet she could not name what she saw in those hooded eyes—anger? cruelty? lust? She was glad she had tied the drawstring high on her linen chemise so it peeped out modestly above the neckline of her jacket; nevertheless, she felt almost soiled by his regard.

"Lovely," he said softly. "I admire your taste, my dear Comte du Crillon." He lifted a heavy chestnut curl and played with it idly for a moment before resting it on her bosom, where it seemed his hand lingered for just the fraction of a second.

Marielle bit her lip. Her heart was pounding in trepidation, and she looked helplessly to André. He still seemed to loll idly in his chair, but the muscles of his jaw had begun to work, forming a hard line on the handsome contours of his face.

"It is so warm in here, Mademoiselle, after that damp cell. Permit me!" With slow and deliberate fingers, Gravillac began to unfasten the hooks on the front of Marielle's jacket. She took a step backward, trying to pull away, to avoid those intruding hands, but he pressed toward her again and she felt trapped. When he had undone the last fastening, he began gradually to pull off the jacket, both sleeves at the same time. To do so, he put his arms around her, pinioning her arms behind her back, and holding her very close to his body. She closed her eyes and turned her head away, trying to shrink back from his odious contact. She knew she trembled in fear and loathing, and she cursed the weakness of her woman's body. Loosing the sleeves, he let the jacket fall to the floor, and stepped back, a malevolent smile playing on his lips.

"Better and better!" His glittering eyes traveled hungrily over her body. The soft linen of her chemise clung to each curve, revealing every contour of her heaving breasts. The room was very still, save for the logs crackling in the grate. A guard coughed nervously. Barrault passed his tongue across his dry lips. Marielle looked desperately to André who sat now far forward, his hands gripping the arms of his chair so tightly that the knuckles gleamed white. Gravillac chuckled softly, maliciously, enjoying the moment, his sense of superiority. Almost without looking at her, his left hand suddenly shot out to Marielle, and with one swift movement he grasped the neckline of her chemise and wrenched it away from her body, tearing the drawstring. The soft folds of fabric fell about her waist, and for one terrible moment she stood frozen, her naked breasts exposed to his lustful eyes. Then with a small cry she wrapped her arms tightly in front of her, trying to shield her body while waves of shame stained her creamy flesh.

There was a terrible choking sound. Panic-stricken,

she looked to André. At this last indignity he had bolted from his chair, his eyes murderous, only to be stopped by a pike, held from behind, pressing against his windpipe. The guard increased the pressure on the pike, forcing André back down into his chair, winded and gasping.

"Damn you, Gravillac!" he spat out. "She can tell you nothing!"

"Perhaps not, my friend. But you can, I think!"

Gravillac snapped his fingers and two of the guards seized Marielle, snatching her arms from off her breasts and holding them away from her body. She writhed and twisted, trying to escape their grip, to break free, then cringed in horror as Gravillac turned and slowly removed a red-hot poker from the coals where it had lain.

"It seems a pity to mar such perfection," he said regretfully.

"Enough," said André, and his voice was tired, resigned. "There is no need for her to suffer. The King and Richelieu will attack at night."

"Where?"

"From the woods."

"They will cross the river?"

"Yes. Above Digne."

At this, Gravillac looked triumphantly at Barrault. Their strength?" he asked.

"I do not know."

"When?"

"I do not know."

Gravillac brandished the poker menacingly. "I like not your answers!" he burst out. "Will the wench's screams jog your memory?"

"Confound it, man! My orders were to meet the

King's forces on the west. The time of his arrival, the strength of his forces—that all depended on what he could muster in Italy!"

"But you attacked, you did not wait!"

"The Chevalier was impetuous. I could not prevent him giving the order to his men," said André in disgust. Even now the thought of it made him sick, lending credence to his words.

Satisfied, de Gravillac turned, placed the poker back into the fire, and waved away the guards who held Marielle.

"You are fortunate, Mademoiselle, to have a lover who prizes you so highly!"

"Villain! Pig!" she hissed, and clutching her cloak to her bosom she ran to throw herself at André's feet. He lifted her by the elbows and tenderly wrapped the mantle around her soft shoulders, murmuring soothing words. Gravillac had turned away and was once again leaning over his maps, talking heatedly with Barrault. Although the guards watched the doors and there was no escape, within the Hall itself no one seemed concerned with them any longer. André led Marielle to a small bench against the wall where she might recover herself. She leaned against him, feeling still the shame and humiliation, and he winced as her head touched his raw wounds. She gasped, noticing them for the first time. Her eyes widened with pity and guilt, comprehending what his silence had cost him.

"You would have said nothing," she said, weeping. "But for me, you would not have spoken. Ah, that I had not been here to break your resolve!"

"Softly, my love," he whispered, placing a gentle finger on her lips. "God willing, they will not guess I lied until after the attack comes." Relief flooded her face, and she pressed his hand to her mouth, covering it with her kisses.

"Marielle Saint-Juste! Can it be you? Barrault, what is this girl doing here?"

Marielle looked up in surprise. The Duc de Bonfleur had come into the room, and was eyeing her now with alarm and astonishment. She had not seen him for some months now, and was shocked to see how he had changed. He had been a hearty man, strong and robust; now the ruddy face was lined and worn, with a haunted look about the eyes. She would have pitied him, but she remembered her father, and despised him instead.

"They are prisoners, Bonfleur, that is all," said Barrault impatiently.

"Nonsense! That is Marielle Saint-Juste! Her father is the doctor! She cannot be a prisoner here. It is absurd. Is it not so, Marielle?"

She looked at him with contempt. "My father is dead. My brother is dead. I do not choose to recognize you!"

His eyes filled with remorse. "Can I do nothing to help, to make amends?"

"When you might have helped my father, you did not. I cannot forgive you for that," she said with finality.

"These are my prisoners, Bonfleur," said Gravillac dangerously. "I warn you not to interfere."

Bonfleur's shoulders drooped. He turned to go, seeming to age and shrink with every step. André had been eyeing him reflectively, deep in thought. Now he stirred himself.

"Wait! There is a small service you might perform. Bring the priest here, if you will. I should like him to marry us. I trust, Monsieur le Marquis," he said, turning to Gravillac with a mocking smile, "you can find enough compassion in your heart to allow it!"

"Do you expect to live long enough to enjoy your happy state?" asked Renard coldly. "Very well. It matters little to me." He turned impatiently back to his maps and charts.

Marielle smiled up at André. Her beautiful face radiated love, wonderment, joy. If he had had doubts before, they were washed away in the glow of her eyes, the tears of happiness that sparkled on her cheeks. He laughed softly, remembering her misgivings of the night before.

"If I am to have you, my lovely virgin, if only in God's heaven, I think you would come to me more willingly with a ring on your finger!"

He removed a golden circlet, old and worn, from his little finger. Long years of wear had flattened the crest and polished the edges to a luster; Marielle had difficulty discerning the figures engraved thereon, a lion and a hound standing erect, supporting between them a bunch of grapes.

"My father's," he said simply. "The hound is for fidelity." He slipped the ring onto her left hand; she fingered it gently with her right, turning it, admiring it, noting how it fit exactly, as though it had always been meant for her hand.

"I have nothing to give you," she said wistfully. He laughed at that, filled with wonder and awe. Nothing, he thought, but unspoiled love, a pure heart. Nothing! *Mon Dieu!* He felt suddenly, achingly, as though he had been searching for her all his life.

The ceremony was brief, hurried. Bonfleur watched the marriage of his old friend's daughter with a face that spoke of regret, and grief and a weariness with life. At the end, when he turned to lead the priest away, André stopped him, shook his hand, thanked him. He looked pleadingly at Marielle, who touched his arm briefly then turned away. Even in this moment of joy, forgiveness came hard.

The hall was a flurry of activity. Vautier arrived, and Molbert, Gravillac's lieutenant. Bonfleur, who had been the nobles' leader, now seemed incapable of making a decision; by tacit consent, Gravillac took charge. It was arranged for a patrol to ride north to Digne and bring word of the King's arrival. Barrault was dispatched to see to the defenses of the west wall, and deploy the musketeers more efficiently. Vautier, concerned with a sky that now seemed to threaten rain, had gone to gather the scattered gunpowder stores and house them in a small shed that lay up against the southwest corner of the stable. Bonfleur was shunted to the river bank.

"What about those two?" asked Molbert, indicating André and Marielle, who, ignored until now, had been blissfully lost in each other's eyes. Gravillac shrugged the question impatiently aside, then stopped and turned. He thought again of André's unflinching gaze— the lack of fear in those clear blue eyes—and hated the man anew.

"Take him to the stable for now," he said, pointing to André. "When the signal comes from Digne, hang him, and string up his body from the west parapet. I want the King to be greeted by his noble general!"

Marielle gasped in horror and clung to André.

"What about the woman?"

Gravillac smiled cruelly. "Put her in the small prison with the other whores!" André's face fell. He held

Marielle tightly for a moment, drinking in her beauty, as if he would memorize her lovely face forever.

"Before God, André, I swear it!" she whispered. He smiled sadly, longingly.

"I shall wait, *ma chère!*"

The guards led him out; the door closed on her love, her husband. Marielle turned, sobbing, to de Gravillac. "Let me be with him!" she begged.

"Take her away." he said, impatient, annoyed.

They seized her, struggling. For a moment, her cloak flew open, revealing her naked breasts. Something flickered behind Gravillac's eyes.

"Wait!" he said. "On second thought, a bride should have a wedding night. Put her in my quarters!"

They dragged her shrieking, horrified, up a narrow stone staircase and threw her roughly into a small bedchamber, slamming and locking the door behind her. She felt she would surely go mad. It had all been too much! She screamed and pounded on the door, tore at the bed hangings, kicked wildly at the furniture. She threw herself to the floor, buried her face in her hands and sobbed uncontrollably. At last, her frenzy spent, she felt her panic subside. She sat up, wiped her face and tried to think clearly. If Gravillac had not come by now, he surely did not intend to bother her until evening. There was time—to collect her thoughts, to make some kind of plan, to keep a cool head. Time even for the King to arrive, God willing!

She examined her torn chemise. Better not to tempt the animal in every man! It was not badly ripped, only the drawstring would need repair. Her hands were still shaking, but at least it was something to do, to keep busy, to recover her balance. She set about the task as quickly as she might, uneasy at being even temporarily more naked and vulnerable. The mending finished, she dressed rapidly, and set about to explore her prison. It was a small chamber, and like all the others in this ancient fortress, stone-walled and dark. There was only the single oaken door and a small window high up on one wall. Even were the door not bolted, the guards in the corridor and the constant activity outside would make escape impossible. She looked again at the window, and wondered if she might find freedom that way. No. It was too high, too narrow. And no assurance that, once having squeezed through the opening, she would find anything but a sheer drop to the open courtyard below. No. Escape was not the way. A weapon, perhaps? She prowled the room, searching. It was sparsely furnished: the large bed, a massive armoire, a heavy oaken chair. What few personal effects the Marquis de Gravillac had brought to the room were useless for her defense. Even the two bronze *torchères* were too heavy for her to lift.

She paced the floor, thinking. If she could beguile Gravillac, play the submissive maiden long enough to get out of the room, she could find Bonfleur. He would not countenance the Marquis' savagery! A feeling almost of serenity came over her at last; André would be proud of her. André! Ah *Dieu!* Let the King come in time!

There seemed a great deal of noise and tumult from the courtyard. She was aware suddenly that it had been going on for some time; now it grew in volume. Men shouted. There was the crack of a musket, then another. From somewhere far away there came a booming sound. She pulled and tugged at the heavy chair, straining to drag it to the window. By standing on tiptoes and leaning forward on her elbows, she could just look out onto the courtyard. There was much excited activity, shouts, calls, men running in every direction, buckling on swords, priming flintlocks. Across the courtyard and slightly to the right was the stable where she and André had been, and where now he must be again. She could see clearly the corner of the building where they had spent the night, and knew that he would have returned to that self-same spot. Her heart ached with dismay and longing. She heard the booming sound again, louder and more insistent, and a peculiar whistling noise. It was coming from the right, out of her line of view, from the direction of the river. Cannon! From the east! And de Gravillac and his men poised on the western parapet! She laughed aloud, relief and happiness flooding her being. A cannonball whined through the air, landed in the courtyard, and kicked up a spray of dirt that sent men scurrying for cover. A horse reared up in fright, his rider desperately trying to keep his seat. Another cannon blast. The King's cannoneers were finding their range. The ball struck the chateau itself, somewhere below Marielle. A man shouted in pain. The third cannonball whistled through the air and landed squarely on a small shed tucked up against the corner of the stable. There was a terrible explosion. Another. And a third. The whole corner of the stable had vanished. From the gaping opening came tongues of flame, as the mounds of straw were ignited one by one. From within came awful screams, smoke-racked coughing; the whole stable was a mass of flames.

Marielle screamed. "André!! No!!" And then she was falling, falling, down, down, striking her head, and from thence to blessed oblivion.

PART II

THE NIGHTMARE

Chapter Five

LOUISE DELOCHE NAVIGATED HER AMPLE GIRTH UP THE broad oak staircase. *Bon Dieu!* She was getting too old for all this running and fetching! Puffing, she stopped for breath and, hands on wide hips, scolded the two young pageboys struggling up the steps behind her. Between them, they carried a large tub filled with hot water, which they took great pains to keep in balance.

"Pierre! Georges! Come along! Do you think I have all night? And if you spill one drop, just one, I'll box your ears!" She hitched up her homespun skirt, shifted the bulky armload of clothing she was carrying and continued on up the stairs. Outside the windows, the heavy rain still beat down, and the drafty staircase was cold and damp. She shook her head. Who would think it was nearly May? And what a night for the master to come home! Pounding on the door in the dead of night, drenched to the skin! The horse foaming and exhausted —*Mon Dieu!*—he must have ridden straight through from La Forêt. Thrusting that sodden little waif in her direction—"Take care of her!"—and storming into the great hall to stand by the fireplace and shout for wine. Well, she wasn't about to ask him what had happened. Best to leave him alone. Let Molbert handle him, if he ever showed up, Devil take him!

She pushed open the door to the large bedchamber. The poor creature was still sitting where she had placed her, on a little stool in front of the blazing fire. The tray of food in front of her was untouched. Louise showed the boys where she wanted the tub, then sent them, yawning, back to bed. She put down her bundle and turned her attention to the girl.

She was young, no more than nineteen, the same age as her own daughter Adèle had been. But where Adèle had been small and dark, this one was tall, slender, fair, with hair the color of ripened chestnuts, rich and burnished. She was pretty, that was clear, even with her hair hanging damp and matted about her face. Poor little thing! She looked exhausted, numb, shivering still from that long cold ride. A hot bath, a good meal, a night's sleep—that would put her to rights. Louise fussed about, stripping off the wet chemise, the mud-stained skirt, the heavy country shoes. The girl neither helped nor resisted; she seemed bewildered, lost on some distant shore. Strange. She reminded Louise so much of Adèle. Which was absurd! But perhaps it was the sadness about the eyes, the vulnerability, that made Louise's heart ache. She felt needed, motherly, the way she had not felt for these two years. Not since she had buried her dear Adèle, the stillborn baby at her side. She eased the girl, uncomplaining, into the hot tub, happy to see her trembling stilled at last. How strange this one was! The master had brought more than one pretty creature to stay at Quiòt: bright, gay ladies of the

Court; tempestuous, dark-eyed vixens from the south; even a country maid or two. This one had the clothes of a provincial but the proud bearing of royalty. Lost as she was in some faraway world, she yet thanked Louise for every kindness, murmuring her gratitude in a soft and cultured voice. The bath over, Louise dressed her in the warm nightdress she had brought, fed her a few mouthfuls of soup, and led her gently to the large bed. The poor child was asleep before Louise had finished smoothing the coverlet.

It was night again before Marielle awoke. She struggled up from the layers of mist that surrounded her, trying to clear her head, to remember. It had all been a dream, of course. She could think about it—Gervais, André, the burning stable—but it was a dream. She could picture it all, vague and distorted like a dream, but it did not touch her, it was not real. She could remember it all dispassionately, the images flickering behind her closed eyelids, her heart unmoved.

That dreadful ride in the rain—hours and hours—balanced precariously behind de Gravillac, her hands clutched tightly to his wide sash. He rode like a madman, never slowing his pace, even as the mountains rose before them and the horse threaded its way through narrow, stone-strewn paths, slippery with the rain. She dared not nod, dared not sleep lest, falling from the horse, she tumble into a rocky gorge or slip under those flying hooves.

La Forêt—waking in a sheltered corner of the courtyard with Gravillac saddling his horse, arguing with Molbert, his voice filled with fury. All around them was death, destruction, smoking ruins.

"Damn them all, Molbert! What care I for the rest? Shall I wait with Barrault for Louis to enter in triumph?

Shall I kneel in the dust with Vautier and beg the King's mercy? Bah! I'm for Quiot! If the King wants me, let him seek me there! I expect you to bring the troops back as soon as you can." He looked at the devastation around him, his face purple with rage, and pounded his fist against the stone wall. "Curse André du Crillon! Let him rot in hell! I should never have believed him!" His eyes took in the gutted stable, then swept Marielle, and he laughed bitterly. "At least I shall have some revenge, if only on his specter in hell!"

Bonfleur appeared, his face smudged with soot, weary-footed, distracted. He watched Gravillac mount his horse, then, divining his intention, ran at horse and rider with a strangled curse. Gravillac turned and, with his booted foot, kicked savagely at Bonfleur's head, again and again, until the old man fell and lay groaning in the dust, blood running down his face.

Then Molbert had picked up Marielle, kicking and struggling, put her up on the horse behind Gravillac and the wild ride had begun.

No. It was not real, not any of it.

This was real—this cozy room, fire singing in the hearth, the bed larger and softer and far grander than anything she had ever seen before. She ran her hands along the fine sheets. They were smooth and cool and smelled of lavender. Gravillac must be very rich. Gravillac. He was real. She thought of the way he had looked at her, at La Forêt, and a sense of uneasiness began to creep through her. No! Best not to think of yesterday or tomorrow. She swung her legs quickly out of bed and padded, barefoot, around the room, forcing herself to concentrate only on her surroundings.

There was a soft knock on the door and a robust woman entered, carrying a small tray with food. Marielle recognized her as the woman who had tended her the night before.

"Good!" she exclaimed, nodding her head to Marielle and putting down her tray. "You're awake! Come, eat! 'Tis best you stay here in your room." She shook her head. "He's in a rage, he is! Molbert rode in from La Forêt. The cause is lost. Vautier is dead. Bonfleur has lost his wits. The fortress has been leveled to the ground. And him," here she thrust with her chin toward the closed door as if to indicate the absent Gravillac, "and the rest of the nobles, banished from Paris and the Court for five years. Exiled! And his pension cut too. A hundred-thousand *livres* he must give back! And God knows how many men will drag back here to work the land." She shrugged her shoulders. "Well, I cannot say I'm sorry for him—it was a wild scheme; he wanted too much power. Even when he was a child. . . ." Her face darkened with some unpleasant memory, then she shook off the mood. "Well," she said with a sigh, "my family has always served the de Gravillacs and I expect to die here at Quiot."

At Louise's insistence, Marielle managed to swallow a few mouthfuls of food, but the talk of La Forêt had stirred up some uneasy current deep within her, and she had no appetite. Without warning, the door burst open and Renard de Gravillac strode into the room. He had removed his doublet and riding boots, and was clad now only in soft shoes and breeches, his linen shirt hanging open carelessly. His hand held a cup of wine. His languid eyes traveled the length of her body, then slowly back again to her face. She confronted him proudly, her chin held high, but a small pulse of fear had begun to throb in her temples.

He jerked his head in Louise's direction. "Leave us!" he barked, but his eyes never left Marielle's face. She tried desperately to read his look, to guess his intentions, but his eyes were unfathomable. Anger? Would he kill her out of bitterness, frustration? He was drunk, that was apparent. Surely not rape! Dear God, not rape! He was a gentleman, a nobleman, raised on chivalry—it was unthinkable!

The door closed behind Louise. They were alone. He smiled and bowed unsteadily. "Madame la Comtesse!"

She frowned. Why did he call her that? Ah yes. She felt the ring on her hand, remembering. André. The priest. A small finger of panic scratched at her insides. She shook her head, willing the images to vanish. That was just part of the dream . . . wasn't it? Wasn't it?

"I'm sorry Louise did not bring you some wine," he said suavely. "I should send for more, but it takes her so long to climb the stairs. You must have some of mine." He crossed the room and stood before her, proffering the cup. She thought at first to refuse, but something in his glittering eyes made her suddenly unwilling to cross him. Besides, it would give her time to think. She drank slowly, holding the cup in both hands, arms pressed protectively against her bosom. Stupid. She had hardly eaten for three days, and the wine burnt her insides and made her feel dizzy.

"Madame, I grow impatient," he said, his voice smooth, silky. A slow smile lit his handsome features, but his body was a coiled spring. He pulled the cup away from her, flinging it aside, then lifted her hands to his lips, turning her palms upward and pressing soft kisses into her flesh. His eyes were dark and smoldering as he drew her closer to him. She loathed him. She wrenched her hands from his grasp, backing away, shaking her head.

"Please," she said, her voice low, "I beg you. Do not make me hate you."

He laughed softly. "Even the vanquished deserve rewards after the battle. Besides, my trembling pigeon, I can make you forget your hatred; I can play you like a lute and make you sing. A body like yours begs to be loved!"

Inexorably he advanced, his eyes filled with desire, his body tense and rigid. She felt sick. The wine burned in her belly and panic clutched at her throat. She stepped back, back, her nerves taut, until her shoulders touched the large armoire and there was nowhere left to retreat. Smiling, triumphant, he stretched out his hands and placed them firmly on her full, ripe breasts. She shuddered, feeling his hands through the soft fabric, fondling, caressing. No! By *le Bon Dieu*, he would not dare! Her anger boiled up within her, driving out the fear. She pushed him away with all her strength, and swung her hand in a great arc across his face. André's ring left a fiery welt on his cheek.

"I belong to André!" she shrilled.

The coiled spring snapped. He slapped her face, once, twice, anger contorting his handsome visage. She twisted away, eluding his grasp, and headed for the door. She was halfway across the room when he lunged, catching her by the arm and dragging her back. Savagely he twisted her arm behind her, drawing her toward him until she could smell the wine on his hot breath. With his free hand, he ripped open the front of her gown, his eyes narrowing as the torn fabric fell

71

away and revealed the creamy smoothness of her rounded breasts. She gasped in horror at the naked lust in his face, and twisted vainly in his cruel grip.

"I'll make you forget du Crillon!" he panted fiercely, and bent his burning mouth to her bosom, covering her with hot kisses. She could feel the scratch of his beard on her flesh, and trembled in fury at her helplessness. She pounded on his back with her fist, all the while heaping curses on him, deriding his manhood, comparing him scornfully with André. His eyes burning angrily, he twisted her back until she cried out in pain. She could feel the hardness of his desire against her body and with a sudden thrust she lifted her knee and drove it into his groin with all her might. With a groan he released her and doubled up, cursing under his breath and writhing in pain. For a moment she stood frozen, aghast at what she had done, appalled at her own ferocity. Then she started for the door again.

With a roar he overtook her, grabbed her fiercely by the arm and flung her across the room. She collided heavily with the armoire, its massive corner catching her between her shoulder blades and knocking the wind out of her. She slid to the floor, half sitting, gasping for breath. Gravillac, his eyes still murderous, was in front of her in two strides. Cursing, he struck her again, full in the face, his fist doubled up in fury. She could feel her lip split against the edge of her tooth, hear a roaring in her ears. His frenzied hands tore at her nightdress, ripping it to shreds, til she lay naked on the floor. With a grunt of satisfaction, he picked her up roughly and threw her onto the bed, where she lay still gasping, dazed from his blow, her head spinning from the wine. She lay exhausted, vaguely aware he was stripping off his garments, too weak to offer resistance. Then he was on the bed, beside her, on top of her, his weight pressing against her body, his knee forcing her legs apart. She struggled feebly, arching her back, trying desperately to push him away. He had abandoned his passionate kisses; now there was only the ache in his loins that cried out to be eased. Savagely he thrust into her, feeling the momentary resistance of her maidenhood. She gasped in shock and agony as waves of pain and nausea swept upward from her thighs. Ah, *Dieu!* This was real, it was all real! And André had been real! André! Her love, her husband! She scarcely was aware now of the figure who heaved and panted above her, as a huge sob rumbled in her chest and she trembled violently. At the very moment his passion was spent, the sob broke from her into a wail, a terrible keening moan, as her reawakening memories flooded her with grief. Startled, Gravillac moved away from her, hastily jumping off the bed and pulling on his clothes.

Damn the wench! Must she cry so? He had had too much to drink—his head hurt. He made for the door and his own room, bellowing for Louise to come and see to Madame.

Louise hurried into the room. One look at the moaning figure crumpled on the bed told her all she needed to know. That animal, she thought, furious, and aloud, "Let Louise help you." She moistened a small towel in a basin and, seating herself on the bed, dabbed at the bloody lip, the bruised jaw. She wrapped the shaking body tenderly in the coverlet and held Marielle in her lap, rocking her gently and steadily. Marielle looked up at her, her face swollen with grief, eyes filled with despair, disbelief.

"He's dead!" she sobbed over and over. "He's dead. He's dead. He's dead."

Chapter Six

THE BRIGHT SPRING SUNSHINE GLOWED THROUGH THE casement window. Marielle sat up in bed, every bone and muscle crying out in painful protest. She fingered her swollen lip and groaned, dropping her aching head into her hands. Her brain felt as though it would explode, and there was a tender spot along the line of her delicate jaw. Her shoulders throbbed, her back twinged. On the irreparable damage to her chastity and the dull pain in her heart she dared not dwell. Louise bustled into the room carrying her breakfast. She placed the tray on Marielle's lap and smiled brightly.

"A lovely morning, Madame! The sun is warm—I think we shall have spring at last! Come. A little breakfast to cheer you up. No need to dwell on what is done. Eat."

Marielle bent to the food. A piece of bread, cheese, a slice of cold lamb. A large cup of wine, thinned with water and sweetened with rich honey. It seemed impossible that she could eat, but her appetite was young and healthy and she wolfed down the meal despite the heaviness of her heart. Louise busied herself about the room, directing the placing of the bathtub, carrying in armloads of clothing to be folded neatly into the oaken armoire. ("They are old, Madame, but of good quality"), throwing wide the windows to the warm breeze. But ever her glance turned to Marielle, eyes filled with maternal concern. While Marielle soaked away her aches in the warmth of the tub, Louise fetched in armfuls of bright spring forsythias, yellow blossoms ariot on the supple branches, and arranged their cheerfulness about the room. By the time Marielle was bathed and dressed in a smoky green silk gown that just matched her eyes, she was beginning to feel a great deal better, both in body and spirit. Louise combed her hair until it shone, and arranged it full and loose about her face, heavy tresses cascading down her back. A knock on the door, and the pageboy Pierre announced that Monsieur le Marquis was in the garden this morning, and wished Madame la Comtesse to join him. Her heart thudding, Marielle allowed the boy to lead her down the staircase and out into the bright sunlight.

Gravillac was standing on the edge of a terrace that fronted the river far below. The neat order of the terraced garden was separated from the wild vegetation below by a stone retaining wall, surmounted by a carved balustrade. Gravillac turned and smiled as she approached. He was dressed for riding, high leather boots that cuffed at his knee, brown velvet doublet, a wide red silk baldrick sashed at his waist. His eyes swept her graceful form approvingly, filled with open admiration. She eyed him coldly, guardedly, puzzled to find not a flicker of lust nor even of uneasiness in his frank stare. Could he have forgotten last night?

"I would have preferred you to wear your hair up in the back," he said smoothly. "The ladies of Paris have dressed their hair that way for several seasons now. The back of a woman's neck is too charming to hide!"

She felt flustered, disarmed. She had never dressed so grandly in all her life, and was flattered by her reflection in his eyes. He smiled warmly, and offered her his arm. She hesitated, bewildered. No word of apology, no acknowledgment of what had happened, nothing. Had he been so drunk he did not even remember?

"As you wish," he said, and lowered his arm. "I shall be gone most of the day. I must see to my estate. You have the freedom of Quiot, of course." Then he was gone.

She spent most of the day exploring the house and grounds. Quiot was situated on an isolated promontory overlooking the Saône River. The nearest town was some leagues distant, reached by a single narrow road through the hills. On the river side, with its steep bank, the chateau was virtually inaccessible. The fields dropped away on either side, planted with early wheat that would soon begin to sprout under the May sun. To the south, where the mountains rose high and steep, Gravillac's tenant farmers herded their flocks of sheep. The front of the chateau was approached by a wide avenue that cut through a broad lawn dotted with formal flower beds. The chateau itself was no more than fifty years old, built, no doubt, on the site of previous Gravillac holdings. It was a fine house, paneled with rich, dark woods and high Italianate windows, almost incongruous in this wild secluded setting. On reflection, Marielle decided that perhaps it suited Renard de Gravillac; both were charming, attractive, with a guarded aloofness that neither touched nor was touched. One lived in this house—one never belonged to it. She was aware during the afternoon that Molbert seemed to appear rather frequently; she wondered idly if he were watching her, guarding her. No matter. With the expanse of open fields, there would be no way to leave without being seen.

Gravillac had insisted that she join him at supper. They sat facing each other across a massive oak table polished to a high luster. He seemed in fair enough spirits, although Louise had said his tour of the estate had been disappointing; far too many fields would lie fallow this spring, their tenants buried in the soil of La Forêt.

Marielle ate sparingly, her green eyes cold as a wintry sea, unable to forget his violation of the night before. For his part, Renard was pleased to have this lovely creature sharing his table. It had been a difficult day; it did a man good to look at someone as exquisite as this wench. They had begun to talk of politics, of France and Spain and what was happening in England. At first he only watched her as she spoke, her eyes flashing, bosom heaving in anger when she disagreed with him, but in a bit he began to listen more carefully to her words. What was it that Bonfleur had said? A doctor's daughter. Well he could believe that. She had a fine mind, sharp and logical as a man's, a mind to match her other merits as a woman. Frank admiration showed in his face.

Marielle found her anger softening under his courtly attentions; his open approval pleased her in spite of herself. She could never forgive him, of course, but perhaps she could understand. The loss of his cause . . . exile . . . and surely he had been very drunk. A man might forget himself under those circumstances. She could perhaps prevail upon him to help her get to Paris; there must be people there who remembered her father, who would befriend her. She thought of Claude, Gervais' friend. She knew he would marry her in a moment, and after all, what did it matter? After André, she no longer expected a man to make her heart sing. Lyon, after all, was not so far. Surely Renard would be willing to help her find Claude. She felt optimistic, almost happy, as they left the dining salon.

Renard gripped Marielle's elbow, and guided her firmly to the foot of the staircase. He motioned to Louise, who had just come in from the kitchen.

"Attend my lady," he said. "I shall be up presently." There was no mistaking his meaning. Marielle's heart sank.

In the bedchamber, Louise bestirred herself about the room, closing the casement against the chill night air, turning down the coverlet and sheets. Marielle paced the room, wringing her hands, her eyes purposely avoiding the huge imposing bed, feeling helpless and trapped. She stood quietly, lost in unhappy thought, while Louise removed the soft lace collar and unhooked the front of the green silk bodice. Their eyes met briefly and a wave of sympathy passed from the elder woman, a look filled with understanding and dismay. The green silk skirt fell about Marielle's ankles, then she sat and removed her dainty brocaded shoes, the silk stockings. She stood up, slipping the soft white chemise over her head. Louise hurried to fetch a nightdress as she stepped out of her linen petticoat and stood there naked, shivering with a chill that had less to do with the night air than with the heaviness in her heart. With a start, she saw that de Gravillac was at the door; how long he had been watching her she could only guess. Scooping her petticoat off the floor, she clutched it to her and shrank back against the heavy bed hangings, her pulse racing. Louise approached with the nightgown, but Gravillac motioned her away, then followed her to the door, closing and locking it securely when she had left, and pocketing the key.

He was sober tonight, and smiling, thoroughly enjoying Marielle's helplessness. The pig! She could not make excuses for him this evening. Her fear turned to cold fury. By *le Bon Dieu,* she would fight him tonight! It would cost him dear to take her, she would see to that!

He smiled smugly, confidently, content to savor every moment.

"I could wish you were not so modest, my dear," he said. "You are exceedingly lovely to look upon, and it occurs to me I only have glimpses of you through tattered garments."

"That is all you shall ever have," she said contemptuously. "If I could, I would dress in heavy furs, though it be summer, to keep myself covered against your hateful eyes!"

He laughed aloud. "You should consider yourself fortunate that you look so charming in silks and velvets, else I would be tempted to keep you always locked in your room, with no garments at all!"

"You are vile!" she said stamping her foot in fury. "I wonder not that you need to rape a woman to get what you want. Only a fool would come to you willingly!"

He smiled languidly, desire smoldering in his eyes. "I have had many women—mostly willing. And I always get what I want. And what I want now is a spirited wench with green eyes—willing or no!" His eyes swept hungrily over her, and she cringed farther back against the draperies of the bed. "You are worth the sport, *ma petite.*"

He began then to undress, slowly, carefully, unwinding the long baldrick sash about his waist, slipping off the brown doublet. Marielle leaned into the bed, powerless, transfixed, her eyes darting wildly about the room—a trapped animal desperate for escape.

"If I were a man I'd kill you!" she said boldly, and was dismayed to hear the quaver in her voice.

He laughed wryly, pulling his shirt over his head. "As I recall, you very nearly did, last night!" He stepped closer, enjoying himself thoroughly. The sight of his hairy chest, black and thick and matted, made her stomach churn. She glowered at him, eyes burning with hatred.

"Come, my little tiger, show me what you are guarding with such modesty!" He circled warily around her, ever mindful of her dangerous kicks, and grabbed her suddenly from behind, pulling the protecting petticoat from her grasp. She flailed furiously with her arms, catching him in the ribs with her elbows, and pounding against his shins with her bare heels. She shrieked and cursed him furiously, trying to turn in his steel grip, to use her punishing knee as she had before. The more she struggled, the more he laughed, exultant, enjoying the challenge, the certainty of ultimate victory.

"*Dommage!* Am I not to see you plain, then? Will you deny my eyes their feast?" He laughed, as though struck by a thought. "Ah, no, my lovely flower, there is a way!"

So swiftly that she hardly had time to marshal her defenses, he bent down, picked up his long sash and looped it skillfully around her narrow wrists, binding her hands in front of her. With one strong arm slipped about her waist, he lifted her, kicking and wriggling, and carried her to the bed. He threw her on her back and swiftly tied the other end of the baldrick to the bed post, stretching her arms cruelly above her head. She sobbed in rage and frustration, twisting and writhing while his eyes burned into her, shaming her with his lascivious stare. His gaze never left her body as he removed boots, stockings, breeches, his eyes traveling hungrily from her full ripe breasts to her flat smooth belly and the patch of chestnut beyond. He stood before her in the full vigor of his manhood, lean and hard—a powerful body, strong, potent, brutal. She knew her struggles only added fuel to his ardor; with a great sob, she lay still, knowing she could not escape the unavoidable, but wanting to hurt him as much as he hurt her.

"And is this how your father begat you?" she said with contempt and bitterness. She saw his passion die instantly, and a look of such violent rage came into his eyes that she cringed in terror. Seething, he cast his eyes around the room till they lit upon the forsythia branches. He snatched up one supple twig, stripping it of leaves and blossoms in one swift gesture, then, using it as a switch, slashed at her tender body again and again. She shrank against the bed, drawing up her knees to protect her breasts, twisting and turning to avoid that flailing arm. The restraining baldrick cut into her wrists, and the punishing lashes stung her shoulders, legs, buttocks. She yelped in pain and outrage, humiliation cutting her more deeply than the switch. Finally, his anger abated, he snatched up his clothes, unlocked the door and stalked from the room.

Louise, hearing Marielle's shrieks, was waiting impatiently outside the door. As soon as Gravillac vanished into his own room, she rushed swiftly to Marielle's side, to untie her, to soothe her, to still the racking sobs.

In the morning, Marielle spent a long time in her tub. She felt dirty, soiled, degraded more by the whipping and by his laughing enjoyment of her plight, than she had when he raped her in anger.

Louise knelt beside her, gently soaping the milky shoulders, rubbing as softly as she might where ugly red welts yet remained. If there were only something she could do to help this poor creature. She knew with certainty that, family tradition or no, she would leave Quiot tomorrow but for this girl. But she was a practical woman, and perhaps that was what was needed most.

"Eh bien," she said finally. "Maybe it is none of my concern, my lady, but what is so bad after all in going down for a man? Women have always done it and it's soon over—and what's the harm?" She smiled tenderly at the look of surprise on Marielle's innocent face. "It leaves no scars, *ma petite*—unless you struggle! He will tire of you soon enough, and then you will be free!"

"To do what?" asked Marielle with bitterness in her voice.

"He has brought beauties from Paris, grand ladies, but none could match you in face and form."

"Shall I then go to Paris and be a harlot?"

"Nay!" said Louise. "But in Paris a woman's past is

of no matter. No one cares. They make much of beauty and wit. You could be the toast of the Court, and marry well in the bargain!" She sighed with exasperation. "But you can be nothing if you are maimed and crippled."

"Aye, marry well," said Marielle, and a tear coursed down her cheek. "And bestow on my husband the gift of my virtue."

"'Tis gone, and no calling it back. Would you die for it?"

Despite herself, Marielle knew there was wisdom in Louise's words. How ridiculous to go on suffering. For what? She was no longer a virgin, and no amount of tears and rage could change that. There was something else as well. Gravillac's temper was wild and uncontrolled; he could be a dangerous man. Louise was right. Only a fool would provoke his murderous moods. She resolved that, come what might, she would endure with fortitude, praying he would weary of her in good time.

In spite of her resolve, she was glad he was gone for the whole day; the thought of facing him still made her uneasy. She asked Louise for a small piece of needlework, and spent much of the afternoon sewing in the spring sunshine, glad to have something to keep herself busy, to forget André, Gervais, her grief. She was aware that Molbert watched her from time to time—a cunning prison, this! The air had become chilly; she shivered slightly and came inside, minded to ask Louise for a shawl. Just as she reached the staircase, she heard Gravillac's voice behind her; she had not seen him in the shadows. She took a deep breath, willing her tremulous heart to be stilled, and faced him.

He bowed courteously. "Good evening, Madame la

Comtesse. I was about to go in to supper. Will you join me?"

She eyed him coldly. *Dieu!* How she despised him! "I should prefer to take supper in my room, Monsieur. My head troubles me this evening—a slight *malaise.*"

He took a step toward her, and placed a hand gently on her arm. He smiled disarmingly, his face filled with concern.

"You understand," he said with an apologetic shrug, "I like to have my way. I am used to it. There is no need for things to be difficult between us. I should regret a repetition of last night." He smiled magnanimously. "I shall send Louise to your room with your supper. I will join you later."

She escaped up the stairs, happy to be free of him, if only for awhile. At the landing, his voice, sharp and willful, stopped her abruptly.

"Tomorrow, wear your hair up!"

She fled to her room, sobbing. What kind of man was he? Nothing in her background had prepared her for this. Trusting and guileless, she could not cope with his duplicity. He played with her as a spider with its victim, and she felt helpless. The vile temper—that she could understand. He was like a cruel, spoiled child, frightening and dangerous, but not unfamiliar to her experience. But what thoughtlessness could make him ugly and abusive one moment and then smile, be charming, act as though nothing had happened? Was he so unfeeling as not to know the grief he caused, or so selfish it mattered little to him?

She picked at her dinner; her head had begun to throb. When he came to her room, she submitted with cold anger and disgust, turning her head away, trying to keep her lips from his loathsome kisses. Afterwards, alone, she thought of André and the sweetness of his kiss. She felt overcome by her loss; large, bitter tears welled up in her eyes and she wept softly, curled up and shivering in the big bed.

In the morning, her fever was raging.

Chapter Seven

RENARD DE GRAVILLAC WATCHED FROM THE WINDOW AS Louise helped Marielle into the daybed laid out below in the May sunshine. The girl was terribly thin and pallid, her face pale and translucent as alabaster. He felt an unexpected pang of concern; she had been so terribly ill. A prison fever perhaps, or the chilling ride in the rain. For nearly two weeks she had lain in her room, teeth chattering against the chills that racked her, writhing with fever, her face flushed and hot, eyes glassy and unseeing. Sometimes she muttered unintelligibly or sobbed bitterly or cried aloud the name of André. Always du Crillon! Would the man haunt him even dead? He remembered with frustration those unflinching blue eyes, the clash of wills between them, the lies that had cost him the battle at La Forêt. He gnashed his teeth in fury. He had thought that taking Crillon's woman would even the score, would make him the victor, if only over a dead man, but the remembrance of the nights he had spent with her brought him no satisfaction. He tried to concentrate on those traits of hers that he usually found so arousing in a woman—the fighting spirit, the voluptuous body, the pride that begged to be subdued. He had beaten more than one woman into submission, and found that, despite her protests, it served to inflame her passions. But not Marielle. He turned impatiently from the window and muttered an oath. It was useless to try and remember her soft body under his—his mind dwelt only on her heartbroken wailing, her horror and disgust. Well, perhaps it was because she had been a virgin. He allowed himself a small surge of satisfaction over that; so much for du Crillon, who had not been smart enough to take her when he could! Still, a man's body was new to her, and perhaps frightening. He must proceed more slowly, delicately. She was a flower to be plucked gently, not ripped brutally from the ground. It suddenly seemed important to eradicate that loathing from her eyes.

Mairelle walked slowly along the hall to her room. How tired she felt! Perhaps Louise had been right. It had been too soon to come down for supper. After so many weeks in bed, the effort of dressing, of sitting at the table, trying to eat, had exhausted her. But Gravillac was becoming testy, impatient. She had begun to fear another violent outburst. What a strange man! He had been so pleased to see her, so delighted because Louise had twisted her hair into a thick rope and piled it high atop her head. He had gently fingered the curls and tendrils that still hung soft and loose about her face, and when he had seated her at the table had bent and kissed the nape of her neck with such a triumphant air that she was tempted to unpin the whole mass and let it cascade down her back, just out of pique. *Mon Dieu,* but she was tired! She hoped that her appearance at supper tonight would not serve as the signal for him to resume his visits to her room. Though she had submitted passively enough that last night before her illness, she yet feared his violence. *Le Bon Dieu* knew her body still creaked and ached enough from her fever without risking a beating from him! And it was so difficult to guess what might anger him.

What was keeping Louise? She was too tired to wait for her, and began stripping off her clothes herself, leaving the silks and linens in a heap upon the floor. She had just slipped her nightdress over her head and was adjusting the drawstring, when there was a soft knock on the door. Louise! At last. Perhaps she would forego the nightly hair combing, and simply unpin her coif; the thought of sleep was uppermost in Marielle's mind. It was not Louise. It was Renard, clad in a long brocaded dressing gown.

"I dismissed Louise tonight," he said. "I could not bear to wait whilst she clucked over you like a mother hen." His voice was low and throaty, and his eyes burnt into her. He held out a small vial. "Perfume. From Paris. Wear it for me tomorrow. It is the last I have, but perhaps when Molbert goes to get supplies and the latest news from Versailles he can fetch more."

Silently, she took the bottle and turned to place it on her dressing table. In one soft step he was behind her, his arms gently about her waist, his hands cupped on her breasts. He held her very tightly for a moment and she could feel the heat of his body against her back, the hardness that betrayed his passion. Then, stooping slightly, he bent his mouth to her vulnerable neck, letting his lips stray softly up to her ear and burying his face in her fragrant hair.

"I could not keep my eyes from you at supper. You drive a man to madness!" His hands moved upward from her breasts, releasing the drawstring on her garment, loosening it til it drew away from her body, then sliding it down to the floor, while his hands followed its course from the firm breasts to her slim waist and the softly rounded hips. He released the pins from her hair and watched the glowing tresses ripple down over her velvety shoulders, then turned her to face him, slipping his hands beneath her buttocks and holding her tightly against his hungry loins. She felt strangely unmoved by his attentions. Although she was dimly aware that he expected her to respond, that his caresses were supposed to ignite some flame within her, she felt only discomfort, unease, wishing he would stop. She could tell by the glow in his dark eyes, the way his breath came short and hard, that she excited him, and she prayed that, in his impatience, he would have done with her quickly. He scooped her up in his arms and carried her swiftly to the bed, laying her down tenderly and flinging aside his dressing gown. She found his nakedness repelling, frightening; a wave of nausea flicked at her insides. He seemed in no hurry tonight. He lay beside her, touching, caressing, letting his fingers stray to every part of her body. She felt degraded, shamed, as though he violated her privacy with his rapacious hands. Finally he pulled her body under his and entered her. She shuddered. It was so unpleasant, distasteful. She thought suddenly of André. Was this what he had wanted of her? Renard strained above her, the muscles of his neck hard and knotted with his exertions. It was all so ugly. Surely André, her beloved André, would not have expected this of her! Renard gave a groan of pleasure, a final thrust, and collapsed against her, his passion spent. He sat up then and looked at her, eyes narrowing, curious, trying to gauge her reaction. She was too tired to care. She pushed his weight from her body, plodded heavily across the room to pick up her night-dress and slipped it over her head. She hardly cared if he stayed or went; she climbed wearily into the bed, pulled up the sheets, and was fast asleep while yet he gazed at her in frustration and dismay.

"Coward!" whispered Marielle into her mirror. Her reflection gazed back at her, the pale cheeks less drawn and tired after her night's rest. What had happened to her pride, her spirit—that she should have allowed him so easily to resume his assaults on her body, on her dignity? She had been exhausted from her illness, true enough, numb with grief because of Gervais, André. Still . . . "Coward!" she said again, her voice sharp with self-loathing. It was foolish to fight him openly, as Louise had said, but surely there were other ways to resist his attentions. To escape even!

She fretted impatiently as Louise helped her into her gown; when the elder woman, her hands clumsy, fumbled with the lace falling band, Marielle snatched the wide collar from her and tied the strings herself. She was impatient to be out of doors, to walk in the gardens and the grounds of Quiot with more direction than she had shown before. Surely there was a way to leave! She spent the morning in mounting frustration and anger, finding herself stopped at every turn. The terrace dropped steeply to the river—impossible! The wheatfields, unprotected and open to view. Once, during the morning, she managed to reach a small stand of trees at the edge of a field, only to be startled by one of Gravillac's tenants who firmly guided her back to the chateau, under orders from the master to see that the fine lady did not stray from Quiot. And Molbert—always Molbert—skulking around every corner! By the time a pretty young serving girl came to announce the noon meal, Marielle was filled with a savage desperation that showed in her green eyes, and the servant curtsied humbly in response to her testy mood.

Gravillac was waiting for her, smiling and at ease, lolling in his chair while the servants spread a cloth on the table before him and set out platters of food and wine and cutlery. He looked up when she entered, but did not rise; his eyes scanned her face with such sharpness that she wondered if he could read the hatred written there. Nervously she averted her gaze and paced the room until the servants had withdrawn, her thoughts in a turmoil.

He indicated a chair and she sat, picking indifferently at the food as he offered each platter, scarcely listening to his casual conversation, so intent was she on her own thoughts. She would reason with him, make him understand that she did not welcome his attentions, that he would be better off to let her go back to La Forêt, or Lyon—or Paris even. Her hatred would only cause him needless grief—surely there could be no joy for him in a woman who could not return his ardor! And if reasoning failed? . . . Almost involuntarily her eyes strayed to the cutlery upon the table, the sharp knives meant to carve the slab of beef. She would kill him. God forgive her, she would kill him. She dragged her eyes away from the blade and looked up to see him smiling oddly at her.

"Will you take more wine?" he asked softly.

"No, I thank you. I am content." Still agitated, Marielle rose quickly from the table and went to stand by the window. Could I really kill him? she thought, her eyes traveling once again to the knife. As though he read her thoughts, Gravillac rose from the table in his turn and ambled to the cold fireplace, seeming almost deliberately to turn his back to her as he leaned against the mantel. Now! she thought, moving quickly to the table. Dare I do it now? She stood for a moment, her hand poised over the blade.

Suddenly Gravillac whirled, transfixing her with his malevolent glare. Despite the smile that twitched at his mouth she could see cold fury in his dark eyes. He had seen. He knew.

With trembling hands, Marielle reached for her wine cup and drained it in one gulp.

Gravillac selected a hefty stave from a large basket of kindling on the hearth. "You must have fresh wine," he said silkily, and gave the floor a sharp rap with one end of the rod. In a moment the pageboy Pierre appeared carrying a large jug; at Gravillac's order he refilled Marielle's goblet. "Wait," said Gravillac, as the boy made a move to retire. Though his tone was mild, there was something in his manner, the tension in his body, that made Marielle shiver. "Did you lay out the table?"

The boy bobbed politely and nodded his head. "Yes, Monsieur."

"The knives as well?"

"Yes, Monsieur."

"Have you the sense that God gave you, boy?" The voice low but edged with cold steel.

The boy trembled. "Monsieur?"

"Do you not see the knives are too sharp? Madame could harm herself, and you would bear the blame!" All pretense of civility was gone now as Gravillac scowled fiercely at the boy.

The poor lad began to shake with fear, "Monsieur . . . I did not think . . . it will not happen again . . . I . . . ."

Gravillac gripped the rod more firmly in his hand. "Indeed it shall not! And you shall have a reminder!" He pointed toward the table.

Whimpering, the boy leaned over the table, his fists clutching tight to the cloth, his face screwed up in pain as though he already felt the blows.

"No!" cried Marielle, as Gravillac's arm rose and fell. Pierre gave a muffled squeak, his small body twitching at the force of the stroke on his rump. "The knives are not too sharp! Do not harm the boy!" Another blow. This time Pierre cried out. Marielle was near tears. "Please. I shall not touch the knives. I swear it!" Gravillac, unmoved, continued the punishment. An ugly red welt appeared as the rod struck the lad's bare leg. "I beg you!" cried Marielle, clutching at Gravillac's arm.

He turned to her, his eyes burning. Rage had carried him beyond the edge of reasoning. "Would you take his place?" he growled. Aghast, Marielle hesitated, half-minded to endure the beating herself, if only to spare the boy. Gravillac delivered one more stroke, then jerked the lad upright by the scruff of his neck. "Get you gone!" he ordered. "But do not forget there are to

be no more knives at table when Madame sups!"
Shaking, Marielle watched the boy limp away, then
made for the door herself. "Wait!" thundered
Gravillac. "I have not said that you may go!"

She whirled toward him, her chin outthrust in defi-
ance, though her heart pounded at the sight of the
threatening staff yet clutched in his hand. "Have I your
leave to retire?" she asked coldly. At his stiff nod, she
fled to the safety of her room. She sank onto her bed
feeling drained and exhausted, her heart heavy with
remorse. There was a flurry of light taps at her door,
then Louise entered and hurried to her side.

"You are well, Madame? He has not harmed you?"
The simple face creased with concern. She sighed in
relief at sight of Marielle, then frowned again in
disgust. "That poor lad . . . ."

"I was the cause," said Marielle in an agonized voice.
"It was to make me suffer that he beat the boy."

"No. You must not reproach yourself. He beats the
boys often—Pierre . . . Georges . . . all of them. He
would have found a reason soon enough! There is a
cruelty to him. . . . I have never understood it. He can
be kind, generous, gentle . . . like his father was. They
were so alike. Hot-tempered, quarrelsome—Quiot
rang with their battles. But the father never saw the
cruelty in his son—mayhap that is why I stayed with
him so long, thinking the cruelty was a childishness that
would pass." She sighed deeply. "Ah, me! Pierre's
bruises will heal—and Gravillac will be charming once
again. Will you stroll in the garden this afternoon?"

Marielle shook her head, remembering her frustrating escape attempts of the morning. "I shall rest here
for a little. See to the lad, for my sake." She lay back on
her bed, meaning to close her eyes only briefly, but

when she awoke it was evening and the young serving girl was shaking her gently and inviting her to join Monsieur le Marquis at supper. Marielle hesitated. "I shall sup in my room. But . . . tell Monsieur, most kindly, that I should like to . . . receive him in my chamber . . . after he has dined, if it so pleases him."

She scarcely touched her food when it was brought, rehearsing again and again the words she would say to him. Louise said he could be kind, reasonable—it was she herself who had provoked his rage at lunch by her intemperate courting of murderous thoughts. Surely she could appeal to his reason. After an eternity of waiting, a soft rap announced Gravillac. He strode into her chamber, his face beaming, a large red rose in his hand. At sight of her, the smile faded and was replaced by a puzzled scowl.

"When a lady invites me to her room, I expect to be greeted with more warmth!" His black eyes raked her figure. "And you have not even sent for Louise! Am I to strip the gown from you myself?"

Marielle gasped, dismayed that he should have read acquiescence into her invitation. "N-no," she stammered. "I . . . I wished to . . . speak to you, merely." She took a deep breath before continuing. "You must see that I cannot stay here . . . it is not seemly . . . it is an affront to God. Surely you will release me!"

"No!" he said sulkily, clearly disappointed in his expectations.

"If I plead with you," she said humbly, "if I beg you on my knees . . . will you let me go?"

"No!"

"Is there no way to soften your heart?"

He chuckled maliciously. "Will you offer yourself in rags and covered with ashes next?"

She bit her lip and turned away, angered by her own servility. "You have no right to keep me!" she cried, her voice firm and proud.

He shrugged. "I have every right! The spoils of war. Had I bested du Crillon in a duel, I should have claimed his sword—I took his widow instead! You are far more . . . useful . . . than a blade!" He laughed softly, but there was a hard glitter in his dark eyes.

"How dare you! I am not chattel to be treated thus! You have abused me, raped me, kept me here against my will! I am not yours to do with as it pleases you!'

"Yes!" he thundered, throwing down the rose. "You are mine—just as Quiot is mine! And everything, everyone here! You are mine for as long as I want you!" He pounded a fist on the table, his dark eyes glowing; Marielle drew back before the savagery of his onslaught. "Shall I send for Pierre that he may instruct you once more in the ways of obedience?"

She gasped, her hand flying to her mouth. "You would not beat that poor child yet again . . . ?"

"I would beat him every day in your presence, so you may learn that I am to be obeyed!" He paced the room for a moment, and when he turned back to Marielle some of the fury seemed to have drained from his face. "I do not wish to be cruel to you, but . . . the choice is yours."

"What can you want from me," she said tiredly, "knowing I am unwilling?"

"I ask only that you grace my table with your beauty, give me the pleasure of a pliant disposition . . . and allow me to make love to you when I wish it!"

"Ugh! Love!" Marielle spat the word, her lip curling in disgust. "You call it love?"

Gravillac's eyes narrowed, and he took a menacing

step toward her. "There are other . . . practices . . . which please me from time to time. Mindful of your sensibilities and virtuous nature, I have not asked them of you. There are other women here who satisfy my . . . coarser appetites. *That,* mayhap, is not love. I have no thought for their delicacy at such times—I please only myself. But, with you, it is different. Would you have me treat you like all the rest?"

Marielle frowned, mystified.

He laughed shortly. "Not only a virgin, but naive as well!" Softly, enjoying the look of horror that spread across Marielle's face, he began to tell her what he meant, describing acts that made her burn with shame, his language deliberately crude and ugly. When at last she could bear no more, she clapped her hands to her ears and turned away, her face drained of color, her body shaking. Gently he turned her about and smiled softly, his finger stroking the line of her collarbone, seeming not to notice that she cringed away from his touch. "I ask none of this from you, my charming flower—only your sweet agreeableness. In exchange, I give you fine clothes, food, shelter . . . for as long as you please me. Could you ask for more? Does the world beyond Quiot offer you finer?" He brought her hand to his lips in a lingering kiss. "I shall leave you to your solitary bed tonight, that you may think well on my words." He turned and strode from the chamber, his booted foot crushing the fragile rose on the floor.

Still trembling, Marielle sank to her bed, feeling the terror well up within her, aware suddenly that she was more frightened of him than she had acknowledged. And she could not kill him. After all her years of nursing, of seeing life as sacred, she had not the heart to take a life—even his. Besides, would he ever allow her the opportunity? After this morning, he would be on the alert, never trusting her for an instant, poised to retaliate should she be so foolish as to try to destroy him.

What does it matter, she thought, suddenly overwhelmed with grief. Where would she go, even if she were free? Except for Louise, was there anyone to care? Her soul was dead, had died at La Forêt, snuffed out in Gervais' pain-filled eyes, drowned in the shrieks from the flaming stable. "André!" she sobbed aloud. How few the hours they had shared—yet every word of his, every gesture, the feel of his lips on hers, was seared into her brain. She had lived a lifetime in the prison—there was no past, there was no future. "Before God," she had said to André; now there was nothing save the weary time until sweet Death should reunite her with him.

What does it matter? she thought again. She would submit to Gravillac. And if she were cold, though compliant, would he not soon find her tiresome and let her go? And if her coldness should enrage him? What grief could he visit upon her that was crueler than her own painful memories?

"André!" she cried again—and the word echoed mournfully in the silent room.

May unfolded slowly into June. The shepherds herded their flocks higher up into the mountains to nibble on the young spring grass, the newborn lambs frolicking and bouncing around their dams. The wheat grew tall enough to catch every passing breeze, and rippled with each soft breath that blew up from the river. Marielle's life fell into a monotonous rhythm. Most of her days were spent on the terrace overlooking the river, Molbert close at hand. Occasionally she could prevail upon him for a game of backgammon; more often she sat with her needlework until weariness overtook her and she closed her eyes, the piece dropping from her hand. She found herself still tired and weak—the fever had assuredly taken its toll. When it rained or the air was cool, she wandered into the kitchen and helped the cook and Louise. This diversion was short-lived. Gravillac, his dark eyes throwing sparks, made it clear she was not to play the servant; besides, the kitchen was hot and suffocating and made her dizzy. Renard was gone most of the day, tending to his diminished holdings. With his royal pension cut and fewer tenants to work his lands and pay rents, his fortunes had declined.

Moreover Marielle soon discovered that Philip of Spain had been paying Gravillac a considerable pension, a practice common to the Spanish King, consolidating his power by maintaining adherents in foreign countries, men of influence who could be helpful. With the disappointing results of the Languedoc campaign, Gravillac had ceased to be useful to Philip and his pension had been cut to the bone. He sat at supper pensive and distracted, but Marielle knew that within his breast he seethed at his predicament, and she took great pains to keep their conversation light, lest she touch the spark to ignite his fury. When he came to her bed at night he was gentle, charming, cajoling, the perfect courtier wooing his lady love. Sometimes he brought her presents—a lace handkerchief, a delicate pair of embroidered gloves, and once a string of milky pearls, creamy and opalescent. She accepted his gifts and attentions with cold indifference, suffered his body with anger and revulsion, turning aside his kisses as best she could. She could not bear his lips on hers. Kisses meant love and warmth and André. She had been right all along: the things that a man did with a woman's body had nothing to do with love. They were merely in response to the basest urges, obscene and repellent. She knew that he chafed in frustration at her reactions, and he grew sullen and petulant at her lack of warmth, renewing his efforts like a wounded suitor. To placate him, she carried the handkerchief, let Louise dress her in each of the half-dozen gowns in the armoire, doused herself with the perfume he had given her, though it was cloying and sweet and made her sick. A great many things made her sick lately, but she refused to think about it, putting unwelcome thoughts out of her mind. She was not a fool, after all—a doctor's daughter! She had been aware for several weeks now that her female cycle had been disrupted, but it was easier to pretend to herself that perhaps her illness, the loss of her virginity and the shocks to her system that followed had upset the normal course of her body's functions. It was not until the June morning that Louise entered her chamber carrying a breakfast tray of rare beef, and she fled the sight and smell of it, leaning over and retching into a hastily-fetched basin, that she forced herself to face the truth. Pale and shaking, her skin tinged with green, she looked into Louise's face and saw the same conclusion written there. Sobbing in despair, she leaned on that ample bosom, hungry for warmth and comfort.

Louise rocked her, and rubbed her back, murmuring soothingly, remembering again her daughter. Adèle had been newly widowed when she learned she was with child; her poor husband had been swept down the river while trying to rescue a friend. Adèle had carried the child in a cloud of grief, finding little comfort in the knowledge that the child would be legitimate, conceived out of love, sanctified by marriage. How much less comfort was there for this trembling girl. The man she loved was dead (shyly, timidly, Marielle had told her of André), the child she carried had been conceived in pain and misery, and the father—ah *Dieu!* The good Lord alone knew what he would do or say when he found out!

Marielle spent the next weeks in despair that deepened with every passing day. She trembled lest Gravillac discover her secret, and was grateful at least that her nausea was confined to the mornings, that she might sit at table with him without gagging over her food. She dreaded the moment she could no longer hide it from him. She might hope that he would then be content to be rid of her, but it seemed far more likely that he would kill her in his rage or, worse, delight in her misery and mock her condition.

And what of the child? Once, in the first few weeks at Quiot, sunk in black despair, she had thought briefly of flinging herself out the wide casement windows to the pavement below, ending once and for all this nightmare she endured, but she could not. It was contrary to everything she had ever been taught; it was against God's will. How much worse to take the life of an innocent creature, the small spark of humanity growing within her womb. No. Though it brought her misery, she could do naught but persevere, for the sake of the child. She began to convince herself yet again that things would be well; he would be glad about the child, he would be kind. She knew he would not marry her—even to give the child a name, but mayhap he would let her go away, to Paris, or back to La Forêt. She might even persuade him to provide a small pension for his child. Yes, all would be well. Had he not made every effort these last weeks to please her, despite her coldness to him?

And then he struck her.

They had been strolling on the terrace in the cool of a June evening, a soft night that hinted at the summer to come. He had admired her in the blue silk gown she wore; it had belonged to his mother, he said, though of course she had worn it with many more petticoats and a stiff farthingale underneath, as was the fashion then.

"And was she pretty?" she asked, surprised. He had not spoken of his mother before, though he mentioned his father often, in tones that made it quite clear that father and son had been at odds with one another.

"She was lovely," he said with a smile. "A saint. I could always count on her to soften up my father when I came home after some escapade. She always allowed me to do what I wanted, knowing it would please me, then kept my secrets from the Noble Sire!"

And did she also allow his childish tantrums? wondered Marielle to herself. "She must have loved you very deeply," she said aloud. "I wonder your father did not sometimes feel excluded. Did he love her very much?"

"What does it matter?" he said. His voice sounded odd in the darkness; she wished she might see his face. "What does it matter?" he repeated. "She was his wife!"

"And that is as it should be!"

"Little fool!" he roared. "What do you know?" and swung at her with such savagery, striking the side of her head with his fist, that she fell heavily to the ground and lay there, gasping for breath while tears of pain sprang to her eyes. Immediately he was contrite, and bent to help her. Angrily she shook off his hands and struggled, unaided, to her feet, swaying slightly and clutching at the balustrade for support. Her head was spinning, her thoughts in a turmoil. She pitied him and wondered what kind of mother the Marquise de Gravillac could have been—to deny her son nothing . . . nothing . . . except first place in her heart.

She held the side of her head where it still throbbed, kneading her palm against her temple to ease the pain. Dear God, he could have killed her! She gasped. He could as easily have struck at her belly and harmed the baby! And what if the child were a boy? Would he hate him? Would he compete with his own son as his father had done? Ah, no! She shuddered.

"I am going to my room," she said, drawing herself up and trying to still the quiver in her voice. "My head hurts! Pray do not trouble me tonight!" She marched determinedly up the terrace to the house, but her heart thudded in fear that he might come raging after her to strike her again, to drag her to her bed, scorning her plea for solitude. He walked slowly behind her up to the chateau. As they reached the large glass doors of the salon, she turned. By the candlelight from the room she saw his face. The look he cast on her surprised and astonished her; she saw tenderness, concern, remorse. She felt bewildered, confused, like a ship on a stormy sea, buffeted and tossed one moment, deceptively becalmed the next. She had to leave this place, or go mad.

Chapter Eight

MARIELLE SAT ON THE TERRACE WITH MOLBERT, THE backgammon table between them. She found it hard to concentrate on the game; her mouth was dry and her hands felt so clammy that the dice seemed reluctant to leave her damp palms. Again she questioned Molbert, the same questions she had posed over and over for the last week, since, reading a grain of sympathy in his face, she had begged his help for her escape. Would the rope ladder be put under her bed during supper? And what of the rope leading from the balustrade down the embankment to the river? Would Gravillac notice it if they strolled the terrace after supper? Had he looked today? Was the boat waiting below, hidden in the rushes? Ah, *Dieu!* Why must it be tonight, with the moon bright and full? Molbert explained impatiently yet again that all was in readiness, that tonight was the only time, since he was leaving for Paris after supper. And besides, he had not wanted to be anywhere near

Quiot when the master found out she was gone. And what about the payment she had promised him? He was not about to risk his neck for nothing, no matter how sorry he felt for her!

She put her hands up to her neck, and unclasped the pearls she wore.

"Oh, no, my lady!" he exclaimed. "Those pearls belonged to his mother! Unless you want him coming after you, you'd best leave them here when you go! If I take them, and he finds out, he'd nail my thumbs to the stable and skin my hide! Oh, no. Not those pearls!"

"But I have nothing else to give you!" said Marielle in dismay.

"What about your ring? It's gold, is it not? I could sell it or melt it down—it's worth something to me!"

Biting her lip, Marielle twisted André's ring on her finger. It was worth a great deal more to her, but if it remained on her finger, she would be trapped here at Quiot.

"André, forgive me!" she whispered, a tear catching in her throat. Pulling the ring off her finger, she thrust it quickly at Molbert; it was best done before she had a chance to change her mind.

Supper was an eternity. Renard was jaunty and spirited, filled with amusing stories, plying her with more wine and keeping her at table till she thought she must scream with impatience. Never had she been more anxious for him to come to her bed and leave it quickly, for her mind was already carrying her down from the window and to the river, and from thence to Lyon and—God willing—Claude. She felt a momentary doubt. If Claude were not there? If she could not find him, where would she go? How would she live?

What matter? 'Twere better to beg in the streets of Lyon, or be a whore, than endure another day in this prison.

Though she chafed with impatience, she lingered overlong at her toilette, suddenly reluctant to have Louise leave too quickly. Dear Louise! Marielle had told her nothing of her plans; Gravillac would be fearsomely cruel if he thought Louise had any part in them. Marielle had come to love the older woman; she was her friend, her comfort, her mother. She said goodnight, then called her back and hugged her tightly, while Louise shook her head at this excess of feeling and wondered if the girl had had too much wine at supper.

She was glad that Gravillac seemed impatient too. He made love to her perfunctorily, indifferently, seeming as anxious to leave her company as she was to see him go. She heard his footsteps plod across the hall, and his door slam. Good! That meant that in all likelihood he would sleep now, rather than going below to walk the terrace as he was sometimes wont to do on these warm summer nights.

Swiftly she extinguished the last few candles and dashed to the open casement. She was in luck. The moon was behind a thick roll of clouds. If she made haste, she could reach the river before the sky cleared. She hurried to the armoire and rummaged through until she found her own clothes, the homespuns she had worn to Quiot. She donned them quickly, tucking up the heavy skirt on one side to free her feet for climbing. Under the bed she found the rope ladder. Bless Molbert! She tied one end of the heavy knotted cord to the window frame, and played out the other end to the ground, holding her breath lest one of the heavy knots

should swing against a windowpane below, and shatter
the glass noisily. It was a pity she could not use the door
and the staircase, but the door was heavy and creaked,
and the sound would be too close to Gravillac's room.
And there might be a servant about in the passageway.
Best not to chance it. Carefully she swung her leg over
the sill and eased herself out the window, her feet
finding the first of the knots. She hung suspended there
for a moment, listening. The warm night was alive with
sounds. Crickets chirped loudly, and from the river
came the croaking and singing of a chorus of frogs;
their harmonies carried clearly through the night air,
heavy with the scents of linden and honeysuckle. She
took two more steps down, her feet searching out the
vital knots, then stopped, gasping. One of her heavy
shoes had slipped off her foot, and went clattering to
the pavement below. Ah, *Dieu!* Surely someone would
have heard that! She strained her ears and peered into
the darkness. Nothing. With a sigh of relief, she
continued her descent, wincing as the rough rope
scraped her bare foot. Reaching the terrace at last, she
dropped to her knees, searching frantically for the
missing shoe. She cast a glance at the sky; the clouds
seemed ready to break, the moon would soon illumi-
nate the whole garden. She would have to hurry to
reach the grassy terrace overlooking the river. At last!
Her fingers touched the shoe, and she slipped it quickly
back onto her foot. She sped through the garden,
wishing Molbert had told her where on the balustrade
he would tie the rope; she would have to search the
whole long line of balusters in the dark. She began to
run her hands along the stone railing, seeking, anxious.

"You will not find it tonight, I fear!"

She whirled in panic as the moon burst from the

clouds, silvering the implacable form of Renard de Gravillac. His eyes were unreadable. She choked back a sob of disappointment.

"In the name of God," she begged piteously, "let me go!"

"Ah, no, my dove, I have not tired of you yet!"

She drew herself up, proud, imperious. "Then know I loathe and despise you! Your every touch makes my flesh crawl! I pray each night that you will not come to me, and when you do, I am filled with disgust and horror. I can only endure you by praying to *le Bon Dieu* for strength, by dreaming of André, while you stain the virtue that was meant for him alone! Do you think I did aught but laugh at you—playing the eager suitor, making a mockery of love?"

Seething, he grabbed her fiercely by the shoulders, his rage boundless. Strangely, she felt no fear, only contempt.

"And will you beat me now, you coward, you debaucher of women?" she spat, her voice heavy with scorn.

He seized her fiercely by one arm and began to drag her toward the chateau, his brain whirling.

Damn the wench, he thought. Her words stung him, wounded his pride. He had been kind to her, gentle, far more patient than he had ever been with any woman. And yet she lay there, night after night, cold and unresponsive, avoiding his kisses and making him feel foolish, frustrating his every attempt to arouse her. And there was something more. He had begun to look forward to her company at supper as much as he hungered for her in bed. There was something so honest, so direct in her temperament that she was incapable of dissembling. Just as she never hid her revulsion in the bedroom (which hurt him mightily), she could not hide her enthusiasm and interest when they engaged in spirited discussions. She was wise and well-spoken, and he knew that somehow his admiration had long since deepened into feelings that were new to him. He had wanted to please her. He had looked at her soft belly, her nurturing breasts, and wondered if she could bear him sons. He had even toyed with the idea of marrying her. Now here she was trying to leave, heaping scorn upon him, challenging his rage. He felt helpless, impotent. Well, by God, he'd make her pay, and pay again! If he could not win her love, he would see that she played his game! No slip of a girl was going to confound him, wrench his heart, scorn his manhood!

He dragged her, protesting, up the wide stairs, pushing aside a worried Louise who, filled with dread, had run to the landing at the first sounds of trouble in the garden. He swept up a lighted candelabra in the hall, and pulled Marielle to her room, flinging her inside with venom in his eyes. Then he put down the candles, locked the door firmly and turned on Marielle, his face a mask of cold rage and vengeance. Now she knew fear, as she never had before, fear for herself, for the baby. She longed to take back the words she had hurled at him outside, words that seemed not to have hurt him, but only inflamed his fury. Swiftly, he tore off his clothes and stood naked before her; his power and force were unmistakable.

"Well?" he said, in a voice that was cold and hard, dangerously so. "Well?" It was a command, not a question.

Her eyes searched his face, terror gnawing at her insides, as she sought even a spark of pity in that dark visage. There was no pity there, no warmth. She suddenly felt beaten, numbed. With trembling fingers, she loosed her garments and let them fall to the floor, feeling helpless and vulnerable. His desire as strong as his anger, he grabbed her roughly in his arms and bent to her mouth. She turned her face away; his kiss caught her on her cheek, now stained with shame and humiliation.

"No! Curse you!" he roared. "I will have your kisses!" The words were measured, angry, determined. One hand went around her waist, pressing her body so tightly to his loins that she shuddered at the contact. The other hand swept behind her head, clutching savagely at her curls and pulling her head back until she gasped in pain. He took her mouth then, cruelly, possessively, forcing her lips apart and pressing hard, harder, while she felt his passion mounting. Abruptly, he picked her up and threw her roughly on the bed. Ripping her legs apart, he entered her with brutal force. She cried out. She was used to his lovemaking by now—repellent, distasteful, something to be ignored, endured, that was all. But this was different. There was no love here, no ardor—only hatred, the desire to punish. He took her viciously, cruelly, and when she tried feebly to wriggle away, he put his hands beneath her hips and forced her body ever closer to his heaving loins, till she felt she must scream out in torment.

It was a night filled with pain and terror, of unspeakable acts and brutal assaults. When he left her chamber in the morning, she prayed for death, that she might forever be joined with André.

July was hot, the air heavy and close. Not a breeze blew from the river, not a breath stirred the ripening wheat. Marielle spent her days like a sleepwalker, numb, defeated. All the spirit seemed to have drained out of her. The heat, her existence, the child—they sapped every ounce of strength from her body. Molbert had returned from Paris and by the look on his face, the way he avoided her eyes, she knew he had betrayed her. She demanded André's ring back, but he insisted he no longer had it, and besides, he had done what she paid him to do—the ladders had been there, hadn't they? She had not the strength to argue; she hardly had tears left to weep anymore.

She still had the freedom of Quiot during the day, though she was watched more carefully, and at night Gravillac locked her in her room, with a guard posted on the terrace below. She and Renard no longer dined together, and when he came to her bedchamber the scenes were repetitions of the night she had tried to escape. Each time, some small new humiliation, some fresh cruelty, until she felt stripped of her dignity and pride, and obeyed his orders like a whipped dog. She no longer wept; she no longer blushed.

She began to wonder how long she could deceive him about her condition. It had been easy enough at first to put him off for a few days every month, claiming female disability so he would not guess. Now she had begun to fill out slightly, her breasts fuller, her hips rounder and softer. She feared for the child when Gravillac should notice the changes, and one thought tormented her to the core of her being: he would never let her go. Never.

Gravillac lived in his own world of torment, chafing and dissatisfied. He sought in vain a sense of victory, a feeling of triumph in his power over her. Did she not do his bidding? Did she not bend to his every whim, surrendering her mouth to his kisses, though hatred burned in her eyes? Still his discontent gnawed at him. He knew, with a certainty that only increased his anger and cruelty, that though she submitted without a struggle, he was—for the first time in his life—being denied what he wanted. He could break her spirit and ravage her body. He could never have her heart.

Chapter Nine

HE SEEMED TO SWIM UP FROM A GREAT DEPTH, HIS BODY on fire, his lungs reluctant to function. He gulped great mouthfuls of air, feeling the searing pain race through his shoulder and end in a throbbing at the base of his neck. With great difficulty he opened his eyes. There were stripes, blue and red and gold, nothing but stripes above his head. It seemed peculiar, yet vaguely familiar. He frowned, trying to clear his thoughts, closed his eyes, then opened them again. The stripes were gone. In their place was a face, a young grinning face bisected by large mustaches, the whole surmounted by flowing curls in the most preposterous shade of orange. The face was familiar too, but recollection took too much effort, and his head ached. He groaned aloud. The grin deepened.

"*Mon Dieu*, André, I thought you would sleep through the whole month of May!"

He laughed unsteadily, a hoarse grunt that seemed

not to come from his own tortured chest, closed his eyes and slept again. When next he woke, the stripes were still there, but now he knew them for what they were, the canopied roof of a military tent, a Royal tent. Louis! La Forêt! He struggled to rise. Jean-Auguste, Baron de Narbaux, he of the remarkable curls, rushed to help his friend, to press him gently back upon the bed.

"Come, come, *mon ami,* would you kill yourself? You have lain here long enough while I played nurse-maid to your half-dead carcass! I would not see my effort wasted now!"

André rubbed his forehead and winced as his fingers came in contact with the tenderness of a freshly-healing wound.

"What took you so long?" he growled. "Had you come in good time, mayhap my head would not feel so swollen!"

"The Huguenots were more difficult than Richelieu had anticipated. We swept down the Rhône, and the towns fell easily, sometimes without a fight, but even capitulation takes time. *Mon Dieu,* André, you should have seen that army! Four thousand infantry, five thousand men on horseback, four of the finest Italian cannon that the Piedmont could provide!"

He stopped as a young page brought in a flagon of steaming broth, and beamed his approval as André sipped the healing liquid.

"He wept, you know. The Cardinal. When we met the remnants of your forces retreating from La Forêt. He wept. I've never known a man to cry like a woman the way that one does! And made his flowery speech to Louis, the way he always does, about the bravery of all those fine men, but I think he was furious about the

Chevalier. The King was more mournful than usual, whether because of his poor judgment in choosing du Trémont for the campaign, or because he does not look forward to the wailing of his newly-widowed cousin, I could not tell! We knew you were alive. Several of your men saw your horse go down during the battle. *Eh, bien!* It did not take us long to avenge your defeat! A cannon has a loud voice! And Bonfleur seemed to have placed most of his musketeers on the western parapet. What are you grinning about, you big ape?" he exclaimed, as André began to chuckle.

"I am grinning at a fine jest, the way to twist the tail of a rattlesnake!" He fell silent, thinking. Gravillac. And remembering Gravillac made him recall more. An angel's face, a ripe mouth and misty green eyes that looked at him with trust. Marielle! With a start, he sat upright and felt a thousand agonies in his chest and shoulder, ripping a cry of pain from his lips. Alarmed, Narbaux rushed to still his friend.

"And La Forêt!" gasped André through clenched teeth. "What happened to La Forêt? The town, the fortress!" His blue eyes burned urgently into Narbaux's face.

"Why, we destroyed them!" said Narbaux, mystified. "Barrault, Tapié, the other nobles, came out and handed their swords to Louis. Vautier was killed. Gravillac fled. We did not find Bonfleur for days, until one of the guards discovered him wandering through the ruins, all reason gone. The fortress was reduced to rubble. The town—God forgive us all—the town was sacked, although Richelieu swore no orders were ever issued. It was a night, I can tell you! Butchering, raping; they set fire to the houses and trampled the crops and gardens, to make them unusable. They attacked the women, tied up the men and threw them in the river to drown. It was the kind of horror that you expect of mercenaries in Germany and Bohemia; but that French soldiers should visit such cruelty upon French families. . . ." His face mirrored his disgust and revulsion. "The King gave Bonfleur a large pension for reparations, but the old fool hasn't enough wit left to administer it, and his peasants will suffer. Louis exiled all the rest for a time, and cut their pensions. He and the Cardinal are off again, marching the army toward Nîmes and Alès. They left me here to patch you together and send you home, and restore as much order as I can to this town and its unfortunate people."

"But what about the prisoners?" demanded André.

"Ah, *Dieu*, my friend. Whoever of your men were in the cell are gone now. We hardly saved a one. Bonfleur must have stored the gunpowder near the prison, and the whole thing exploded. You were lucky not to be in there. We found you in the courtyard, with a dead man across your body. He very likely saved your life. There were enough fragments in his body to kill half the King's men-at-arms. As it was, I'll wager I dug a dozen pieces of cannonball out of your chest and arm!"

"But what about the dungeon?" André persisted, as Narbaux looked mystified. "There was a small prison within the chateau itself! What happened to the prisoners?"

"André! My friend! Calm yourself! Let me think . . . ah yes. There was a dungeon. Mostly women . . . whores, I remember. They would have been released before the castle was razed, but if they were young enough to satisfy a soldier's lust, they would not have got far." He laughed shortly. "Without a *sou* to show for a night's work!"

André groaned, and clapped his hand over his eyes to hide the tears that threatened to unman him. Marielle! Marielle! If only he had got to the dungeon in time, he might have saved her! He had been overjoyed upon reaching the stable to hear the guard call the old jailer by name . . . Jacques! Of course! It was after noon—the old man had returned to his post. Hastily André had explained to him about Marielle, their marriage, everything. It was too late to release her now, Jacques had said. If they now treated her like a prisoner in the Great Hall, then she was a prisoner. André begged him then—for her sake, for the old doctor's sake—to put him in the small dungeon with her, that they might at least be together. He remembered crossing the court-yard with Jacques, his heart light, his step jaunty; then chaos, and darkness. Oh, Marielle! The thought of her sweet innocence at the mercy of a ravaging army overwhelmed him. My poor Marielle! The bitter tears scalded his face; he wept unashamedly. Narbaux, shaken by his friend's grief, could only turn away, helpless, until André recovered himself.

"Here," he said gruffly, thrusting a cup of wine into André's hand. "A woman?"

André nodded.

"Who was she?"

"My wife."

"Mon Dieu! Wife? You? Who romped through half the bed-chambers of France, leaving a trail of broken hearts? She must be remarkable!"

"I want her found. Marielle Saint-Juste. The doctor's daughter. They know her well in La Forêt. She must be here!"

"Ease yourself, my friend," said Narbaux, settling André upon his pillows. "You have been close to death these past weeks, closer than you may know. I would not see the poor girl widowed before we have found her!"

André smiled gratefully at Narbaux. A great weariness overtook him. He was about to close his eyes, when a sudden thought struck him. "Jean-Auguste," he said hoarsely, reluctant to say what was in his thoughts, "find the priest who married us. If Marielle were . . . if he had to say the words . . . over her . . . body, mayhap he would have recognized her. . . ." He closed his eyes and slept.

Narbaux proved a diligent friend. For days he scoured La Forêt, sending out his men to question the townspeople, to inquire of the remnants of the King's army who yet remained behind: had they seen Marielle Saint-Juste? Had they found a pretty girl with chestnut brown hair? He searched the *hôtel de ville,* which had been turned into an infirmary for the wounded and convalescent. It was useless. Marielle seemed to have vanished from La Forêt.

The priest was found. Yes, of course he remembered André and Marielle. No, he did not remember burying her, but there were so many who needed him in that long night of death and horror. He would say a prayer for her, and for Monsieur's recovery, and should Comte du Crillon wish it, he could provide him with a copy of the marriage document that he had been careful to enter into the church's registry.

Narbaux found a woman who knew Marielle and had been in the small *donjon,* and he brought her to André; he questioned her closely, his eyes burning with the fever of dread. She could not help him. She had been asleep until the soldiers came to free the prisoners, and thus she would not have seen when Marielle was brought in. Her eyes dark with the remembrance of the horror, she told him of the things the soldiers had done, how the women had screamed and struggled, how she was too fearful for her own safety to have noticed if Marielle were there or not. Her voice rose shrilly with the terrible recital of the night's agonies, until André could bear no more, and dismissed her abruptly, motioning Narbaux to give her a few crowns.

Meanwhile, André ate and slept and felt his strength returning. He still found it difficult to lift his left arm, and the piece of steel that had passed through his lung had left a wound that still made his breath catch with too much exertion, but he was young and his body was strong. There came a morning that Jean-Auguste entered the tent and found him dressed, and puffed with satisfaction, although, in truth, he wobbled slightly as he swaggered back and forth. He was impatient to be out and, in spite of Narbaux's protestations, insisted on being taken to the ruins of the chateau where, leaning heavily upon his friend, he examined the rubble of the dungeon, the gutted stable. Thoughts of Marielle crowded his mind; he felt suddenly exhausted. Narbaux led him gently back to his bed, wondering if the pain he saw in those blue eyes came from the body or the heart.

But the following day, he was up again and dressed. This time he wished to talk to Bonfleur who, after all, knew Marielle well and had been in the chateau that day. Perhaps he had seen her. No matter that the man had lost his reason; if he had but one lucid moment it might be enough for André to get answers. They found Bonfleur in a small cottage where he lived with one of his former tenants and his wife. The old man was sitting in the garden, idly plucking the petals from a rose he had picked. André had seen him a few times at Versailles, and then at La Forêt, but he was not prepared for the wreck of a man before him. Bonfleur's hair had gone white, hanging loose and matted to his shoulders. The flesh sagged on his hollow cheeks, and one eye twitched; his fingers shook constantly as they worried the rose, and he muttered to himself. He had sustained a terrible blow to the head, explained Narbaux, but André, remembering the old man's distraction at La Forêt even before the battle, wondered if his loss of reason were not God's way of shielding him from unendurable pain.

André began to speak then of Languedoc, of the nobles, the quarrels with the King, trying to lead Bonfleur down a familiar path in which his memory might be suddenly awakened. The old man sat quietly, his eyes staring and vacant, his hands still trembling. As André described the battle that day, he began nervously to rub his palms together, clasping and unclasping his hands. Suddenly, with a sob, he burst out, half rising from his bench.

"Oh the deaths! All the bright young people! The waste . . . .the waste . . ." His voice trailed off, and he sank again into his own world, lost and distant.

"Marielle!" said André. "Marielle Saint-Juste!" The old man's eyes were blank, hidden behind a mist. André shook him roughly by the shoulders. "Do you not remember? The doctor! Marielle!"

Bonfleur smiled. "Yes! Marielle! Mark my words, she'll be a great beauty some day. I vow I'm tempted to marry her myself when she grows up!"

André turned away impatiently. Narbaux put a restraining hand on his friend's arm, then addressed Bonfleur.

"But she married. Remember? The day of the King's attack. Can you remember?"

Bonfleur sighed deeply and frowned at Narbaux. He looked then at André, and the mist seemed suddenly to lift from his eyes.

"Crillon!" he exclaimed. "Is it you?"

With a cry of relief, André knelt quickly at the old man's side. "Do you remember Marielle?" A nod of recognition. "Do you remember that we married?" Again the nod. "Now, think, man! Did you see her again that day?" The old man closed his eyes, pain written large across the face.

"Ah!" he groaned. "Alas! Alas!" He opened his eyes, and André could see, with rising panic, that reality was slipping away.

"Bonfleur—please!" he said desperately. "Marielle! Remember!"

"She is lost to you forever!"

"Is she dead?"

Once again the curtain dropped over the old man's eyes.

"Is she dead?!!" shouted André, beside himself. "Speak, man!!" The breath caught in his throat as a sudden spasm gripped his chest. He began to cough violently, doubling over on the ground. With a cry, Narbaux sprang to his side, fearful lest he rupture his lung.

"Come away, André! *Nom de Dieu!*" With Narbaux's help, André rose to his feet, still gasping. Bonfleur was rocking back and forth on his bench, wringing his hands in agitation, his eyes rolling wildly in his head. The farmer's wife came rushing out of the cottage to stand near him and try to quiet his unhappy moaning. Narbaux pulled anxiously on André's sleeve, leading him quickly out of the garden. As they passed through the gate, they could still hear the old man's tortured cry.

"Forever! Lost forever!"

There seemed no longer any purpose for remaining at La Forêt. It was time to go home to Vilmorin. In spite of André's protests, Jean-Auguste sent along half a dozen of his own men, to see to André's needs on the long trip and, quietly, to restrain his friend from exerting himself beyond his still-limited strength. They traveled through countrysides sweet and rich with the sights and smells of June. Every breathtaking vista was an affront to André's sensibilities: if Marielle were dead, such beauty ought not to exist. The warm sienna tones of the rich earth recalled for him the glory of her hair; the dew-sparkled rose at dawn reminded him of her sweet mouth, lips parted in welcome. He rode through the sunlight, her face ever before him, his heart black with despair, and envied Bonfleur his oblivion.

Chapter Ten

CLOTHILDE LANCOURT SMILED AT HER REFLECTION IN THE
large Venetian mirror. She tugged at a curl half-hidden
under her linen cap, pulling the golden tress out until it
curled beguilingly in front of her ear. She pushed up the
sleeves of her chemise until her dimpled elbows
showed. She laced again the bodice of her jerkin,
pulling her waistline in and pushing her full breasts
upward until a rounded *décolletage* peeped above her
neckline, then accented the line even more by loosening the drawstring and lowering the chemise almost
to the tips of her breast. The snugness of the lacings
made her catch her breath, and she wished she were a
little more slender, but, by and large, she was satisfied
with the effect.

The master was coming home. One of Baron Narbaux's men had ridden in ahead last night to announce
his arrival, and Vilmorin had been in a frenzy of activity
all day as Clothilde directed the polishing of the marble
stairs, the airing and dusting of the rooms, the scrub-

bing of floors and windows. The chateau was redolent with the scents of roasting meats and pastries bursting with ripe June cherries. In the little smokehouse behind the kitchens, the cook was busily preparing sausages from the freshly butchered hog, and Clothilde had sent Grisaille to the chalk caves to fetch a large keg of wine and store it in the cool cellar.

She herself had seen to the master's room. The floor had been scrubbed until the tiles fairly sparkled and the heavy velvet bedhangings and coverlet had been shaken and beaten unmercifully, filling the kitchen courtyard with clouds of dust. She rubbed the fine oak furniture until it glistened, and filled the room with roses from the garden. Every garment in the armoire had been aired and brushed by her own hands; she handled the doublets lovingly and marveled at the shoulders that would fit such a span of fabric. They said he was handsome, Grisaille and the rest, and she felt a tingle of anticipation. Perhaps he was what she had been waiting for. They said he was no stranger to women. She flung herself down on the bed, clutching his doublet to her bosom, feeling the soft velvet coverlet beneath her, and, closing her eyes, gave herself up to her fantasies. She knew how to please a man, and if he was as attractive as they said, she would please herself in the bargain. Moreover, he was important at Court. They said he had distinguished himself at La Forêt, against great odds—and in spite of the Chevalier's stupidity—and the King admired him very much. To appear at Versailles in his company would give importance to her at once. And, once at Court, who knew what liaisons she might form? She thought with bitterness of her father. How she would make him crawl then, when she was the toast of Paris! She would enter his shop, and call him "storekeeper" and make him beg for her trade! He would regret the way he had treated her, the sanctimonious old hypocrite! He was rich. He had made his money selling diamonds to the aristocracy, cheating them when he could, fawning on them for favors, hiding his profits from the tax assessors. He had even bought a title! Baron Lancourt he was now. And he called her whore!

She thought then of Perrot. Even now, after all these years, she could not regret what she had done. Her father had arranged a marriage with a threadbare viscount, who was attracted to her by her large dowry as much as anything else, but he came from good stock and had fine connections at Court. It would have been an advantageous match. And then . . . Perrot. She had not thought she could love anyone so deeply; she would have followed him anywhere. She even persuaded herself that he might eventually marry her; when he abandoned her, she wept, knowing herself barren and bereft even of the child she might have had to remember him by. And her father called her whore, and disowned her, and went to visit his mistress!

She was glad now for her barrenness. It had been easier to manage through the years not having to worry about bringing a brat into the world. She certainly would not have wanted a child by that silk merchant in Vouvray! He had been kind enough to her and she did not regret the years she had spent with him, but a child would have meant marriage, and the thought of spending her life as a shopkeeper's wife revolted her. She was out for bigger game. She had been raised in the city; she could put on airs as well as the next one, and a man with a title was just the benefactor she needed. She had a few crowns and lengths of silk put aside, and twenty-five was not too old to catch a good title. She'd take marriage, or whatever she could get! When Grisaille, who was the silk merchant's friend, had mentioned that the old housekeeper at Vilmorin had died, Clothilde persuaded him to install her in her place.

And now Comte du Crillon was coming home to recuperate. He would need nursing, tender care and a fine soft bosom to rest his weary head upon. Catching sight of herself again in the mirror, she laughed aloud. Perhaps he would find her restless hips more to his liking! She laughed again. He would be her *passe-partout* to Versailles!

The days grew warm and drowsy. The grapes flowered, dense clusters of fragrant green blossoms, and the hum of a thousand bees filled the air. André spent his days in the fields, wandering up and down the long rows of staked vines, examining the leaves, watching the sky for signs of bad weather, agonizing when it did not rain and suffering when it rained too much. His wounds troubled him less and less, and he forgot he was a soldier and settled comfortably into the life of farmer and landowner. It felt good at the end of a long day to fall into bed, too tired and bone-weary to think of Marielle, except briefly in those few moments before sleep overtook him. Then the memory of her sweetness and purity flooded his soul and pierced his heart, and he welcomed sleep gladly. In the daytime, he would stand on the rise of a hill and look out over his lands that rose in gently undulating fields, long rows of vines rolling away softly from the river valley. He had described this very scene to Marielle in prison, and he could no longer gaze upon it without the pain of remembrance. Then it was that he would bend to his tasks with more diligence, eager to drive out her memory and be at peace. Clothilde was a great help and comfort to him. He had commended Grisaille on his wise selection of the housekeeper. She seemed always to know when he came from the fields, his throat dry, his spirits low. She would be waiting with a cool draught of ale or a pitcher of his own sweet wine, and a smile and a cheerful word to refresh his soul. Sometimes she came out to him as he labored, bearing fresh sweet fruits, or a dampened cloth to mop his sweat-stained brow. He began to notice her more carefully: a comely girl, a little plump perhaps, with pale blond curls that caught the sunlight. She seemed not to notice his perusal, but bore his eyes unself-consciously. He found it charming. In the evening, there was always fresh clothing waiting in his room, and Clothilde always scampered shyly away as he started to strip off his dirt-stained garments, which made him laugh aloud and tease her about it. She reminded him of Marielle in her innocence.

One afternoon, the grooms had trouble with a gray mare, and André rushed to help, quite forgetting his injuries. It took him and Grisaille together to wrestle the mare to the ground, but the exertion wrenched André's shoulder, and he took to his bed early that night, well-fortified with a mug of spiced wine that Clothilde had thoughtfully provided. It was a long and agonized night; sleep eluded him and his shoulder throbbed unmercifully. His thoughts turned continually to Marielle, while he tasted her kisses in remembrance and his loins ached with a longing he had not known in many weeks. By morning he was short-tempered and testy, filled with self-pity and vague hungers. When Clothilde bustled in carrying his breakfast and a pitcher of water for shaving, he snapped at her and called for a hot tub to soak in. She looked at him oddly, as though gauging his mood, but said nothing and hurried from the room. When she returned with servants carrying the tub, he was already standing at his shaving mirror, the collar of his nightshirt thrown wide, the fine gold hairs on his chest shimmering in the light. She dismissed the servants, but remained herself, watching him shave. Curse the wench! he thought. He was feeling foul-tempered enough, his shoulder twinging painfully, without the added discomfort of her eyes on him. He reached up with his left hand, meaning to hold the skin taut as he shaved his right cheek; a stab of pain shot through his left shoulder and he winced, jerking his head and nicking his cheek with the sharp razor. Damn! He swung round to read the look on her face; her pale eyes were inscrutable. She smiled gently.

"You are in pain this morning, Monsieur. Let me help you." Was she laughing at him? Her mood was so strange. She led him gently to an armchair and sat him down, wrapping a fine cloth around his shoulders and spreading fresh lather on his face. Her hands as she wielded the razor were deft and sure; he relaxed in the chair and allowed himself to enjoy this unexpected luxury. He had never noticed the scent she wore; now the sweetness of roses filled his nostrils and made his breath catch. She had rolled up her sleeves, and he saw the soft roundness of her arms, the little hollows at her elbows. He had never realized before how low she wore her chemise, nor how full and inviting her breasts were. As she bent to her task, the closeness of her body filled his heart with a throbbing that quite outweighed the ache in his shoulder. He found the excitement rising within him. Surely she knew the effect she had on him!

He glanced quickly at her face. She seemed still to be concentrating on her work, unaware of his eyes on her, the way his pulse had begun to race. He did not doubt her innocence, yet he could not shake the vague feeling that she was laughing at him.

The shave finished, she stepped back, pulling the cloth from his shoulders. He stood up and strode to the tub, kicking off his slippers, then giving her time to leave before stripping off his nightshirt. She did not move. He thought perhaps she did not understand. He put his hands on his shoulders and began to gather up the fabric of his garment, as though he would slip it over his head; still she did not move. He frowned. The pale gray eyes that stared into his were cool and steady. Damn her! So much the worse for her! He whipped off his nightshirt and stood naked before her, expecting now the blush, the shy gasp, the fleeing footsteps. She could hardly mistake his intentions, the intensity of his desire. She stood her ground, and now the gray eyes held an answer that was unmistakable. With a groan that bespoke his longing, his great need, he swept her into his arms and carried her to the bed, pouring into his lovemaking all the hungers and frustrations and griefs of the past months. It was clear from her response that she was no innocent, but it hardly mattered. She was here and he needed her. If only his beloved Marielle could speak to the deepest recesses of his soul, Clothilde at least could soothe the hungers of his body.

Toward the end of June, Narbaux returned from La Forêt. He was filled with news. The King was about to sign a treaty with the Huguenots at Alès, the hostilities were at an end and it was fervently hoped that henceforth all the nobility would bend to the common goal: the strengthening of France among the family of nations, and the concomitant weakening of Spain's hold on Europe. Louis would shortly return to Paris, after the signing of the treaty; Richelieu would stay on until August, to see that the religious and civil rights of both Catholics and Protestants were respected. Bonfleur had died without ever regaining his reason again. There was no news of Marielle. Narbaux was pleased to see André looking so well—one look at the fond glance Clothilde turned on her master gave him the cause. When she had gone, he chuckled aloud, his bright orange mustaches bobbing with merriment.

"It would seem, my friend, that you have found a cure that never crossed my mind! I'll wager that rounded wench is a nice handful!"

"There are some things a man finds hard to do without, Jean-Auguste, though I must confess I should have preferred not to involve myself with Clothilde."

Narbaux snickered at this, but André shook his head, his face serious.

"I speak truly, Jean-Auguste. You should know me by now. I have always avoided, if I could, bedding a woman from my own estates. It becomes difficult and tiresome. What is to happen when finally we tire of one another?"

"It would seem, André, from the look on her face, that she might desire something more permanent!"

André's blue eyes flashed. "Marriage? Ridiculous! She cannot think such a thing! I have not pretended feelings to her that do not exist! She fills my needs, that is all."

"And what are you to her?" asked Narbaux.

"She was no virgin when she came to my bed. I feel

no obligation nor loyalty to her. And frankly, *mon ami,* she leaves my bed satisfied. Perhaps I fill her needs as well!"

"Arrogant dog!" laughed Narbaux, cuffing the side of André's head. His voice dropped. "And what of Marielle, my friend? Do you still think of her?"

André turned away, and when he spoke, his voice was muffled.

"Constantly. She haunts my every moment. I feel the pain of her loss more sharply now than I ever did. Sometimes, in bed with Clothilde, I try to imagine that she is Marielle." He laughed bitterly. "Then she whispers something coarse and vulgar, and I remember how Marielle blushed at my slightest glance. . . . Oh my friend! Give not your heart away lightly in love, lest you live with a ghost as I do!"

"Still," said Narbaux, "it is in this world that you must dwell. If I were you, I would proceed cautiously with Clothilde. A woman is a peculiar creature, more especially if she has determined to catch a husband!"

"Then I shall tell her what I tell you. As long as there is a shadow of hope that Marielle may be alive, there will be no other Comtesse du Crillon!"

"I wish you well, my friend. I'm bound for my chateau. I only hope my vines are as robust as yours! Come and visit me, if you can tear yourself away from Mademoiselle *la Docteur!*"

In mid-July a messenger rode in from Paris. His Majesty Louis XIII, King of France, sent his compliments and trusted that Monsieur le Comte was quite recovered from his wounds. His Majesty wished to thank his loyal subject for numerous services to the realm, and Monsieur le Comte was forthwith invited to come to Versailles, in the company of his great and good friend and comrade-in-arms Jean-Auguste, Baron de Narbaux. It would please His Majesty greatly to enjoy their companionship for a week or two. Furthermore, it had come to His Majesty's attention that Comte du Crillon had been recently bereaved, and it was His Majesty's fervent hope that the good fellowship of the Court, and the many charming ladies therein, would provide surcease to his sorrows.

It seemed a good enough idea. The vineyards were thriving, and their soundness in the next few weeks would be as much in the hands of *le Bon Dieu* as any *vignerons* in the district. He had begun to weary of Clothilde; having dropped her mask of innocence, she had become simply another conquest—and a bawdy one at that. He laughed at her coarse jokes and romped unrestrainedly in her bed, but the contrast to his memory of Marielle disturbed him vaguely. And there was something more. Despite his attempts to be frank with her regarding his intentions, she had begun to be possessive, jealous of the time he was not with her and imperious with the rest of the servants, as though she already fancied herself mistress of Vilmorin instead of just housekeeper. He regretted ever having taken her to bed, and then, recalling her cool gray eyes that first day, laughed ruefully and wondered which of them had been the seducer. Still, it was clear that she cared for him a great deal more than he fancied her; his conscience chafed him, knowing that she might in all innocence have mistaken his great need for love. A week or two at Versailles would give him an opportunity to sort out his thoughts; when he returned it would be soon enough to tell her gently that the affair was at an end.

The long ride to Versailles was a pleasant one. Narbaux was in high spirits. He had not been at Court since January, having accompanied the King on his Italian campaign, and there were several lovely acquaintances he was anxious to see again. André laughed and reminded him that since Versailles had no more than two or three dozen rooms, the company would be small and the only sport he could expect would be a rousing hunt or two. The most charming ladies of the Court would scarcely choose to ruin their complexions in a day of falconry out in the open, and unless Narbaux favored some buxom Amazon, the pickings at Versailles would be slim. Of course he, André, would manage to ferret out the gold among such dross, and if he were so inclined, he might deign to share his find with Jean-Auguste. So, laughing, they rode through the flat marshy landscape to Versailles-au-Val-de-Galie. It was one of the King's favorite retreats. He had hawked there as a boy when his father was still King; at length, tiring of the long ride back to Paris after the hunt, he had built a small lodge there. It was a pretty little chateau, all red brick and white stone, the roof tiled with blue slate. It was neither large nor elegant, but it served the King's purposes well, when life at the Louvre, or Fontainebleau or even Blois became too formal and demanding. Here he could hunt and ride, and indulge his passion for cooking, happy in the simplicity and isolation of a country squire's life. Here a man wore his sword for fencing matches, not for parading around like a peacock, and a large hat was for keeping the sun out of his eyes, not for elaborate bowing and scraping, plumes dragging on the ground.

Louis received them in the main gallery, holding out

his hand in welcome to André after the latter's formal bow.

"Ah, Crillon! *Mon vieux!* I am glad to see you up and about," he said, a warm smile lighting up his usually morose countenance. "I should have taken it amiss if my precipitous choice of the Chevalier had cost the realm your services. I should perhaps have trusted in Richelieu's judgment, but never mind. That is none of your concern." He laughed ruefully. "He will remind me of it often enough, of that I have no doubt! I have heard many accounts of your bravery at the walls of La Forêt; thanks be to God, we were able to turn your defeat into victory, though I understand that Bonfleur's unpreparedness for our attack was in part your doing."

André rubbed his chest in remembrance, and laughed. "I had not thought de Gravillac would be so gullible, though I can hardly regret he was so easily satisfied!"

"You have served us well, Crillon, and will, we are sure, proffer your sword once again should France have need of your services. I have already rewarded Narbaux here for his help in the campaign, but I preferred to see you in good health before announcing my decision." He sighed deeply, his thin shoulders heaving. "I must confess to a pang of jealousy. No man should be so newly risen from his sickbed and look as robust as you do! And no man should be as bedeviled by doctors as I am!"

In truth, though Louis was three years André's junior, his constant bouts of ill health had left him thin and sickly, his bony nose and jaw jutting out from a pallid face, making him seem far older than the two young men before him.

"May *le Bon Dieu* smile upon Your Majesty," said André graciously. "All France will welcome the return of your good health!"

Louis beamed with pleasure. "I have asked Cardinal Richelieu to issue letters patent conferring upon you the title of Baron de Verger, together with a pension of three hundred thousand *livres* a year."

Surprised, André dropped to one knee, bowing low before the King, too overwhelmed to do much but murmur his thanks and gratitude. Narbaux's smiling approval added to the King's well-being, and he helped André to his feet, embracing him warmly.

The door burst open, and Anne of Austria swept in. Surprised to see her husband, she stopped, then curtsied quickly to him, her blond curls bobbing.

"Ah, Louis!" she said, a wicked gleam in her blue eyes. "Surely you do not intend to steal André away from the ladies of the Court!"

The shaft hit its mark. Stammering, the King released André and turned away, absorbed suddenly in some vista beyond the high windows. The Queen turned her dazzling smile upon André, who bowed low, surprised again at the innocent young face that masked such animosity. It was no secret in the Court that the royal couple were estranged. Since the plot against the King's life in '26, a plot in which rumors held that the Queen, once widowed, would marry the King's brother Gaston, they had few dealings with one another. Though the Queen had always denied any complicity in the plot, Louis remained suspicious, his pride as a husband wounded more severely than his sense of outrage as the monarch. Anne did nothing to allay his fears, surrounding herself with friends and courtiers who were openly rude and hostile to the King. André found himself hard-pressed to strike a balance between the two camps, but his heartfelt respect for the King's innate decency inclined him towards Louis.

The Queen nodded to Narbaux, who bowed, then turned her attention back to André.

"My dear," she said in her shrill voice. "I hear you have lost a wife! How careless of you! And before anyone had a chance to see her, to make comparisons with all your other choices!" She stopped, seeing the look of pain on André's face. "Ah, forgive me," she said gently. "I did not mean to cause you grief." She glanced venomously at Louis, who still stared out the window. "I forget that, to some, marriage is a pure and holy state!" She swept imperiously from the room, leaving a red-faced Louis to recover himself as best he might.

Still stammering, he excused himself quickly, and hurried away.

Narbaux shook his head. "If I had to bed that viper, that she-wolf," he said in a low voice, "I too might prefer the company of young boys! But come, my dear Comte du Crillon, Baron de Verger! If your fencing arm is not impaired, let us see if I can win some of that pension of yours! One thousand *livres* for a hit. Agreed?"

"Done!" exclaimed André, and the two friends went to fetch weapons, boasting elaborately to one another about their skills.

The weather was fine and warm, and the days passed quickly, filled with fencing exhibitions and wrestling matches and long rides through the beautiful country-side. In the evening, the company would assemble informally to hear the King play upon his lute or sing one of his own compositions, or the Queen would show the latest dance steps from Paris. André rediscovered one of his former loves, a charming little thing whose husband preferred riding the hounds to his wife, and they dallied away many a warm afternoon in some leafy bower, André playing love ballads to her on his guitar while she plied him with sweetmeats and kisses. It was the kind of indolent life he had always led when away from war or Vilmorin, an artificial existence that catered to his senses but left his soul untouched. It had always satisfied him before. Now he played at love while his heart cried out to Marielle.

The King had arranged a hunt for the entire company. Though André would have preferred a romp on the shores of Love to a gallop through the woods, his absence would have been noted. He contented himself with riding as close as possible to his lady love, on the chance that some opportune moment might present itself, and they could slip away into the woods. It was a lovely morning, the bright sun outshining the glittering assemblage. The Queen, clad in emerald velvet and a magnificent plumed hat, sat her mount regally. She was surrounded by her ladies, many of whom were masked to protect their delicate complexions. The King, in snowy lace and rich embroidery, rode out at the head of the company. He was followed closely by the Grand Falconer, the huntsmen and the bearers, supporting on their padded gauntlets the chained and hooded falcons. Most of the company was mounted on horseback, but a few of the women had chosen to ride in heavy gilded coaches that careened dangerously through the woods as the pace quickened. On they dashed through the trees, the dogs barking and straining at their leashes, the horses' hooves crushing the tender blossoms underfoot. In the distance, a deer would start up, disturbed in his forest glade, and vanish deep into the woods. The bugle sounded and the dogs bayed loudly as the whole company raced headlong through the woods, breaking out from time to time into a sun-dappled glade, dashing back and forth through sunlit paths and shadowed groves.

It had been arranged that the hunt should terminate at a chateau some distance away, where the host, having been alerted to the Royal arrival, had prepared a repast. Passing through a particularly dense copse, André saw the opportunity he had been waiting for. He turned off through a thicket, indicating for her to follow, sure in the knowledge that they would hardly be missed now that the hunt was in full cry. He slowed his horse to a walk, and smiled conspiratorily at his lady; then, finding a soft patch of grass beneath a sweet-smelling tree, he dismounted and helped her from her horse, letting his hands linger on her yielding body in anticipation of the pleasures to follow.

By the time they straggled to the chateau, the wine was flowing and the party was in high spirits. No one, least of all her husband, enthusiastically describing the hunt to their host, seemed to notice their late arrival, nor the high color in her cheeks, nor the grass stains on her skirt that she was at some pains to hide.

It had been an unexpectedly pleasant morning. Feeling pleased with himself and at peace with the world, André called for some wine, aware that the serving wench dimpled prettily at his admiring glance. His blue eyes appraised her over the rim of his goblet, taking in the swelling breast, the milky shoulders, the softly rounded arms. Then he started, and the wine cup clattered to the floor. He seized her roughly by the arm, turning the knuckles of her hand upward to face him.

"Where did you get it?" he said, his voice harsh in his throat.

The laughter in the room had stopped. Terrified, she tried to pull away, to cover with her other hand the small gold ring, embossed with the lion and hound, the bunch of grapes.

"A man gave it to me," she stammered, her voice trembling on the edge of tears.

"Where did he get it?"

"He said a fine lady gave it to him!" she wailed.

"What fine lady?"

"I don't know, monsieur, truly I don't!"

"Who was the man?"

"He did not steal it, my lord! She gave it him!"

"Who was the man?"

"Henri Molbert," she said, her voice barely audible.

André groaned, and looked with stricken eyes at Narbaux, who had rushed to his friend's side.

"Gravillac!" he breathed. "I should have known. I could have guessed . . . the way he looked at her. . . ." He released the girl and jumped up. "I'm for Quiot!"

"Wait, André," said Narbaux, quietly pulling his friend aside. "You cannot go alone. If we swing round through Vilmorin, you can pick up supplies, fresh horses, men and swords. You can hardly guess Gravillac's mood since the Peace of Alès—better to travel prepared!"

"There is nothing to prepare," said André bitterly. "I shall kill him, that is all."

"And risk beheading? You know the Cardinal has forbidden dueling! Think, man! Remember Chapelles and Bouteville, executed for dueling, cut off in the prime of their years . . . and for what? That their pride be unscathed? *Nom de Dieu!* You know not if Marielle is there for certain, nor if Gravillac means to use her merely as a hostage, to regain his place at Court!"

Bowing to Narbaux's wisdom, André hastily took his leave of Their Majesties, explaining only that he thought there might be a chance his wife was still alive, and begging their permission to leave Versailles with Narbaux as soon as they could gather their belongings. He brushed past his paramour of the morning, leaving her stricken and abandoned, and rode like a madman back to Versailles, Narbaux straining desperately to keep up with him. On the ride back to Vilmorin he was silent, his mood unfathomable, until Jean-Auguste, hoping for a response, handed him the ring he had redeemed from the serving girl. André murmured his thanks and slipped the ring on his finger; for the rest, they traveled in silence.

It was twilight by the time they reached Vilmorin; the moon had risen ere, changed and fed and mounted on fresh horses, half a dozen attendants armed and ready, they rode out of Vilmorin, Clothilde's troubled eyes following them.

Chapter Eleven

THEY RODE ALL NIGHT, ANDRÉ SUNK IN THE BLACKNESS OF his thoughts, Jean-Auguste dozing fitfully in the saddle. At dawn, only a few hours from Quiot, Narbaux persuaded a reluctant André to rest for a bit and have a bite of food. They turned off the road, seeking a place to tether the horses, and were startled by a terrible racket, a rattling and clatter that made the horses rear in fright. Before them stood a huge fellow brandishing a large cudgel, his eyes darting wildly from one to the other, taking in the fine nobles, the armed men, then steeling himself for a fight to the death.

Narbaux laughed. "Calm yourself, my good man! We mean you no harm! In God's truth, it is we who have suffered this morrow! The sounds you unleashed have surely cost me a year of my life!"

The man relaxed and swung his staff upright, planting one end firmly in the ground and leaning his weight heavily upon it.

"Your pardons, my lords," he said. "I am but a poor tinker, and these woods are full of bandits and the like who prey upon honest men. Thinking me to sleep for a few hours, I set up my pots and pans to warn me of any approach!" He indicated some dozen or so tin vessels now strewn about the glade, scattered by the horses' hooves. The men dismounted.

"Know you Quiot?" asked André.

"Aye, my lord. It is but a few hours' journey from here. I am newly come from there myself. Monsieur le Marquis had work for me in his kitchen. Fine large kettles he has, but sadly in need of repair!"

"Was there a woman there?" demanded André, his eyes burning.

The man gave a grunt and nodded. "That there was, my lord! A fine lusty one. Not so young anymore, but a good handful for any man. I was minded to catch her in the pantry if I could!"

"No, no, man!" said André impatiently. "A young woman!"

"Aye! The handsome one in the garden."

"With chestnut hair?"

"Shining in the sunlight. A pretty thing she was. Far too grand for me. I'd as soon fill my arms with the wench in the kitchen!"

André turned away, relief flooding his heart. He strode headlong into the woods, unwilling to expose his precarious emotions to his men. Marielle . . . alive! Marielle at Quiot! Damn Gravillac! In all the years their paths had crossed, he had never understood the man's animosity and hatred. He seemed always to be competing with André, vying for favors at the Court or wooing André's women. It had never bothered André; until La Forêt he had felt no ill will toward the man, but in some strange way, Gravillac seemed always to consider them rivals. Perhaps it was Gravillac's way—to see every man's accomplishments as a challenge to his own. Though André had paid him little mind when they had been students at the Academy, he remembered the fierceness with which Gravillac had competed with everyone. Now, for reasons André could not fathom, he had abducted Marielle, made her his prisoner, hoping no doubt to force André to come after her and claim her. Perhaps he felt that the grief and humiliation he caused André was a victory over a hated rival; perhaps he wished to avenge La Forêt. No matter. It was only important that Marielle was alive and well. He saw her as she had been in prison, burnished hair falling softly around her lovely face, sweetness and purity shining in her innocent eyes. He wept for joy and thanked God for her life. He would bring his bride home to Vilmorin.

It was Molbert, glancing out the window on the landing, who first saw André's entourage approaching. Their mantles flapped wildly as they galloped across the flat fields that fronted Quiot; they looked like avenging bats out of Hell. By the time the riders reined in and dismounted on the wide front lawn, their horses foaming and snorting and pawing the earth, Gravillac had been notified and was waiting to greet them on the stone steps leading up to the main door. Hatred smoldered in the depths of his eyes, but he smiled and bowed elaborately.

"Ah, Monsieur le Comte! What a surprise! We had heard, some weeks ago, that you had survived the destruction of La Forêt, but I hardly imagined that Quiot held any charms for you!"

André looked at him coldly. "You have, I believe, something which belongs to me. I would reclaim my property!"

Gravillac sighed wearily, but his eyes were guarded and wary.

"I have already given back half my pension to the King. Can there be more that you would take from me?"

"A woman." Thrust.

"There are many women here. Would you care to make a choice?" asked Gravillac. Parry.

"There is a tinker in the woods. He saw a certain woman!" Blue eyes glared challengingly into dark ones. Gravillac wavered. His eyes took in the strength of André's men, gauged the degree of André's confidence. He hesitated. André lifted his fist and displayed the ring. *Touché.*

Bowing to the inevitable, Gravillac shrugged, remembering that Marielle had worn the ring, and wondering when he had first noticed it missing. With a sweeping gesture, he indicated the open door, while Molbert scampered out of their way. Narbaux took a step forward, but André motioned for him to remain. Jean-Auguste spoke quietly as André followed Gravillac into the chateau.

"We shall be here, ready at your call, *mon ami!*"

De Gravillac led André into a small drawing room bright with the morning sun, and moved easily to the fireplace, motioning Molbert to his side. André stood at the window, the sun streaming in behind him, where he could both see and be seen by Narbaux. De Gravillac spoke quietly. Molbert nodded and turned to leave.

"A moment," said Renard. Molbert stopped. "Have her wear the lavender. She knows how I like her in it."

The waiting seemed endless. André fidgeted at the window, trying to hide his impatience. Renard lolled near the hearth, one arm resting casually on the mantel, but his eyes glittered with malice. After an eternity, Marielle appeared. She did not see the figure in the window alcove, half-hidden by the heavy draperies. She stood poised on the threshold, waiting for a word from Gravillac. From where he stood André could not see the lifeless cast in her eyes, only the blooming cheeks, the robust good health that, brought on by her condition, made her positively glow. Her beautiful hair was bound up in a little silk cap on the top of her head, and the lavender dress clung to her sweet young curves. Around her neck was a string of creamy pearls that rivaled the clarity of her flawless complexion. She was more breathtaking, and far more disturbing, than André had remembered her.

"Ah, *ma chère*," said Gravillac silkily. "Come and bid me good morrow!" She moved woodenly across the fine carpet and, at the silent command in Renard's eyes, lifted her mouth for his kiss. With deliberate slowness he slipped his arms around her waist and pressed his lips firmly to hers in a long and lingering kiss; then, a mocking smile on his face, he indicated the figure by the window.

"Perhaps you would care to greet our guest!"

Surprised, she turned. The sun streamed brightly through the casement, making it difficult to see anything but the figure's outline. She squinted slightly at André, then started toward him. She stopped and peered more closely. Another step. A look of disbelief and wonderment crossed her face, her bosom began to heave and she gave a little gasp. Half-running toward him, she uttered a small cry, her hand flying to cover her mouth. She laughed, tried to speak, but could not; she began to weep for joy, astonishment and relief flooding her face.

Gravillac watched from the fireplace, seeming languid and indifferent, but his eyes glittered with envy and malevolence. André's face was like stone, cold and hard, and a muscle twitched in his jaw. Filled with joy and happiness, Marielle had not noticed his look. Finally, with a great effort, she managed to still her trembling enough to stumble out a few words, low and soft, her voice shaking and incredulous.

"I thought you dead!"

He glanced toward Renard. "So it would seem, Madame," he said, his voice heavy with scorn. She saw his face now, and fell back, her hand at her bosom, a look of pain in her eyes. She shook her head in disbelief—the cruelty in his tone tore at her heart.

"Your bridal ring, Madame," he said coldly, lingering mockingly on the word. He thrust it toward her; hands shaking, she slipped it onto her finger. "I can well understand your carelessness. It would seem that Monsieur le Marquis has been more than generous to you." He indicated the pearls around her neck. Before she could collect herself to reply, to refute the terrible things he was saying, he continued. "He seems to have kept you well—you are absolutely blooming since last we met at La Forêt—is it the air of Quiot that does it? . . . Or the company?"

Her face had turned ashen now, all the joy drained out of it. She could scarcely believe what she was hearing. Every word of his stung like a lash, and she reeled as if struck, unable to answer.

"How soon can you gather your possessions together and ready yourself for the journey?"

"Journey?" she echoed, as one in a stupor, still stunned by his attitude.

"You may have conveniently forgotten, Madame, but as Comtesse du Crillon you have obligations and responsibilities of which I must needs remind you! We leave for Vilmorin as soon as you are ready. I await you outside." He turned on his heel and strode from the room.

Gravillac laughed cruelly.

"I will miss you, *ma chère,*" he said with a mocking smile. "I had begun to hope that we were becoming good friends!"

She whirled on him, all the hatred and agony of the past weeks flashing in her eyes. She wanted to scream, to hurl curses at him, to see him lying dead at her feet. Then a wave of nausea swept over her, reminding her of the burden she carried beneath her heart, and wiping out her fury.

"Damn you," she said bitterly. She tore the pearls from her neck and flung them into the fireplace, then turned and fled up the stairs. She threw herself into Louise's arms.

"He lives," she sobbed. "He lives, and he despises me!"

They set out for Vilmorin, a strange and brooding silence hanging over them all. They had brought extra horses for the journey, which provided not only for Marielle's needs, but also for Louise, who had rushed out of the chateau and begged André that she might be allowed to accompany Madame. She would ask for no recompense, only to be able to serve her lady. Lost in his own dark mood, André shrugged his assent.

Pale and drawn, Marielle rode with her own

thoughts. Even now, her brain whirled. The joy she felt at his being alive battled with the agonies she suffered at his greeting, until she thought her head would burst. She had begged Louise to say nothing of what had happened at Quiot—she could not bear for André to know. Moreover, knowing, he might try to kill Gravillac, and she could not have him risk his life.

Narbaux watched them both in bewilderment. He could not understand his friend. Here was André's wife, the woman he had ached for, alive and far lovelier than he had described, and he ignored her. She seemed so pale, so fragile, and André so cold and distant, that Jean-Auguste rode close beside her, feeling responsible for her well-being. They stopped briefly for lunch, but Marielle was not hungry.

As the long afternoon wore on, André was filled with pangs of remorse. He had been so cruel to her, assuming the worst because of one kiss, because she looked so heartbreakingly beautiful, but so different. Because she had not looked like his own Marielle with her glorious hair hidden. Because she wore the lavender gown, though he was hard-pressed to know why that had disturbed him so. By evening he had softened enough so that when Louise rode up to him and said that Madame was weary, and begged that they be allowed to spend the night at an inn they had just passed, he reluctantly agreed. In truth, he had to admit that Marielle did not look well at all. Several times she seemed as though she were about to swoon and fall from her horse. A warm meal and a good night's sleep would suit them all—he suddenly remembered he had not slept in two days.

At the inn, Marielle refused supper, begging instead to be shown immediately to her room. Insisting that

Louise remain below to finish her meal, she followed the innkeeper's wife and mounted the stairs heavily, intending to sleep without bothering even to undress. As she crossed the threshold, a searing pain tore at her insides, and then another. She felt a warm rush of blood and doubled over in agony, half-crouching on the floor, and screamed for Louise. André burst into the room, aghast. As the full import of the terrible scene struck him, he stumbled from the room, defeated, his world crashing around him. Louise rushed to tend Marielle.

André sat in a corner, near the hearth, his brain reeling, until at length the innkeeper's wife came to tell him that Madame would survive, God willing, but that she had lost the child. He laughed crazily, bitterly, until she fled in fear, then he stood up and addressed the empty room.

"Now she will have nothing to remember him by!" and threw his winecup into the empty fireplace.

PART III

THE AWAKENING

Chapter Twelve

ANDRÉ STRODE ALONG THE WIDE CORRIDOR THAT LED TO HIS bedchamber. *Mon Dieu,* but he was tired! After a day of riding the countryside, he was ready for fresh clothes, a good supper. He passed Marielle's door quickly, glad to see that it was closed. As he neared the sitting room that separated his room from hers, he glanced through the open door. It was a fine evening, the sun still glowing amber in the sky, and the large windows had been thrown open to the breezes, so the sheer gauze curtains rippled gently. He stopped for a moment, then entered. He had forgotten how much he liked this room, with its gilded paneling, delicate frescoes and pale blue ceiling strewn with gold stars. For the last two weeks he had felt like an exile from his own home. By choice, perhaps, but an exile nonetheless. He crossed to the window and leaned out, breathing deeply, letting the calm and the beauty of Vilmorin fill his soul. Since that terrible day they had brought

Marielle here, borne on a litter, her eyes dark and tearless and unreadable, he had spent as little time as possible in his own home. True, Marielle passed most of her days in her chamber, in the company of that woman Louise, but he was reluctant to risk even a chance encounter; thus he had avoided this room, since both his bedchamber and hers opened into it by small doors concealed in the paneling. Perhaps if Marielle had already gone to bed he would take his supper here; it was such a lovely night, and the view from these windows, across the shallow grassy terraces to the wide and placid river, was the finest in Vilmorin. He turned, meaning to send for Clothilde and his supper, then he frowned.

A large velvet armchair had been drawn up to one of the windows, and curled up there, fast asleep, her head dropped to one shoulder, was Marielle. No doubt she had come to admire the view as well. He contemplated her face. It was the first time he had really looked at her since that morning at Quiot. After that he had fled her company, seeking refuge in riding, working the fields— anything to avoid her tears and the cold silence between them. Now he was free to look at her undetected for a while. He felt a sudden pang, remembering how he had watched her sleeping at La Forêt and lost his heart—it seemed like a lifetime ago. Her hair was loose and full; for the first time he noticed how it curled around her cheeks and forehead, the soft tendrils seeming to cling to her velvet skin. Her eyelashes were long and thick, and lay on the pink roundness of her cheeks; her nose in profile was delicate and straight, with just the slightest tilt at its tip, which gave it an elfin quality. The fullness of her lips, soft and rosy and parted slightly as she slept, made his heart stop. He was

minded to bend down as she slumbered and take that
lovely mouth for his very own. His very own! Gravillac
had taken those lips, and more! The thought curdled
the desire within him, and he saw her as just another
woman, no different from the rest, playing with a man,
giving when she wanted to give, using a cloak of
innocence to get what she wanted. Wasn't that how
Clothilde had beguiled him into her bed? And he had
thought Marielle so special, so uncorruptible. He had
promised her marriage, given her his heart and his
love, and she had denied him her body. What temptation had Renard dangled before her to win what he,
André, could not? *He* could hardly have offered her
marriage, knowing André yet lived, but if she had truly
thought André dead, perhaps she was minded to
become the Marquise de Gravillac, and was willing to
chance the giving of her favors as against an eventual
marriage. Renard was darkly handsome, and charming
enough when he wanted to be, and André remembered
with a pang of jealousy and regret that he would have
seduced her himself but for his faith in her purity. His
thoughts tortured him. Surely she must have been truly
innocent at La Forêt, the shy maiden she had seemed to
be. If not, he had married a stranger! And even if she
had been what he thought then, it was clear he had lost
that Marielle, lost her to a man who dressed her like a
princess and lavished her with gifts. He felt his heart go
cold. He could play that game as well! If Renard had
bought her, he was prepared to match the price! He
had already instructed Clothilde to bring in merchants
and seamstresses from the village of Vouvray to see to
all her needs, and had sent some of the finer Crillon
jewels to be cleaned and reset. A man had his pride,
after all—if she wished to be kept like a courtesan, he

would show her he could afford to be more lavish than Gravillac. And without demanding payment in bed in exchange!

He thought then of Clothilde. It was clear he could hardly visit her bed either. With Marielle in the chateau, the situation could be awkward. And besides, he could not take advantage of the poor girl. She had been so terribly disappointed, and tried to hide it, when he had returned with Marielle; it was obvious that she was in love with him. It would be cruel to continue the affair now. He sighed deeply, filled with self-pity. A wife who cared for another man, a housekeeper who cared too much. Caught between the two, where was a man to find his pleasures? Cursing silently, he left the room. The evening no longer seemed pleasant.

She was glad the baby was gone. It would make forgetting that much easier. Then why did she weep so? It seemed that the smallest incident reduced her to tears, charging her emotions with a grief she could hardly explain, confounding André and deepening the gulf between them. Louise said it was just because of her condition, and would pass as her strength returned, but it was so difficult in the meantime. How could she reach André, touch him, when the slightest glance from those cold blue eyes, implacable and unforgiving, would send her to her room in a flurry of tears? She longed to talk to him, to tell him how dear he was to her, but he seemed to avoid her company, spending time with her only when Louise or Clothilde was present, or when his friend Jean-Auguste rode over from his chateau to while away an afternoon. Then he was polite, civil, a kindly stranger. He smiled, spoke to her, put his arm casually around her waist—but it was a sham, a mockery. The smile was cold, the voice was hollow and the encircling arm was simply to establish ownership for the world at large. Otherwise he was away most of the time, inspecting his vineyards, collecting rents and taxes. She was surprised when tradespeople began to appear with clothing, perfume, lovely things she had never dreamed to own; André himself had given her a magnificent diamond necklace crowned with a glowing emerald. Delighted, she tried to thank him, but the icy eyes made it clear that for him the giving was joyless, merely his obligation to her position as mistress of Vilmorin.

Under Louise's gentle care, she slowly regained her strength. Until now, she had passed most of her days in her bedchamber, or the lovely sitting room that adjoined or the gardens that overlooked the river Loire. André never dined with her, so she took most of her meals in her room, except when Narbaux came to visit and André made a great show of their closeness. Now she began to explore this estate of which she was mistress.

She was struck at once by the contrast between Vilmorin and Quiot. The latter had been aloof and proud, built for show; grand, certainly, compared to the ancient stones of La Forêt, but a cold, unwelcoming place.

Vilmorin was different. Perhaps it was the valley, gently rolling hills clothed in tender green, or the placid river, wide and glassy, that murmured along the stones near its grassy banks. The air had a sweetness that was almost palpable, shimmering and golden under a clear blue sky. The chateau was old, built nearly a hundred years ago during the reign of Francis I, when the aristocracy of France had first discovered the beauty of the valley. It was like a fortress built for toy soldiers, with miniature turrets and rounded towers, long airy galleries and pointed roofs. It was a large chateau, but it was set so perfectly in the narrow valley—as though it had grown there, its golden stones the color of pale amber—that it gave one a sense of warmth and intimacy. Within, the rooms were large, their walls covered in plaster frescoes or wood paneling, or hung with tapestries and tooled leather from Spain. Marielle took especial delight in the ceilings, beamed and gilded and painted, striped and flowered . . . she had never seen such lovely rooms. Above the fireplace in each room was carved the Crillon coat of arms, the same lion and hound and grapes that were etched into the ring on her finger.

There was something about Vilmorin that was so happy, so normal, that she began to wonder if Quiot had ever happened. Surrounded by the laughter of Vilmorin, it was easy to forget Gravillac. She prayed that she could make André forget him too. She knew she loved her husband more than ever; surely with patience she could make him understand, she could wipe out his jealousy of Renard without having to tell him of her shame. She tried to tell herself that what she saw in his eyes was not hatred, only wounded pride. She would win his love again.

At first she thought to begin meeting him as he came from the fields, letting her presence indicate her interest in what he did, but as often as not Clothilde had already climbed the path to the vineyards to meet him with a flagon of ale, and they came back down together, laughing, the girl bent attentively to his every word. Clothilde made her uneasy. She was an efficient housekeeper, careful, competent, devoted to André and

Vilmorin, but there was something about her attitude that made Marielle feel like an intruder, and a provincial one at that. She took great delight in telling Marielle about her own upbringing in Paris—with every new detail that brought expressions of wonder and awe to Marielle's face, she smiled with a superiority that almost bordered on insolence. And there was more. It seemed as though she always gave the orders for the cleaning of the bedchambers in Marielle's presence; something in her tone would suggest that she knew André did not sleep with his wife, a note of triumph that disturbed Marielle. She tried, once or twice, to speak to André about Clothilde, but how could she describe feelings that were so vague, so ephemeral? Perhaps she only imagined Clothilde's attitude—she still had not completely mastered her emotions since her miscarriage.

In mid-August the weather turned unexpectedly cool. Though there was little danger of frost, the budding clusters of grapes were young and tender, and if the cool days remained, their growth would be stunted. That would mean that the harvest yield would be less ripe and mature, and the wine produced would be thin and sour. Although there was little to be done about it, André eased his frustration by riding out early every day and inspecting the long rows of vines, looking for the damage of the previous night, and riding back late, often after sundown. Marielle felt useless. Clothilde seemed to anticipate his every need—a warm doublet against the chill, a hearty meal packed and ready for his saddlebag. After the second evening, when Marielle had sat up late in the sitting room, the door open, awaiting his return, and heard

Clothilde greet him on the marble staircase below, she persuaded herself that he did not need her. The next night she went to bed early without waiting for him to come in. She did not know how late it was when she was awakened by noises in the corridor outside her room. Throwing on a peignoir, she rushed to see what was amiss.

A sleepy and terrified pageboy was holding a large candelabra in his shaking fist. By its light Marielle could see that Clothilde and Grisaille between them were half carrying, half dragging André. His clothes were dripping wet and his face was covered with blood. He seemed barely conscious, and he stumbled along, sometimes going limp in their grasp. All the while terrible sounds came from his chest, gasping and wheezing, and a racking cough that would have pitched him forward on his face but for the restraining hands. Marielle took in the dreadful scene at a glance, then snatched the candles from the trembling boy.

"Fetch Louise!" she said. She glared at Clothilde. "Why was I not awakened?"

"Madame, it was not necessary," said Clothilde coldly. "I am quite used to taking care of things. We do not need Louise," she said to the boy, who still hesitated.

Marielle bristled at the challenge, her temper rising. "You may take charge of things," she said evenly, "but I am mistress here, and I gave an order! Go!" she shrilled at the boy, who fled in the direction of Louise's room. Her eyes flew to Grisaille. "What happened?" she demanded.

"Ah, my lady. Monsieur's horse must have slipped near the river's edge, and thrown him. I found him in the water, half-drowned. And he hit his head! He must have swallowed a lot of water . . . he keeps coughing and choking!"

"Get him into his room," she ordered, thinking quickly. Narbaux had told her of the wounds to André's chest; she knew that his lung must still be weak. If he coughed too much, or took a chill and came down with fever, the lung might rupture and kill him. Putting down the candles, she whipped the coverlet from the bed and placed it on the floor, a small distance from the fireplace.

"Place him here! Grisaille, I want the fire built up as quickly as possible. Ah, good!" she said, as Louise bustled in. "I need a basin of water and some soft cloths." She turned to Clothilde, who stood glaring at her, the challenge now open and unmistakable in her eyes.

"I do not think—" began Clothilde, her mouth hard and stubborn.

Marielle stamped her foot impatiently. "If he dies, I shall be mistress of Vilmorin! I scarce think you would find that to your liking! I would not be won over by soft blandishments!" Clothilde's eyes wavered. "Now," said Marielle, "I want you to make me a mixture of herbs and oils that I shall name for you—I need a warming salve for his chest. When that is done, fetch a straw pallet and a fresh coverlet to place nearer the hearth. He must be kept warm."

As she spoke, she knelt beside André, taking the basin from Louise. Gently she sponged the blood off his face, and was grateful to see that the injury to his head, just within his hairline, was neither as large nor as serious as she had at first supposed. The bleeding had already stopped, and she decided that a bandage was probably not necessary. Of far more urgency was the racking cough, which had continued almost unabated, despite the fact that he was still almost insensible from the blow to his head. She began to unbutton his wet doublet, indicating to Louise to remove his boots, while she listed the medicines that Clothilde was to mix. By this time Grisaille had a good fire going, and she sent him off again to find some hot broth, hoping that André would be alert enough to swallow a few mouthfuls. She and Louise stripped off the rest of his wet clothes, and when the pallet and dry coverlet had been brought, they transferred him carefully, wrapping him well in the warm blanket. The salve was so strong it made her eyes water, but it eased his wheezing, and after a few sips of the hot broth he dropped off to sleep. She had Grisaille place a small chair for her, that she might sit by him all night in case he had another attack; she then dismissed them all, ignoring Clothilde's protests.

The fire was warm and he slept peacefully. It was strange. She had never noticed before how extraordinarily handsome he was. These last few weeks they had neither of them really looked at one another, and in prison he had been drawn and tired and badly in need of a shave. Besides, she had hardly been able to see anything but those riveting blue eyes. Now she took in every detail: the tawny hair, spun to pale gold by long hours in the sun; the burnished copper of his skin, stretched taut over the strong jaw; the wide forehead. His nose was straight and thin, and flared proudly at the nostrils, and the corners of his wide mouth were crinkled from frequent laughter. His lips, firm, sensuous, made her heart catch, and she closed her eyes, wondering if he would ever kiss her again. The memory of his kisses still stirred her with a strange excitement;

she ached to throw herself in his arms, to return to what had been between them before Gravillac had poisoned everything. Heavy-hearted, she dropped off to sleep at last.

She was awakened by the sound of his coughing. She dropped quickly to the floor by his side, but the spasm had already passed, and he had fallen back to sleep. She yawned and stretched, feeling the creaking in her bones; it was nearly dawn and she had slept the whole night curled in the chair. He did not seem to be feverish—she was glad for that. Still, it might be a good idea to rub more of the salve on his chest, in case there was still congestion. She folded back the top of the coverlet and scooped up some ointment in her hand, rubbing as gently as she might so as not to disturb him. She scarcely knew at what point he ceased to be a sick man in need of tender care and became a sensual male whose closeness filled her with an unfamiliar excitement. She was conscious suddenly of his bare flesh under her hand, warm and slightly moist from sleep, the feel of the powerful muscles just beneath the surface. It was ridiculous! She had helped to care for scores of injured men; why should this be different? Yet try as she might to erase the image from her mind, her thoughts returned again and again to the sight of him, as she and Louise had wrapped his naked body in the coverlet. She remembered again the fine golden hairs covering his chest and limbs—powerful shoulders and long legs—which glinted and shimmered in the fire-light. Her breath caught in her throat and, all unaware, she rubbed more vigorously, disturbed by the intensity of her feelings. She dragged her eyes away from his body, forcing herself to look at his face; her heart leaped in her breast. Clear blue eyes were staring at her and the lips held the hint of a smile. She wondered how long he had been awake and if he had read her thoughts, and she sat back quickly, briskly wiping off her hand and busying herself with the pallet to hide her agitation. His hands seemed to be exploring beneath the coverlet and he looked at her questioningly.

"Your things were wet!" she said sharply. Again the quizzical look, the glint of mockery in the eyes.

"Louise and I," she said as casually as she could, afraid now to look at those blue eyes that suddenly disturbed her more than his body. He began to laugh then, a laugh that was half a cough, and left him gasping but still merry.

"Ah, yes," he panted, "I had almost forgot! The doctor's daughter. In the interests of medicine, of course! Though there be women at Versailles who would give their rouge pots to have such a reason to get a man so quickly out of his breeches!"

Stung, she would have risen, but one strong hand, emerging from the coverlet, stopped her. The mockery had faded from his eyes and he looked at her seriously.

"I thank you for your concern. The memory of last night is dim, but I know I could not breathe and you lifted the weight from my chest. Come. Sit by me a while longer and be my nurse."

Relenting, she bent again to the salve, rubbing in a fresh portion while he breathed deeply, letting its strong aroma clear his lungs.

"So many scars," she said suddenly. "Jean-Auguste said you were grievously wounded at La Forêt, but . . . so many!" Her soft fingers gently traced the marks on his shoulder and chest, solicitude written large in her eyes. She touched the two scars on his breastbone that were different from the rest, her green eyes hazy with remembrance.

"A small price to pay," he said. "They believed the lie."

"I saw the stable burn," she said softly.

"I found Jacques. He was bringing me to you when we were hit."

For some moments they were silent, lost in memory, in the past, in what might have been and was no more.

"Vilmorin is lovely," she said at last, for want of something better to say. It was safer if they did not talk about the past.

"Have you seen the vineyards and the caves?" he asked. She shook her head. "In a day or two then, when I am fit. And since it seems that I am also beholden to that Louise of yours, we shall take her along and treat her to a goblet of fine wine!" She smiled. They lapsed into silence again, trying to read each other's eyes. Something trembled in the air between them.

"Marielle," he said softly, questioningly. His hand reached up to touch a curl that lay on her shoulder.

There was a knock at the door, and without waiting for an answer Clothilde burst in, smiling brightly.

"Ah, Monsieur! I knew you would be better this morning! I have brought you breakfast and good news! The sun is bright, the air is warm and Grisaille says the grapes are safe!"

Pleased, André struggled to his feet, wrapping the coverlet about him, and stood unsteadily, while Clothilde, having deposited her tray on a table, rushed to give him her shoulder to lean on, and guided him gently to his bed. She settled him against the pillows and brought him his food, fussing over him while he basked in her attention. Marielle felt suddenly tired. It had been a long night in that chair; she arose wearily from the floor and went out, her eyes burning with tears, aware that Clothilde's triumphant smile followed her to the door.

Chapter Thirteen

AT MARIELLE'S INSISTENCE, ANDRÉ SPENT THE NEXT THREE days in his bed, until he could breathe freely and no longer wheezed. But it was Clothilde who took it upon herself to tend him. She seemed always to be with him when Marielle wished to assess his progress, she served him all his meals and supervised the steaming baths which eased his coughing. Since the night they had brought him home, she no longer made a pretense of even liking Marielle, though she was careful to be polite and subservient, particularly in André's presence. For his part, André was not inclined to ask Clothilde to leave, even when Marielle was there; indeed it seemed almost as though he welcomed her intrusion to forestall any closeness with Marielle. Although he no longer treated her with coldness, there was still distance in his attitude, an air of sadness tinged with regret. It matched Marielle's mood. It dismayed her to see Clothilde fussing over him with such possessiveness, all the more so because he seemed to enjoy and welcome her attentions. For the first time she felt the pangs of jealousy, wondering what they had been to each other before her arrival. It heartened her little when Clothilde, remarking on the speed of his recovery, smiled smugly and said, "Monsieur is a very strong man . . . in every way!"

The day came when he announced that he was well enough and it was time to take Marielle to see the caves. While she went to fetch a shawl, he marched into the kitchen, bellowing loudly for Louise.

"I am hardly deaf yet, my lord, and do not wish to be," she said tartly.

He laughed aloud. "It seems I am to show you the caverns, and then, minding myself of the other evening, methinks you will have seen all that Vilmorin has to offer!"

She snorted loudly. "Do not praise yourself overmuch, my lord! I was not struck dumb by the sight of you! I have seen enough knaves in my time!"

"Aye, and bedded them too, I'll wager! What a devilish wench you must have been!"

"I would have been a match for you, my lord!"

He roared with laughter and delivered a resounding whack to her ample bottom. She smiled broadly and followed him out to the wide front lawn where Marielle was waiting.

Chateau Vilmorin had been built close to the river Loire, on a narrow and verdant strip of land, rich and loamy, the soil built by the river for eons. Beyond the chateau, a few hundred yards from the river bank, were overhanging bluffs and cliffs, chalky limestone outcroppings that had marked the river's edge in some prehistoric time. These cliffs were honeycombed with caves, some built by nature's hand, others dug out by men from the dawn of time. Cool and dark, the caves were used as storage for the kegs and casks of wine, the chill air helping to stop the fermentation process. Curious houses had also been built into many of the caves, serving as living quarters for the *vignerons* who worked in the fields. Above the cliffs, and stretching for many miles away from the river, were the rich plateaus of the province of Touraine, gently rolling hills woven with the neat patterns of the vineyards.

Grisaille, the chief *vigneron*, met them as they mounted the paths to the caves. He greeted Louise with particular warmth, and Marielle was surprised to see the flustered look upon her face; while André suddenly remembered that in the last few weeks Grisaille had found countless reasons to go into the kitchen. His eyes glittering wickedly, he whispered something in Louise's ear and was gratified to see her redden, feeling revenged for the jibes she had directed at him.

Grisaille lit a large candle and led them through the caves, pointing out the large fermenting vats that would be used for this year's harvest, and the oaken casks in which the wine was aged, large wooden kegs stoppered with straw and clay plugs. André explained the peculiar quality of the Vouvray grapes which produced wines noted for their *petillement,* a slight effervescence that left a tingle in the mouth. Marielle had already noted it when she dined, and had found the wine very agreeable. She was surprised now to discover that, unlike the wines of the Languedoc region on which she had been raised, the quality of the Vouvray vintage fluctuated radically with the differences in the weather. When the summer was rainy and cool, the wine was thin, a sharp acid taste that made Marielle wrinkle her nose and shiver. Moderate years produced a light, refreshing wine, pale and golden, while a good summer, hot and sunny, rewarded the vintner with a strong, fruity wine, of a light rose color, heavy but not overly sweet. Because of the caves and the unusual quality of the Vouvray grapes, the wines lasted remarkably well, some living to a great age. There were many vintages to be sampled, discussed, enjoyed, while André beamed with the pride of ownership. Grisaille had been very generous with Louise's samples, and her eyes had begun to sparkle, her cheeks a bright pink, while she giggled like a young maiden. André suggested that perhaps Grisaille would like to offer her one more glass of the finest vintage; he and Madame would walk through the vineyards for awhile.

Marielle was glad to be out of the caves at last; she had begun to feel chilly. The air outside was warm; it was a pleasant afternoon, with the hint of hot days to come. It would be good for the grapes. André gave her his hand, helping her up the narrow path that ran alongside the caves, until they reached the top of the plateau, with the fields stretching out before them. The touch of his fingers brought her back to reality, and, remembering Clothilde, she drew her hand away, suddenly shy and vulnerable. As for André, the glow of the wine had faded, and he seemed lost in a strange melancholy. They walked silently through the rows of vines, each vine staked to its own forked branch, reaching almost to a man's waist.

At the end of the field they came upon the cottage of one of André's tenants. The farmer and his wife were delighted to see the Seigneur and his lovely Comtesse, of whom they had heard so much. They insisted on sharing their meager supper, setting a small table under a fruit tree and waiting on Marielle as though she were the queen herself. It had been a long time since Vilmorin had a mistress, let alone one as lovely and gracious as this. When they rose to leave, André thanked the farmer and suggested that he come up to the chateau in the morning; the cook had a fine smoked ham that his family might enjoy.

They strolled back toward the edge of the bluffs, warmed by the goodness of the peasants. Marielle marveled at André's kindness, a generosity that could give without leaving obligation or embarrassment. She felt suddenly proud, glad to be the mistress of Vilmorin.

"How long has it been," she asked suddenly, "since Vilmorin had a lady?"

"My sister married some eighteen years ago," he said curtly.

"Do you never see her?"

"She is many years my senior; we were never particularly fond of one another."

"And your mother?"

He was silent, quickening his pace so that she had to take a little skip to keep up with him. There was something about the set of his jaw, his rigid expression, that made her almost regret asking the question. Finally he spoke, his voice so low she had to strain to hear.

"I was twelve when she . . . died." There was something in his tone that touched her heart, a note of pain that she longed to ease. She reached out her hand to comfort him, then stopped. The blue eyes turned toward her were cold and hostile, filled with jealousy and suspicion. She bit her lip and turned away. What had she done to remind him of Gravillac? Would the man haunt them forever?

They descended from the bluffs and passed the grove of fruit trees leading up to Vilmorin and the broad front lawn dotted with flower beds and gently splashing fountains. By the time they reached the wide front door, André's black mood had passed. He stood aside for her to enter, and then they both stopped, riveted by the sounds of howling and wild laughter that seemed to come from somewhere above them, echoing down the marble staircase that spiraled upward through the chateau. The sound bounced down the polished stone steps, reverberating against the tile flooring of the vestibule in which they stood. Clothilde, hands on hips, was standing at the foot of the stairs, a look of disgust on her face; at the sight of Marielle, she sneered and flounced into the kitchen, slamming the door loudly behind her. André and Marielle raced up the staircase. At the first landing they stopped, struggling to hold back their laughter. Louise, her apron askew, her eyes glassy, had plopped herself down and was steadfastly refusing to budge, despite the earnest entreaties of Grisaille, who was desperately tugging at her arm. She was very drunk. It was he who howled, and she who laughed, a wild cackle at every frenzied attempt of his to lift her. It was an uneven contest. Even sober, she stood half a head taller than he—and considerably wider. In her present condition, she was just so much dead weight, and she sat and laughed and grinned, shaking her head at his feeble attempts.

André roared with laughter.

"Louise, you wicked woman!" he crowed. "Drunk! And trying to seduce Grisaille as well!"

Grisaille looked horrified and shook his head vigorously.

"Nay, my lord! I was just trying to get her to her bed!"

André roared all the louder, and Marielle smothered her laughter with her hand.

"You see, Louise?" said André. "If you were not so drunk, you could at least help the man!"

Louise glared at him through red-rimmed eyes, and her voice was thick and slurred.

"You are a wicked devil, Monsieur! I am a good woman, and perfectly sober besides!" She nodded her head for emphasis. "But if you would be so kind, Monsieur, as to help me to my feet, I should like to go to my room!"

Still laughing, André gripped her firmly by one arm, motioning Grisaille to take the other. Marielle scampered on ahead to fetch a candle, as the evening was falling and the staircase had grown quite dim. By the time she returned with light, they had managed to struggle almost to the top of the staircase, André and Louise engaged in a ribald battle of words that had poor Grisaille blushing; all the while they shook with laughter so that André was hard-put to keep a grip on her. The sight was so ludicrous that Marielle, at the top of the stairs, burst out laughing herself, too convulsed to do more than point a finger at Louise, while the candle shook in her hands. Seeing Marielle, Louise broke into fresh fits and let her whole body go limp. Before they realized what was happening, Louise began to slide backwards down the smooth and polished stairs, her own weight carrying her down. André and Grisaille, caught off guard, felt themselves being dragged down, and hung on desperately while they shouted to Louise to help herself. She would have none of it. Like a child on an icy hill, she was enjoying the sensation of sliding, and in a moment all three were heaped upon the landing, roaring and shouting, while Marielle, watching from above, laughed till the tears sprang to her eyes.

It took all their powers of persuasion to convince Louise to cooperate, but at last they got her up the stairs and into her bed, where she bristled at André's sly suggestion that he help her undress, and promptly rolled over and fell asleep, snoring noisily. Mortified by the whole episode, Grisaille fled to his cottage, while Marielle and André, exhausted from the laughter, collapsed against one another.

Marielle sighed deeply, trying to recover herself. André wiped a tear from the corner of his eyes, and grinned down at her, his eyes warm and gentle. Absently he brushed aside a stray lock that had fallen across her forehead, his finger tracing a gentle path around the curve of her cheek.

"I like Louise," he said. "I should pay her a wage. If she is sober enough in the morning, tell her so, and send her to me." She smiled back at him, noticing how white his teeth were against the rich tan of his face. His blue eyes burned into her, making it difficult to speak or to concentrate on what he was saying. He seemed to be having the same trouble, and spoke distractedly.

"Where did you find her?" he asked, his eyes on the eager rosiness of her lips.

"Quiot," she answered, wondering why she found it so hard to breathe. "Her family served there for generations." Would he never kiss her?

"And she would leave?" he asked, a small unwelcome thought beginning to nag at the back of his mind.

It seemed foolish to talk. She gazed up at him, love and longing shining in her pale green eyes; then stepped back as his face darkened and all the joy drained out of it.

"And are all of Gravillac's women so fickle?" he said bitterly, and turning on his heel, strode away.

Chapter Fourteen

True to the promise in the air, the weather turned hot. August was nearly over and the fields basked in the sunshine. The road beyond Vilmorin turned to dust, sending up little puffs and eddies with each stray breeze. André returned from his rides covered with a fine powder, his throat parched and dry. Marielle found a willow tree near the river where she could sit and read or do her needlework, shielded from the glare. An uneasiness hung between them; they no longer went out of their way to avoid each other, but neither did they spend much time together. By tacit agreement, Marielle took her meals alone in the dining salon before André returned. Occasionally he rode in early, joining her for a glass of wine while she finished her meal, but their conversations were guarded and awkward, punctuated by long silences, while they avoided one another's eyes. Fearful of being hurt, they met only on neutral ground, discussing the weather, the grapes, anything that would not poison the air with regrets and recriminations.

In spite of the heat, they were glad to receive an invitation from Narbaux to visit him at his chateau. It was something to do, to break the tension that had begun to build up between them, exacerbated by the sweltering weather. It was only a short ride, an hour or so, and the path took them through cool glades and a large stand of pine, following the course of the river that never flowed more than a few hundred yards from where they rode. They traveled slowly, letting the horses set the pace. Marielle was glad she had worn only a sleeveless doublet over her chemise, and a cool linen skirt; nevertheless, by the time they arrived at Jean-Auguste's they were both flushed from the ride.

Narbaux met them at the long, tree-lined avenue leading up to his chateau. He was in his shirtsleeves, his bright red mustaches drooping with the heat. He greeted them warmly, his face wreathed in smiles, and shook André's hand as he alit. Turning to Marielle, still mounted, he put his hands around her waist and guided her gently to the ground, his eyes full of frank admiration.

"I hope you are taking good care of this wife of yours, André!" he said, smiling benignly at them both. They exchanged pleasantries as they strolled to the chateau, while Narbaux's grooms led their horses away.

"I thought we might have a picnic," said Jean-Auguste. "We can boat across the river. There is a very agreeable spot downriver that should prove cool and inviting on this warm day."

He led the way to the bank, where a small boat was already waiting, a large hamper of food aboard, and a small mound of pillows in the bow upon which Marielle was soon comfortably settled. Jean-Auguste stood in the stern, holding a large pole, and André sat between the two. They drifted gently downstream, Narbaux content to let the current work for him, and chatted pleasantly about their vineyards, the weather and the latest news from Paris. Richelieu had returned from the south of France, and the King was preparing to leave Versailles for Fontainebleau. With the coming of autumn, the Court would be gay again. No doubt there would be royal invitations for them both, especially since the King would want to meet Marielle. They regaled her with stories of the festivities at Court, while her eyes opened wide and she clapped her hands in sheer joy. They were like children. With Jean-Auguste to break the tension, they laughed and joked, reality forgotten. They beached the boat in the shallows and sat in the shade of a large oak tree, gorging themselves on the food and wine, while the river gurgled happily over the smooth rocks nearby. When they had finished, André stripped off his doublet and rolled up his sleeves, putting his hands behind his head and leaning up against the tree with a contented sigh. Narbaux kicked off his shoes and pulled off his stockings. He waded into the water, urging the others to join him.

"Indeed, it looks inviting!" cried Marielle. She quickly removed her shoes and stockings, then hitched up her skirts almost to her knees, while Narbaux made a big show of pretending not to look. André watched them idly, too lazy to join in.

"I like your wife, André," said Jean-Auguste. "And she rides well too, I noted." He turned to Marielle. "How does a country girl who has never even been to Paris—*Mon Dieu*—learn to ride like that?"

Marielle laughed in fond remembrance. "If she is fortunate enough to have a big brother to teach her. . . ."

"And what else do big brothers teach little sisters, then?"

With a superior smile, Marielle rolled up her sleeves and reached down into the clear water, groping until she found a large flat rock. Holding it in her thumb and forefinger, she swung her arm horizontally, releasing the rock so it skipped across the surface of the water.

"Three!" she announced triumphantly.

"Ha!" shouted Narbaux, as he too danced a stone on the water. "Four!"

"Five!" said Marielle, as her stone skipped across the river, raising five ripples that fanned out in ever-growing rings. The challenge was too much for André who, rapidly casting aside his footwear, plunged into the river beside them. Narbaux was groping frantically in the riverbed, complaining bitterly about the size and shape of every rock that he dredged up. André scooped up a large stone and sent it flying across the water.

"Six, Madame! What have you to say to that?" he crowed, a satisfied grin on his face.

She shrugged in seeming disinterest, but her green eyes gleamed wickedly. Stooping down as though to pick up another stone, she scooped up a handful of water and splashed it into his face, while his look of triumph turned to surprise. The battle was joined. By the time the three of them had struggled back to the bank and lay exhausted, gasping and chuckling, André's shirt was soaked through, Jean-Auguste had lost a lace cuff, and Marielle, despairing of ever finding her hairpins, was trying to arrange the masses of chestnut curls that swirled around her face in a tangled cluster.

On the ride back to the chateau she dozed, her riotous hair spread out on the soft pillows like a brilliant halo, one hand thrown over the side of the boat and trailing gentle fingers in the water. Narbaux poled against the current, while André, his back to his friend, contemplated Marielle's lovely face with a mixture of awe and desire. Shaking off her spell, he turned to speak to Narbaux, then stopped. Oblivious to his friend, Jean-Auguste was gazing fixedly at her, a look of naked longing on his face. Disconcerted, André turned quickly away. By the time they reached the chateau, Marielle had awakened. André and Jean-Auguste scrambled ashore, and André turned to help Marielle; Narbaux was already there, lifting her smoothly out of the boat and swinging her onto the land. She thanked him smilingly, and skipped off to the chateau, minded to find a comb and some hairpins. Both men watched her go.

"You know, André," said Jean-Auguste lightly, "if you do not treat her well, I shall steal her away from you!"

At André's frown, Narbaux laughed. "As I recall, you did not mind poaching on another man's territory. Take care now, lest you become the cuckold!"

André whirled on Narbaux, clutching his shirt front with both his fists. His eyes glowed with anger.

"Don't be a fool, *mon ami*," cried Jean-Auguste. "I did but jest! I could not win her away from you if I tried! Surely you must see that!"

André growled an apology and turned away. When Marielle returned, they took their leave curtly, while she wondered what had transpired between the two friends to cast such a pall on their lovely day.

The ride home was a quiet one, André sullen and

brooding. As they passed the pine grove, they heard the sound of a child weeping and a man crying out in pain. Following the cries, they came upon a little child of six or seven, who sobbed helplessly; nearby sprawled a peasant, writhing in pain and thrashing his arms wildly about. Across his chest and torso lay a huge tree. It appeared that he had been chopping it down when the large trunk, dry from the rainless days, had cracked too soon and pinned him to the ground. A thin trickle of blood came from his mouth and he raved like a madman, his eyes two black pools—as though he already saw Death's approach. They jumped from their horses, Marielle to comfort the child, André to lift the tree trunk if he could. It soon became apparent that the man, in the frenzy of his pain, was impairing his own rescue, for every time that André came near, the peasant clutched at his arms and legs as though he would drag him down.

"Wait, André!" cried Marielle. "Mayhap I can be of help whilst you clear the tree!" So saying, she fell upon the peasant, struggling with all her might to hold his arms above his head. He was strong, with the strength of madness and desperation. He freed his hands and clutched at her fiercely, his fingers bruising the soft flesh of her bare arms. She murmured softly, stroking his forehead, his cheeks; soothing, comforting, until some of the madness passed from his eyes and he lay still, groaning in pain, his breath coming in soft gasps. In the meantime, André had managed to loop his horse's reins around that portion of the tree that lay across the farmer; now he urged his horse on while he himself strained to raise the trunk. Dragged and lifted, the tree rolled away, freeing the unfortunate man. Marielle bit her lip and looked hopelessly at André. It was clear to them both that nothing could help the farmer. His body was woefully mangled, the chest stove in; already he was beginning to cough weakly and pant for air, his eyes glassy and faraway. Leaving André to make him as comfortable as possible, Marielle scooped the child up in her arms and cradled him against her breast, rocking him, kissing his tear-stained face, giving what comfort she might. André arose from the farmer's side; his face told Marielle that the man was dead. He helped her into her saddle, then handed the boy up to her. In silence, they rode to the nearest cottage, where André arranged for the man to be buried. The boy would be cared for and returned to his family.

They rode back to Vilmorin in silence, each lost in his own thoughts. André marveled at her quiet strength, at a spirit and capability only dimly perceived until now. He had thought of her as a sweet and lovely girl; it was clear now she was a woman, with depth and understanding. He remembered suddenly how she had seemed to read into his heart at La Forêt. Strange how the Marielle he had conjured up when he thought her dead had so lacked the substance of the real woman.

"Take supper with me," he said when they arrived home. "Tonight. Every night. I should be glad of your company."

She smiled gently. "I have no thought for food this night. But I will take a glass of wine with you."

They walked into the long gallery, where André took two glasses and a flagon from a small cupboard. He brought the wine to Marielle; she stood at the window, gazing pensively out at the star-filled night. They drained their glasses in silence, but as Marielle reached out and put her empty cup on a small table, André saw her bare arms. They were scratched and red from her struggles with the farmer. He held them gently and kissed their sweet softness, his eyes filled with tenderness and consolation. With a sob, Marielle turned away, covering her face with her hands.

"Why should I weep for them?" she cried. "What were they to me?"

He folded her gently in his arms, holding her trembling body to his breast, his face buried in her fragrant hair, until her tears subsided and her quivering ceased.

"Life is so fragile, Marielle," he said, his voice husky, muffled by her tresses. He hesitated, groping for the words. "We are foolish, you and I. Do you remember La Forêt? How we vowed our friendship? Can we start anew, Marielle? Can we be friends at least?"

Slowly she lifted her eyes to his face, peering deeply into his eyes, trying to read an answer written there.

"Ah, André," she sighed. "And will you be able to forget the past?"

His gaze wavered, clouding with doubt; he tried to speak, agony and confusion crossing his face. He groaned and turned away.

"God knows!" he said wretchedly.

The heat became oppressive, sultry, the air so heavy with moisture that Louise puffed when she climbed the stairs, and mopped at her forehead with her sleeve. Marielle and André had discarded doublets and jackets, spending their days in cool shirts and chemises; nevertheless, by the end of the day the fabric clung damply to their bodies. When the rain came, they welcomed it, but joy turned quickly to dismay. It brought no relief from the suffocating heat, adding only to everyone's discomfort. What was more, after two days of steady downpour worry began to show in

André's face. He rode out once or twice, fearing now the grapes would begin to rot, and returned drenched and morose, responding curtly to Marielle's queries and brooding for long hours at a window.

It was thus she found him, one late afternoon, in the sitting room that separated their chambers, sunk in despair, watching the persistent rain.

Her heart ached for him. How much she loved him! She wanted to comfort him, to smooth the frown from his brow, to ease his dismay. Crossing to the window, she stood beside him and touched his arm, at a loss for words. He smiled gently at her, but the cloudy blue eyes mirrored his helplessness and frustration. On an impulse, she reached up her hands and locked them around his neck, pulling his mouth down to hers. She kissed him softly, her lips moving gently on his. His arms slipped around her waist and he returned her kisses, his hands playing lightly across her back and shoulders until she shivered with ecstasy and clung more tightly to his neck. Ah *Dieu!* She had forgotten how she thrilled to his kisses, and now she drank hungrily, intoxicated with the sensations his mouth aroused. She closed her eyes, her head spinning, lips parted in desire, while he rained kisses on her face, her eyelids, her velvet throat; her breath caught and she trembled, feeling his mouth burning on her eager flesh. She was hardly aware when he picked her up and carried her through the small door to her room, laying her gently across the bed; she knew only that she wanted his kisses to last forever. His passion mounting, he began to press more insistently, his mouth hard and hungry on hers, his hand groping at the neckline of her chemise and clasping the firm roundness of her breast. She shuddered, a wave of panic rising in her throat. She saw Gravillac's face before her, the hungry cruelty, the animal lust. Oh God! she thought. Not this! Not André! She struggled against him, her terror mounting, as the nightmare of her days with Gravillac overwhelmed her. If she could just explain to André—if he would only be patient, gentle. . . . She tried desperately to hold him back, while he, reading rejection in her eyes, pressed her ever more impatiently, seeking to overcome her resistance with the heat of his passion. His kisses bruised her mouth and she began to whimper, large tears springing to her eyes. He looked at her, bewildered. Did he disgust her? Was she afraid of him? Or was she dreaming still of Renard's kisses? His hunger burned in his loins; his face was a mask of jealousy and rage. He sprang from the bed, hatred glowing in his eyes.

"Slut!" he growled through clenched teeth.

"André," she whispered piteously, "Please!"

He turned on his heel and strode from the room, angrily slamming the door behind him.

"Am I never to be forgiven?" she shrieked at the closed door. She choked and sobbed, throwing herself face down on the bed. In a moment the sobs had turned to anger, cold rage. Forgiven for what? she thought, sitting up suddenly. As though she were somehow guilty—responsible for those months of misery!

By dawn, the rain had stopped and the sun rose on a world dripping and steamy with the heat. For hours Marielle had tossed and turned on her bed, unable to sleep, feeling choked and suffocated. But the heat that she felt had less to do with the weather outside her casement than with the fury that boiled within her. She was tired. Tired of being ashamed and apologetic.

Weary of tiptoeing round André lest the name of Gravillac plunge him into black despair. She had borne the grief of her months with Renard; she resented the burden of guilt that André pressed upon her. Reflected in his eyes, she was a fallen woman, no longer entitled to kindness, gentility, even subtlety. Bitterly, she wondered he had not tried to take her on the sitting room floor, and felt her disgust rise with her anger. Was that all she meant to him? She would be better off with Gravillac—at least he did not pretend a kindness that was foreign to him!

She threw herself from her bed, anxious to be free of her room for a few hours. It was still very early; no one seemed to be stirring. There was a bend in the river that she knew of, a quiet sheltered spot, hidden by trees, isolated from the chateau by the natural twistings of the Loire. She went there ofttimes when she wanted to be alone and knew she would not be found. It beckoned her now. The cool air would soothe her fevered thoughts. Swiftly she slipped out a small door and hurried through the grass, still damp from the rain. Her spot was cool, shadowed. Here and there the morning sun glinted through the thick branches, igniting sparks of light on the crystal water. Not far from the bank, the shallow riverbed dipped sharply, creating a small natural pool that called to her now. Quickly she pinned up her hair and shed her garments, wading in and letting the refreshing water soothe her troubled spirit. She swam slowly, reluctant to see even a ripple disturb her placid retreat, letting the water flow over her body and wash away the memory of the scorn in his eyes, the hateful word on his lips. She glanced up toward the tree. He was there, mounted on horseback, watching her, his face unreadable in the shadows. She stood up in the water, the gentle current reaching to her shoulders and lapping against her skin. She felt cold and numb, remembering still what he had called her, unwilling to forgive him, reluctant even to face him.

"Go away," she said tiredly. "Leave me in peace."

Now she saw the contempt in his face, the ragged pride that turned him ugly and cruel. He dropped his horse's reins and lolled in the saddle, while he unbuttoned his doublet.

"A fine morning for a swim," he said, "and such a secluded spot, where no one will disturb us." He removed his doublet, draping it over his saddle. His eyes narrowed, watching her.

"André, please," she said softly, "try to understand. I never meant for it to happen that way. I did not wish to hurt you."

He laughed shortly. "Hurt me? Why should I be hurt? I have known far too many women like you to be hurt . . . though I seldom call them to their faces what I think in my heart! You must forgive me my lapse of yester-eve."

She bit her lip and turned away. He must not see her weep. After a long moment, she turned to him, her chin held high.

"The water is chilling," she announced as firmly as her trembling lips would allow. "Please be so kind as to withdraw, that I may put on my clothes."

He sneered. "Your modesty hardly becomes you, Madame. Isn't it rather late to play the country maiden? You blushed at La Forêt when Gravillac bared your bosom. Would you bother to blush now? I wonder. . . ." With one quick movement he stripped off his shirt, revealing the strong shoulders, the overpowering arms. She closed her eyes, a look of pain on her face. It was impossible not to read his intent. Would the nightmare begin again?

"Very good, Madame! Very modest! But blushing is for maidens, not whores! Not women of experience!" He spat the words.

It was too much. Her eyes flew open. The fury burst within her. There was little she could do if he was minded to rape her, but if he wanted a whore, by *le Bon Dieu*, that is what he would have!

Coldly, brazenly, she stepped slowly into the shallows, her chin held firm and proud, her eyes never leaving his face. Deliberately she let her hips undulate as she walked, the movement at once tantalizing and defiant, until she stood at the bank glaring up at him, challenging, taunting, enjoying his confusion and dismay.

He sat his horse as one struck dumb, the breath caught in his throat. He had never seen her like this before, beautiful, desirable, with a body to set a man to dreaming. The sun, shining through the trees, dappled her creamy skin with golden patches and kindled the rich chestnut of her hair until she seemed to glow with light. She was slim, but her hips curved beguilingly, and her full breasts were young and firm and rosy-tipped. The defiant set of her chin, the pride in her stance, bosom heaving in anger, dared him and challenged him. He felt his pulse racing and a hungry ache in his loins, but the fury and the arrogance in those hazy green eyes made him feel as stupid and awkward as a mere mortal who had stumbled upon a goddess bathing. She saw the consternation in his eyes, his desire warring with his pride, and pressed her advantage, glad to see him suffer.

"Will you pleasure yourself here, my lord?" she

asked coldly. "Or will you allow me the comfort of my own bed?"

The barb struck home. Frustrated, defeated, he wheeled his horse around and fled in confusion. She remained standing there for a very long time, the bitter tears flowing unchecked. She hated him, despised him. Then why did she feel no triumph—only an aching loneliness in her heart, a sadness that weighed her down?

Chapter Fifteen

HE DID NOT LOVE HER. SHE WAS CERTAIN OF IT NOW. IF HE
had ever loved her at La Forêt, that emotion was gone
now, drowned in his jealousy and suspicion. She had
dragged through the day, her heart breaking, avoiding
Louise's inquisitive eyes, her questioning glances. If
once she let herself weep on that ample bosom, her
tears would never stop; her grief seemed bottomless.
But as the day wore on, her sorrow congealed to cold
anger that he should be so blind. She had loved him
with all her heart, asking only patience from him—how
could he even think that Gravillac mattered to her! As
she dressed for supper, her cold implacable eyes stared
back at her from the silver mirror. Since the day they
had found the woodcutter, they had taken their meals
together, exchanging pleasantries, trying to bridge the
chasm between them. Now, staring at her reflection,
she laughed bitterly. Without any hope of winning his
love, it had been futile. He lusted after her, his basest
passions aroused, but that was all. Even at that, she
knew his pride tormented him—she might be a whore

in his eyes, but she was also Gravillac's leavings. He fought to deny his physical need of her as he had already rejected her love. Whereas before she had trod softly, afraid to hurt him, afraid of being hurt herself, now her blood boiled, wanting to make him suffer as she had suffered. Deliberately she tugged at the neckline of her gown, pulling it low until the soft orbs of her breasts peeped enticingly above the snowy lace. She took her rouge pot and stroked subtle spots of rosy color on her cheeks and in the hollow of her bosom, then doused herself liberally with heady perfume. She nodded in satisfaction, but a sob caught in her throat. She found she could no longer meet her own eyes in the glass. Curse him! She swept from the room and went down to supper.

They dined in silence, cold, correct, polite, but she noticed with satisfaction that his eyes strayed repeatedly to her bosom, in spite of himself, as though he had no will to control his glance. A small muscle worked in the corner of his jaw, and he drummed his fingers absently on the table. He feigned indifference, but she knew he clutched his torn pride around him like a beggar in a tattered cloak. Her heart ached and she almost relented her cruelty; then Clothilde appeared, and he smiled dazzlingly at her, freezing Marielle's heart once more. Tomorrow, she thought with malice, I shall twine flowers in my hair and rouge my lips! By *le Bon Dieu!* If need be I will prance naked before him to torment him!

Supper over, he cleared his throat, finding it difficult to speak, to look at her without seeing that tempting body.

"We have been invited to Court," he said, his voice hoarse in his throat. "Next week Richelieu and Their Majesties leave Fontainebleau for the Louvre. We will join them there. And Jean-Auguste. I expect we shall stay until the end of the month, then return to Vilmorin for the harvest. There are servants aplenty at the palace; you will not need Louise as your personal maid. You may wish more elaborate gowns for Court—arrange with Clothilde for whatever you need. We will go by horseback to Vouvray, then travel by *carrosse* from Vouvray to Paris. The roads are bumpy, but it is a more pleasant ride than in the saddle, and you will have ample space for your trunks and boxes."

Quite forgetting the chill that had hung between them, Marielle smiled in pleasure, her eyes sparkling.

"Paris! Oh André!" she laughed, then stopped, meeting his icy stare.

"I trust you will not embarrass me, Madame. Nor cease to remember that you are a married woman. You will find that the courtiers in Paris are perhaps more seductive even than Renard de Gravillac!" Whirling on his heel, he was gone, leaving her fuming and more bent on revenge than ever.

During the next few days they hardly saw one another. André was seeing to the vineyards, that they should be carefully tended in the weeks they would be away; what with fittings and packing, Marielle scarcely took time for a meal. She chose a pale green watered silk from England, and had it fashioned into a soft gown adorned with clusters of pink ribbons and embroidered rosebuds. A length of creamy taffeta became, in short order, a snug bodice and rustling skirt, sashed lavishly with Italian gold cloth, and bound in gold and silver braid. She packed half a dozen of her existing gowns, newly refurbished with the yards of ribbons that were the rage in Paris. There were wide lace collars and cuffs, brocaded shoes, some with high cork heels, fans to hold or hang at her waist, dainty bejeweled mirrors to suspend around her neck on fine gold chains. Clothilde's eyes glittered with envy, but she had not failed to notice the new estrangement between them and she pressed her advantage. She herself saw to the preparation of André's wardrobe, and she took every opportunity to seek him out and consult about this doublet, that pair of boots, complimenting him on his fine taste until he fairly glowed, making a big show of his pleasure at her interest. All this was not lost on Marielle, who seethed with jealousy and redoubled her efforts to torment and tantalize him. By the time they rode out to Vouvray, the trunks having been sent on ahead by wagon, war had virtually been declared. Locked in by pride, scarred and vulnerable from too many encounters, each sought only to hurt the other, denying the love that tugged at the heart and weakened resolve. At Vouvray they met Narbaux, who noted Marielle's forced gaiety, André's excessive politeness to his wife, and shook his head sadly, suddenly glad to be a bachelor.

The *carrosse,* a large, heavy coach with window glass and curtains, was bumpy and slow, compelling them to break up the journey with a night at a country inn where, much to both Marielle's and André's relief, Madame la Comtesse was forced to sleep in the same room with the innkeeper's wife and two daughters, while the gentlemen shared a bed.

But Marielle could not long deny her natural disposition. As the miles dropped away and they neared Paris, her eyes began to glow in anticipation, and she fairly bubbled with enthusiasm, incapable of hiding her delight. Narbaux beamed, and even André could not maintain his black mood, catching fire from her joy, and looking forward to the first glimpse of Notre Dame's spires as he had not for a very long time.

Since the day was early, they decided to drive around for a bit in a small carriage before settling into their quarters at the Louvre. Paris bustled with activity. More and more, under Louis and Richelieu, it was becoming not only the titular capital of France, but her very heart and soul. The air was filled with the sounds of hammers and saws as new buildings were constructed, and the older houses and churches, encased in lacy scaffolding, were being repaired and refurbished. They passed the Luxembourg Palace, finished barely five years before for Marie de Medici, and still so new it sparkled in the sun. Crossing the Pont Neuf to the Place Dauphine, André pointed out to Marielle the equestrian statue of Henry IV, the father of the present King, who had directed the building of the Place, and the elegant townhouses that surrounded the triangular park at the tip of the Île de la Cité. When Marielle exclaimed that she would like to live there, Jean-Auguste laughed and explained that this was no longer the most fashionable section of the city, and that only lesser government officials and aristocrats lived there. They passed through the old quarter of the city, the wheels of their carriage slopping through the mud and filth, twisting through dark, narrow streets that were ominous even in daylight and, as André explained, positively lethal and crawling with thieves and murderers at night. Used to the relative civility of La Forêt, Marielle was dismayed at the roughness of these streets and their people, where curses and shouts filled the air and every dark corner housed a gambling den or brothel. Harridans stood on street corners singing bawdy songs and offering their wares to the passersby while leering young boys, still in their teens, tendered the lowest forms of obscene literature to every nobleman who ventured into the quarter. At last the cobbled streets and narrow gabled houses were behind them, and they emerged once again into a newer section of the city. Before them was a lovely square, surrounded on all sides by magnificent townhouses, their red and white stone set off by clear blue slate roofs and tall majestic windows. Narbaux announced pompously to Marielle that this, the Place Royale, was the only place to live in Paris, except perhaps for the palaces, and she made an elaborate game of choosing which one she wished to purchase. Passing the Rue Saint-Honoré, where buildings were being razed to make way for the Cardinal's new palace, they drew up at length to the Louvre, sprawled out beside the Seine. It was an imposing structure, a jumble of old and new. The large quadrangle, begun by Henry II and newly completed by Louis himself, surrounded an inner courtyard that had once held the turreted core of the old fortress. Here and there an old tower, a crumbling gate, a sturdy outbuilding stood as mute reminders of the old Louvre, when it had lain outside the walls of Paris, but the new was slowly obliterating the old. Parallel to the Seine ran the Grande Galerie of Henry IV, an imposing wing that stretched for nearly a quarter of a mile in length, almost reaching the Tuileries palace. Since the time of Henry, artists and craftsmen had been allowed to live on the lower floors of the Galerie, and with the unceasing building and repairing that went on their services were always in demand.

Marielle was dazzled by everything. The servants who led them to their apartments were clad in pale blue livery bound in gold braid, and seemed better dressed and well-fed than half the bourgeoisie of La Forêt. The corridors they passed through could have held her father's comfortable cottage within their confines, with room for the kitchen garden besides! She marveled at their apartments: each bedchamber had its own sitting room and dressing closet; a large and opulent drawing room, hung with fine tapestries, served to join their two suites. She danced from room to room, exclaiming in delight at each wonder that met her eyes, chattering gaily to Jean-Auguste and André. But when the servants had retired, taking Narbaux to his own quarters, and she was alone with her husband, her joy evaporated and she retreated behind a cold wall of silence, while André, his eyes an icy blue, withdrew to his own suite. In the presence of others they could laugh, enjoy themselves, be gay; alone together the pain and anger returned like an unwelcome guest to poison everything.

With the help of her maid, Marielle dressed slowly and carefully. Their Majesties would receive them in the Grand Salon; later there would be dancing and a late supper. She had chosen a dark blue silk gown with wide puffed sleeves and a deep slash in the front of the skirt that revealed a brilliant green satin petticoat. A delicate lace collar framed the low bodice, accenting the clarity of her own creamy skin. At her throat she placed the diamond and emerald necklace that André had given her, then told herself that she cared little if he were pleased or not. In spite of herself, she had to admire him as they made their way to the salon—he looked positively splendid. He wore a gold brocaded doublet, close-fitting and slightly widened at the shoulders, which served to emphasize the breadth of his chest. At neck and wrists he had a snowy lace collar and cuffs. His brocaded breeches ended just below the knees and were tied and bowed with ruby satin ribbons, which also adorned the low shoes he wore. A fine, bejeweled sword was buckled on about his waist. Marielle was conscious of the stares and whispers from the women as they passed, and could not suppress a feeling of pride at being by his side.

They were ushered into the Grand Salon, already crowded with members of the Court. It was a magnificent room, the walls covered with handsome frescoes that were framed and divided by carved flowers and fruits in high relief. The huge fresco on the ceiling, illuminated by blazing chandeliers and candelabra on marble tables, was an allegory that showed Louis in a gilded chariot drawn by prancing stallions. Above his head hovered winged seraphim playing upon stringed instruments and bearing a crown of roses for his head, while the Three Graces smiled benignly from an alcove. Marielle found it difficult to keep her eyes from straying to the ceiling, such was its splendor. A small recess off the Salon had been given over to card tables, and it was from there that the Queen, playing cards with the Keeper of the Seals, espied André and beckoned him with her delicate fingers to come forward. His hand beneath Marielle's elbow, he steered a course through the crowded room, conscious of the stir that her beauty caused, and feeling himself torn with jealousy, bitterly aware that she was his in name only.

The Queen smiled warmly as they bowed, then patted the chair beside her, indicating that Marielle should sit.

"My dear," she said in her sharp voice, strong with the accents of her native Spain. "So you are André's missing wife! He chose well, I think. The whole Court is buzzing, you know. That he should have galloped off

across half of France to find you! How very romantic!
There are few husbands in this Court so in love with
their wives they would bother to gallop even through
the Bois de Boulogne, let alone the whole country-
side!" She laughed wickedly as André fidgeted beside
her. "For their mistresses, perhaps—" and here she
smiled conspiratorially at Marielle. "You must beware
those women who seem to dislike you without
cause. . . ." She beamed in delicious malice as André
frowned, clearing his throat, and suddenly found something fascinating in the chandelier to hold his gaze.
Aware at length that a cloud had passed before Marielle's eyes, the Queen lowered her voice and spoke
gently.

"You must forgive me my little games, my dear. We
neglected wives are all filled with envy at your good
fortune. May it be God's will that your husband always
loves you with the same devotion he holds for you
now."

Marielle bit her lip as sparkling tears caught in her
silky lashes. The Queen patted her hand.

"Your sensitivity does you credit, *ma petite*. You are
both very fortunate to have found one another. That
wicked traitor Gravillac! I regret only that Louis did
not have him beheaded! But true love conquers in the
end, *n'est-ce pas?* Now, Monsieur le Comte, take your
charming wife about the room. It will be great sport to
see the faces of envy on the other men . . . and not a
few of the women," she added as a parting shot to
André, who led Marielle away as quickly as he could.

Marielle reflected bitterly on what the Queen had
said. The room must be full of his mistresses, she
thought, yet I have lost his love because of one
unwilling liaison. She was glad when Jean-Auguste

joined them and said that His Majesty wished to meet Marielle. They spied Louis across the room, seated in a dim corner with a young man about the same age as the King. They were deep in conversation, Louis's soulful gaze bent to his companion's every word and gesture, while he held the young man's hand tightly between his own two. André raised a brow quizzically to Narbaux.

"The latest?"

Jean-Auguste nodded. Marielle frowned, then her eyes widened in disbelief as she gazed from one to the other.

"But surely . . . you cannot mean . . ." she stammered. "But the Queen has carried children!" she blurted out. "Not to term, I know, but—" she gulped. "Were they not his Majesty's?"

Narbaux laughed aloud at her frankness.

"Be reassured, country girl," he exclaimed. "Paris is not that much more wicked than the Provinces! As far as is known—and the Court gossips are usually unimpeachable—the King has always been faithful to the marriage bed, as has Her Majesty. But the King is a sensitive man who craves tender companions, male and female, to talk to, to confide in. They play at the emotions of love, with stormy quarrels and tender reconciliations, all very intense . . . and platonic! When the innocent affair has run its course, the King's ministers remind him once again that he has as yet no heir to the throne, and he dutifully fulfills his obligations to Queen and country!" Marielle shook her head. She would never understand the ways of the Court.

Louis dismissed his favorite as they approached, and rose to greet them. Marielle curtsied deeply, touched by the melancholy sadness in his eyes. Perhaps, she thought, a king needs affection more than others do, and she pitied him for being the butt of ugly gossip. When he spoke to her, she responded kindly, gently, wanting suddenly to be his friend. André caught the unexpected note in her voice, and looked at her with surprise and admiration, struck once again by her sensitivity and perception. Louis held Marielle's hand and smiled benignly.

"What an exquisite creature you are, my dear! And since André has chosen you, I have no doubt that your heart is as kind and sweet as your face is lovely! You must dance in the Court ballet in two weeks. We will have you as Venus, I think! Not a word," he admonished, as Marielle began to murmur a protest. "I shall send the dancing master to your chambers to teach you the steps and arrange for your costume."

They chatted pleasantly for a while, Marielle gratified to see the esteem in which André was held by the King. After a time, musicians appeared, carrying lutes and viols, and the center of the floor was cleared for dancing. Marielle was enchanted. The dances she had learned at country fairs, done to the music of an itinerant fiddler, were nothing like the exciting galliards and courantes and sarabandes she now saw. She marveled as the brilliantly clad lords and ladies leapt and spun about the floor, in a whirl of bright satin and taffeta. More than once she had to refuse the young gallants who crowded around, begging for a dance, but her foot tapped gaily to the music and she longed to learn the steps they danced. At last, when the reeds piped out a slow, stately tune and a Spanish pavane was announced, she allowed herself to be dragged onto the dance floor by a persistent young man in scarlet satin, glancing apologetically at André as she did so. Her partner patiently explained the few simple steps of the dance, and in a few moments she was pacing majestically about the floor, the cynosure of every eye. After that she had hardly a moment alone with André, for the young blades, realizing the reason for her seeming reluctance, quarreled with one another over who would teach her the next dance. In a while, laughing gaily, her face flushed with pleasure, she was whirling merrily about the room as though she had danced the steps all her life. André danced with a few of the women, avoiding as best he might those of most recent intimacy, and played the part of the complacent husband, secure in the love of his wife, but he ached with jealousy and desire, wondering which of her partners would catch her fancy. She was too beautiful, too flattered by all the attention, too innocent of the ways of the Court! It gave him little comfort to overhear a courtier comment to a companion that if that lovely thing were *his* wife, he would keep her at home in his bed, or heavy with child! It took all of André's willpower to keep from smashing the man's face with his fist, or dragging Marielle away to her room, and he smiled falsely at the other guests until his cheeks ached.

They withdrew to the dining salon for supper, where Marielle bravely sampled the snails and frogs' legs that had become so fashionable in Paris—much to the amusement of the young man in red satin, who had scarcely left her side all evening. She felt giddy with the wine, buoyed by all the attention, quite intoxicated with her triumph. When at last the evening drew to a close and she and André made their way back to their apartments, she was still sparkling and gay, seeming unaware of the scowl that had replaced André's smile as soon as they had left the salon behind them.

She danced into their drawing room, still humming a

snatch of melody, and was stopped by André's voice behind her.

"A moment," he said coldly. She turned to face his icy blue eyes, angry that he should spoil her happy mood. Advancing toward her, he stared pointedly at her *décolletage*. "You will oblige me, Madame, by covering your bosom when you appear in public!" Surprised and annoyed, she looked down at her bodice, which seemed no lower than that worn by most of the women.

"There is nothing improper in my costume, Monsieur!" She felt her anger rising. "I noted that the other ladies wore their gowns as low! Or is it only your old mistresses whose bosoms you choose to admire?"

His eyes narrowed in fury and he spoke through clenched teeth.

"The ladies who show their bosoms shamelessly are willing to show a good deal more in private than you are prepared to give! Or is your wide-eyed innocence merely a game you play? Do you fancy snaring a duke or prince with your wiles?"

"Do you think I could not?" she challenged, stung by his cruelty. She stamped her foot angrily. "If I chose to, I could have as many lovers in this Court as you have had mistresses!"

At that he flinched and his face turned pale. A hard light glittered in his eyes, but he quickly recovered himself and shrugged.

"Then all of Paris would know what I—and the Marquis de Gravillac—know—that the Comtesse du Crillon is a whore!"

With a vehement cry she raised her hand to strike him full in the face, but he caught her wrist and pulled her cruelly toward him, while she struggled vainly to loose her hand.

"Have a care, Madame," he said, his voice low and ominous. "I have never beaten a woman, but I must confess that the thought of thrashing you like a willful and errant child is suddenly very tempting! Pray do not force me to it!"

Her glance wavering under his withering stare, she averted her eyes and wrenched her hand from his grasp. Fleeing to the safety of her own sitting room, she slammed the door behind her and locked it fast, then leaned her forehead against its heavy panels, weeping bitterly. In spite of everything, she could not even hate him; she could only lock her heart against him and the pain he brought her, as she had barred the door.

Chapter Sixteen

THE DAYS RUSHED PAST IN A WHIRL OF DANCES AND *fêtes*, the nights filled with music and fireworks that brought cries of pleasure from Marielle. True to his word, Louis had sent the dancing master to her apartments, who trailed in his wake musicians and seamstresses and drapers with heavy bolts of fabric. They argued and cut and stitched while the rhythms were tapped out and Marielle sought to remember the complicated patterns of the ballet. The Court picnicked and rode in the Bois de Boulogne, and the great nobles jousted and raced and held fencing matches in the Place Royale while the rest of the assemblage gambled on the winners. André and Marielle spent a morning in the company of Richelieu, seated comfortably in his apartments and surrounded by the cats he loved. The Cardinal insisted that Marielle take a steaming cup of chocolate, a drink that the Spaniards had recently brought back from their outpost in Mexico. Marielle found it rich and delicious, and sat sipping contentedly while the Cardinal, his eyes glittering with intelligence, discussed the Languedoc compaign with André. Trained as a soldier in his youth, Richelieu still gloried in a well-fought battle and, on more than one occasion, had led the King's army himself.

One afternoon, André and Jean-Auguste took Marielle to the theater at the Place Dauphine, though André was reluctant to do so. He warned her she would not find it to her liking, and insisted that she be masked, as was proper for a lady of the nobility. Marielle was appalled by what she saw. It was a silly comedy, involving faithless husbands and wives and lovers, but the language and gestures were crude, the sexual innuendos so coarse and blatant, that she sat in a stew of embarrassment, glad of the mask that hid her face, painfully aware of André's mocking eyes on her.

Most of the time she was surrounded by admirers who praised her beauty and complimented her wit and intelligence. She found it exciting and not a little overwhelming. She had not been raised with vanity about her looks, and she found the sudden attentions flattering and surprising. More than once she would catch sight of herself in a glass and laugh in innocent delight, like a child who has found a new toy. She knew her following of devoted courtiers annoyed André, though he tried to hide it, but it was all harmless fun and it pleased her.

Besides, she was still upset at him for his meanness and bad temper; it was refreshing to be surrounded by young men who smiled and laughed and asked nothing in return. She had not forgotten, however, the look in André's eyes that first night in the Palace. For the first time, she was a little afraid of him, aware that there was a dark corner of his soul that she had come perilously close to exposing, something that seemed to go beyond his hatred and jealousy of Gravillac. She was careful to raise the necklines of her gowns to a more demure level, and when she retired to her rooms at night, though she felt an unfamiliar stirring of uneasiness, she did not lock the door, sensing that it would be for André a challenge he could not long ignore.

For his part, André was aware of the unlocked door, though it might just as well have been a barred gate, for it represented that which no longer seemed attainable. By day he watched Marielle with her admirers, his heart full of jealousy and longing; at night, sleepless, he paced his rooms, consumed by a burning hunger that tore at his vitals, a desire for her that drove him mad. He no longer cared about Gravillac; he yearned for her with a desperation that drove out all thoughts of the past. The thought of his own ugliness and cruelty tormented him. If there had been a chance of wooing her away from the memory of Gravillac he had destroyed it with his jealousy; even when he meant to be kind, sharp and hateful words sprang to his lips and he ended by hurting her. He wished to God they had never come to Paris.

In the rue Saint-Thomas du Louvre, just a few steps from the palace, was the Hôtel de Rambouillet, the most fashionable gathering place in all of Paris. It was here that, every Thursday, Madame de Rambouillet welcomed to her home the noblest aristocrats of the realm, as well as men of letters, poets and scholars. Here, in a large and handsome salon hung with panels of blue velvet bordered with silver and gold, she presided over discussions where wit and intellect held sway, where a man was judged not only by what he said but by the beauty and elegance of his words. A charming and serene woman, Madame insisted on good manners, good taste, courtesy, and imposed her will with such gaiety and wit that the Court shone with a civility heretofore unknown in any capital of Europe.

Marielle found the Salon exciting and stimulating. There were scientists who had known her father, men who could discourse on medicine and philosophy and literature. She listened as lawyers argued points of law and, with a pang of remembrance for Gervais, found herself disputing them with arguments she had heard at home in La Forêt. She basked in the admiration of the intellectuals, finding it a headier wine than the praise her beauty elicited, and was suddenly glad that her father had insisted on educating her beyond the level that was expected for most women.

Madame de Rambouillet, who was in frail health, reclined on a daybed set in a small alcove, and held forth with André and several other gentlemen, elaborating on the latest Court follies with charm and wit. But she was a shrewd and intelligent woman, and she noted with some interest that André's eyes strayed across the room whenever a burst of laughter came from the men surrounding Marielle.

"Tell me, Comte du Crillon," she said suddenly, "have you been to the theater this week?"

André nodded. "I found the play harmless enough, but I fear my wife did not find it to her liking."

A young nobleman leaned forward seriously. "Why should any wife enjoy a play that exposes a woman's inherent susceptibility to the blandishments of other men? It is a cruel attack on every woman's honor and integrity, and suggests that no marriage is safe! A husband would do better to keep his wife at home and free from the temptations and wicked ideas that such plays promote!"

"Nonsense!" laughed Madame. "What has theater to do with it? A woman is more clever than you might suppose! Is there any man alive who can be truly sure of his wife's fidelity? He must simply trust in her faithfulness and virtue. Is it not so, André?" she asked pointedly, as another peal of laughter snapped André's head around. He turned back at once, and smiled disarmingly at Madame de Rambouillet's piercing glance.

"And who can guess?" he said casually. "What transpires in the salon does not necessarily reflect what happens in the bedchamber."

"There you have it!" exclaimed a red-faced gentleman with a large moustache. "A man can but mount and ride his own wife often enough to keep her happily tethered in the stable!"

"Not to mention foals in the barn," said another, slyly, and the whole company burst into laughter. Drawn by the merriment, several other guests joined the group, Marielle among them.

"We are discussing marital fidelity," André said sourly, and watched the smile freeze on her lips.

Madame de Rambouillet beamed at both of them, but her eyes were thoughtful. "How fortunate to be newly-wed as you are. Love is still fresh and unspoiled, and hearts are yet to be broken."

The red-faced man guffawed. "There were more than a few broken hearts at Versailles when the ladies heard that Monsieur le Comte had taken a wife!"

"And a score of relieved husbands!" laughed another guest.

Marielle's eyes flashed. "It would seem that infidelity is only a husband's prerogative!"

"Perhaps so, to judge by the sighs that followed Comte du Crillon in the Grand Salon last evening!" This remark was accompanied by light-hearted laughter, while André squirmed and Marielle glowered.

"If his wife frowns at him like that, mayhap the other women think he is still available!"

"Come!" said Madame firmly, glancing from André to Marielle. "You cannot let such unkind remarks stand unchallenged. You must cast out the lie!" She turned to André. "Kiss her!" she ordered.

André gaped as the courtiers grinned and Marielle turned away uncertainly. Several of the men chuckled among themselves, joking and nudging one another in the ribs. But Madame de Rambouillet would not be deterred. She nodded her head with finality.

"You must kiss your wife and show us that we are all old women who have forgotten what love is!"

Amid much laughter and snickering, André reluctantly approached Marielle and slipped his arms gently about her waist. She smiled uneasily up at him, then closed her eyes as he leaned down and pressed his lips to hers. He felt the tenseness of her body, her rigid mouth; then, without warning, she melted in his arms, her tender curves pressing against him, her lips parting in warm surrender. The laughter behind them died into an embarrassed silence as she swayed against him, her soft arms encircling his neck. He felt the room shake beneath his feet, and the blood pounded in his temples. At last, he disengaged her arms and held her away from him, searching her face and the soft green eyes that sparkled now with trembling tears. He laughed unsteadily at Madame de Rambouillet and bowed, unwilling to risk speech. She smiled gently, a wise and knowing grin that lit up her handsome face.

"You must forgive an old romantic, André. There is nothing so charming, I think, as two young people in love. We can only wish you continued happiness and joy!"

"And many children!" exclaimed red-face, slapping André on the back, as Marielle turned away, flustered. Seeing this, Madame de Rambouillet put her hand lightly on the arm of the serious young man.

"My dear Baron," she said, "have you read Malherbe's last poems? What a great loss France has suffered!" Deftly she guided the company into the new topic, and smiled benignly as André and Marielle slipped away.

It was only a short distance to the palace and the sun had not yet set; they walked slowly, lost in thought. Marielle kept her eyes down, but André stared fixedly at her, as though he would read her profile, his own face a battleground of doubt and confusion and bewilderment. Several times he seemed about to speak and then thought better of it. Finally he blurted out the words, searching her face to gauge their effect.

"I must compliment you, my dear, on your performance. You played the part of the loving wife to perfection!"

Her eyes flew to his face, and he saw the flash of pain in their green depths before she turned away.

"Please, André," she said softly, "don't be cruel."

They made their way to their apartments in silence, André frowning and deep in thought. As Marielle turned to enter her sitting room, he held her arm and pulled her back, slipping one hand about her waist, and tilting her chin up with the other hand until he was staring directly into her eyes. He seemed to be examining her, studying her face, but his own eyes were cold and unreadable. He kissed her then, a long, searching kiss that left her trembling and breathless, her defenses down; but when at last he pulled his lips away his expression had not changed. Deliberately, as though he were seeking answers, he cupped her heaving breast in one strong hand, a gesture that was neither rough nor gentle, only calculating, exploratory. She gasped and flinched under his firm grasp, so brazenly carnal, and he immediately released her and stepped back, his face hard.

"It would seem, Madame, that in spite of yourself you enjoy my kisses." He laughed mirthlessly, a mocking smile on his face. "But you are equally unwilling to pay for them!" His eyes raked her body and she shrank back, filled with dread. "No matter," he growled. "I shall collect the debt one of these days!" And turning on his heel, he strode into his rooms, leaving her pale-lipped and shaken.

Chapter Seventeen

MARIELLE FROWNED WORRIEDLY INTO THE MIRROR. André would be furious with her costume! The dancing master had insisted that Venus always appeared partly draped in her representations, and he had designed a costume in which her chemise had been fashioned of the most transparent silk gauze, so that the rosy pink of her nipples was clearly visible through the delicate fabric. To compound the indecency of the outfit, the bodice of the taffeta gown itself had been cut so low that it did not cover her bosom at all, nor the revealing chemise. She had tried it on in the privacy of her apartments, then changed her clothes and stormed out in a fury, stubbornly shaking her head and insisting to the dancing master that she would not wear such a costume! He had fumed and torn his hair, but eventually they had compromised. The chemise remained, but the offending bodice had been raised to where it covered the tips of her breasts; in compensation for this relative modesty, however, the gown's taffeta sleeves had been eliminated, revealing the sheer chemise beneath, and making her appear almost scandalously bare from wrist to shoulder. It was too late to make any changes now; she could only hope that the other costumes were of the same mode, if only to placate André.

Her maid entered with a small oaken chest, delicately carved. Within, Marielle found a dainty nosegay of pale yellow roses and a brief note. Would the fair Venus wear the favor tonight of one whose heart worshipped at her shrine? It was signed by the Duc de Saint-Denis, the young gallant in red satin who had paid court to her that first evening, and had been one of her most attentive admirers. Marielle smiled fondly. He was a pleasant young man, charming, boyish, sensitive—he had kissed her hand only this morning, then looked hurt when she scolded him for his presumption. How kind of him to send her flowers. *Le Bon Dieu* knew it would not have occurred to André, though her nervousness about the ballet should have been apparent to him! The yellow roses might be just what she needed. She slipped the nosegay into the cleavage between her breasts and was gratified to see that they helped to screen the voluptuous swell of her bosom. Throwing a silken shawl about her shoulders (she did not wish to catch André's eye before the performance!), she hurried to the large gallery in which the ballet would be held.

It was a huge room, some forty-five feet high, with massive stone arches that ran along the two long sides of the chamber. Against the arches had been placed a series of tiers that served as seating for the spectators. Behind the arches was a mezzanine with balconies that looked out upon the hall, and at the highest level of the chamber, traversing three walls, was a large gallery with a stone railing. Since the performance was expected to last at least four hours, smaller rooms adjoining the gallery and mezzanine had been set up to feed the guests who wandered from grandstand to balcony to dining salon in the course of the evening. At one end of the hall was a small dais upon which the King and his party would be seated, and toward which the performance would be directed. At the opposite end of the hall, which served as the backdrop for the ballet, hung a large square of canvas, painted to represent a placid ocean against a vivid blue sky. Behind the canvas were several small antechambers where the rest of the scenery was kept, along with such mechanical devices as were necessary to bring in the various characters on clouds or sky-borne chariots. Since the performers were all members of the Court, high-born lords and ladies, a large antechamber had been set aside with all that was required to see to their comforts during those portions of the ballet in which they were not involved.

By the time André and Jean-Auguste arrived in the hall, the grandstand was almost full, and they hurried up a marble staircase and jostled their way to the front of the mezzanine balcony. Below, *Le Vingt-quatre Violons du Roy,* the grand Court ensemble of twenty-four violins that had played at every *fête* for many years, was already entertaining the early arrivals with a lively air, while musicians carrying lutes and guitars, oboes and flutes, hurried in and took their places in a small alcove to one side of the backdrop.

Amid a flurry of bowing and murmurs, the Royal party appeared, Louis and Anne, Richelieu and Marie de Medici, the Queen Mother. It was a rare evening— they seemed all to be on good terms with one another—

and as soon as they were settled in their places, the King gave the signal for the ballet to begin.

To the accompaniment of a lute, a young man appeared in a glittering costume that identified him for the spectators as Mercury, the messenger of the gods. In a sweet voice he sang a long recitative explaining that the ballet would concern itself with the Trojan War, the battle between Greece and Troy, and would attempt to show the folly of men who warred against one another. Zeus, the king of the gods, was displeased at uprisings that pitted brother against brother, disturbing the countryside and angering all the gods on Mount Olympus. Only when peace was restored could mortals enjoy the benefits that were man's reward for perfect obedience to the will of the gods. It was as much a celebration of the Peace of Alès and the end of the Huguenot uprising as it was a mythical allegory. There was scarcely a veteran of La Rochelle or the Languedoc campaign who did not nod in agreement as Mercury sang in praise of peace.

A chorus of voices now sang a spirited tune as some two dozen women, gorgeously costumed in the colors of the sea, representing water sprites, danced a flowing pattern of loops and spirals that seemed to imitate the movements of the waves. In their midst appeared suddenly a giant scallop shell that rolled silently forward from the backdrop, and upon which stood the Three Graces, holding high a length of shimmering silk that shielded the center of the shell from view. As the oboes played a gentle air, a voice sang of the Birth of Venus from the foam of the sea, and the Three Graces stepped back and allowed their silks to fall to the floor. André drew in his breath sharply, and a murmur went round the hall. There, in the center of the shell, stood

Marielle as Venus. She had never looked more magnificent. Her gown, all sheer gauze and glowing silk, was the color of sea foam, a pale luminous green that enhanced the creaminess of her full young bosom, the soft arms beneath the gossamer sleeves. Her burnished hair was worn long and full, pearls and seashells entwined among the curls and ringlets. Gilded seashells decorated the long flowing skirt and low-cut bodice, snug against her breast. She wore a demure nosegay of roses at her bosom that tantalized as much by what it hid as the rest of her costume revealed.

André was entranced. She was glorious, awesome, the most breathtaking creature he had ever seen. He could not take his eyes from her. A sudden look of pain crossed his face. He *dared* not take his eyes from her! He would have to see the faces of other men, lust and hunger in their eyes. He cursed silently. Why must she wear her gowns so low? Damn them all! They had no right to look at her! His face softened again as she moved gracefully off the shell to a ripple of applause and danced a slow sarabande with the Graces. She carried herself like a princess, head held high, slender body stately and imperious. André felt as though he would burst with pride and longing and jealousy. Watching the emotions at war on his friend's face, Jean-Auguste chuckled softly to himself.

Venus and the sea nymphs now retired behind the backdrop. The violins played a musical interlude, while workmen scurried about, changing the scenery for the next *entrée*, the Judgment of Paris. Against an elaborate background of leafy trees and grottos, Venus now returned in the company of the goddesses Juno and Minerva. A handsome courtier, richly costumed, and carrying a large golden apple, appeared as the Trojan youth Paris, whose task it was to choose the most beautiful among the three goddesses. Hands entwined, Marielle and the others paced majestically about the youth, turning and swaying in a graceful dance. In one of the grottos, announced by a sudden puff of smoke, now appeared a vision of the fair Helen—Paris' reward for choosing Venus—the Greek queen whose abduction to Troy would provoke the war. The youth pantomimed his indecision with such exaggerated gestures, turning from one goddess to the next, that many in the audience began to laugh. Though the myth called for Venus to be chosen as the most beautiful, in truth Marielle was so exquisite, the other women so ordinary in comparison, that there was no contest, no matter what role she played. At length the young man knelt before Marielle, the apple in his hands, and the audience sighed with pleasure. Marielle reached out a slender hand to take the proffered fruit, but at that moment King Louis rose to his feet and strode into the tableau. Snatching up the golden apple, he himself presented it to Marielle, who sank low in a deep curtsy, proud and shy and flustered all at once. The audience rose to its feet, cheering and clapping, and a grinning Narbaux pounded André on the back, while other guests complimented the Comte du Crillon on his good fortune.

He wanted suddenly to have Marielle at his side, to tell her how lovely she was, to beg her pardon for the unkind things he had said. As the *entrée* ended and the dancers left the hall, he made for the staircase, minded to join her in the performers' antechamber; then he halted abruptly, muttering to himself, his plan thwarted. The King had taken Marielle by the hand and was leading her to the dais, to sit among his guests and enjoy the rest of the performance with the Royal party. There was nothing André could do—she was lost to him until the ballet was finished. Restless, impatient, he wandered in and out of the hall, Narbaux at his side, and ate and drank and chatted idly with his friends. Occasionally he paused to look in at the ballet, as the Trojan War unfolded in song and dance and pantomime, but his glance strayed over to Marielle at the King's side. Her face was radiant, eyes shining in pleasure and triumph, soft cheeks flushed with happiness.

The Trojan War had now advanced to scenes of battle, and the great hall was filled with men, gorgeously costumed in glittering armor, who brandished swords and feigned combat to the accompaniment of trumpets and cornets. Though the patterns of the battle had been worked out as carefully as the most elaborate dances, a few of the nobles—skilled in the arts of war—far outshone the others with their masterful handling of sword and shield, and elicited murmurs of praise from the audience. André and Narbaux watched with some interest, leaning over the balcony and nodding their heads in approval at the scene. Behind them, two gentlemen were discussing the merits of the various combatants.

"I fancy that soldier in the red plumes," said one. "I should not mind meeting him in a contest of fencing! One can always take the measure of a man by a sword!"

"For myself," announced the other, "I should prefer to take the measure of that voluptuous Venus!"

"With a sword?"

"Nay, my friend! With my own measuring rod, that which nature has so thoughtfully provided me!" and they laughed together at the ribald joke.

André choked and turned, his eyes murderous, his hand on the pommel of his sword, but Narbaux clutched at his arm and dragged him away from the balcony and into a small room where they might be alone until his friend's fury had abated.

"*Nom de Dieu,* André! If you are going to be jealous of every man who looks at her, you will never have any peace! She is a beautiful woman, every man's desire! Do not trouble yourself with what they may say or think—be grateful she is yours!"

André laughed bitterly. "Is she mine? Is she, my friend?"

Narbaux shook his head in amazement. "Are you such a fool you cannot see the love in her eyes?"

"And what about Quiot?" Narbaux frowned at the question, mystified. "You were at the inn," André continued. "You know what happened!"

Narbaux began to stammer. "But I thought . . . you and she . . . at La Forêt . . . !"

"Not I, *mon ami!* I did not plant that seed!"

Jean-Auguste gaped in surprise and dismay. "Against her will, then," he said gently. "Surely—"

"You did not see the way she kissed him at Quiot!" said André in agony.

Narbaux was silent, at a loss to ease the pain in his friend's eyes. "Come!" he said at length. "I'm for a cup of wine!" He gripped André by the shoulder, his voice low and sincere. "You may never know what happened with Renard de Gravillac. She is yours now . . . she loves you. Be content!"

By the time they returned to the hall, the final *entrée* had begun. The war had ended in victory for the Greeks, and now the various gods and goddesses appeared, Marielle among them, to dance a stately pavane in celebration of peace. The dançers moved in a complicated pattern, interweaving in complex loops and circles until the dancing floor seemed a living thing, pulsating with life and color. From somewhere high above the dancers, lowered on a mechanical cloud, now appeared Louis, magnificently costumed as Zeus, the king of the gods. The chorus proclaimed his pleasure at the outcome of the war, and warned of his wrath if he were disobeyed. As Louis walked among them, the gods bowed to his supremacy, exalting his glory above all other rulers, while the goddesses strewed rose petals in his path. With a final triumphant blare of the horns, the ballet was ended.

In the milling crowd, they sought Marielle. It was odd. They expected to find her the center of attention, surrounded by admirers, but she was nowhere to be found, though they searched the antechambers as well as the hall. At length, one of the dancers, spying André in a doorway, touched his arm lightly.

"Ah! Monsieur le Comte!" she said. "Did your wife find you?"

"Find me, Madame? What do you mean?" His blue eyes glittered.

She smiled wanly. "Why . . . why your message! I thought she said that you . . . oh dear!" she exclaimed and bit her lip, suddenly afraid she might have revealed a confidence. "I am sure she will find you soon enough!" she added as brightly as she could.

"Do you know who brought the message?" asked Narbaux smoothly.

The woman hesitated, her eyes sweeping the room. "There," she said doubtfully, pointing to one of the footmen. "I do hope I have not . . . oh dear!"

Narbaux smiled reassuringly, and he and André

made their way to the servant. Yes, he said, he had given a message to La Comtesse du Crillon. No, it was not a written message, but he was not at liberty to tell the gentlemen what it was, since it was a personal message from the lady's husband. His eyes widened in dismay as Narbaux murmured a few words to him, and he bowed obsequiously to André. He wished to beg Monsieur le Comte's pardon, he had not at first recognized him, the message had been delivered exactly as he had instructed, and Madame la Comtesse had hurried off at once to the tapestry room in the west wing.

"And who gave you the message?" growled André through clenched teeth.

"The Duc de Saint-Denis, Monsieur!"

André whirled and set off for the tapestry room, Jean-Auguste at his side. "Damn! That one! He's a devil hiding behind the face of an angel! Every woman wants to mother him, and ends up, if she is not careful, mothering his brat! Pray God we find that naive wife of mine before it is too late!"

Marielle hurried down the long corridor. It was brightly lit, blazing with the light of a hundred candles, but quite deserted. What an odd place to meet André! Whatever could he want that could not wait until they retired to their own apartments? She hoped he was not angry about her costume! Well, she would know soon enough. She turned a corner; the tapestry room was just at the end of this hall. A small door opened to her right.

"Madame!" She stopped, surprised. It was the Duc de Saint-Denis. Smiling, he stepped from the doorway and took her hand, pressing it softly to his lips.

Reproachfully she tried to pull her hand away, but he sank to one knee, his eyes adoring her. "Nay! You cannot deny me tonight, for I would pay homage with my lips to the most exquisite creature in the world!"

Giggling, she allowed him to kiss her hand. What a sweet young man, she thought indulgently. He rose to his feet, still holding her fingers, and attempted to pull her gently into the small room from which he had emerged. "Come," he said, "sit with me for a little, and let me tell you how I worship you!"

"I cannot! My husband is awaiting me!"

His brow darkened. "Let him wait!" he pouted. "I have not had a moment alone with you these past two weeks! And when you return to the hall everyone will crowd around and I shall not see you again tonight!" He smiled boyishly. "Can I not have but a moment or two of your time to tell you how lovely you are, and how I adore you and how sweetly you danced in the ballet?"

Marielle laughed. "But it would seem you have just told me!"

"How can you jest when my heart is aching with love for you? If you do not come and sit with me, I shall throw myself into the Seine!" His eyes held such misery, feigned though it might be, that she relented and allowed him to draw her into the room. "But only for a few moments," she admonished, as he closed the door and sat on a large settee, pulling her down beside him. His eyes burning, he told her that he loved her, worshipped her, could not live without her. The smile faded from her face.

"Hush," she said gently, seriously. "You must not speak to me in that fashion. It is not seemly."

"Yes, I know." He smiled at her. There was no trace

of the boyish grin. His eyes dropped to the front of her gown, then back to her face. "You wore my favor." He plucked the flowers from between her breasts and touched them gently to his lips. "They are still warm from your bosom!"

"I must go," said Marielle, an edge of uneasiness creeping into her voice. "André will be waiting."

"No."

"What?"

"André will not be waiting!" He smiled, the look of one conspirator to another. Marielle frowned. Whatever was he talking about? "Come now!" he said, with a sly grin. "You must have guessed he did not send the message!"

Marielle gasped in surprise, her eyes wide. One hand flew to her bosom. She started to rise, but Saint-Denis grasped her arm and would not let her leave. He smiled again.

"Such charming innocence—you do it well! But my flowers at your breast gave me the answer I wanted!" He leaned toward her, his free hand reaching for her shoulder. She shuddered. How could she ever have thought him attractive or sweet? She strove to avoid his hands, but he grabbed her determinedly by the shoulders and forced her back upon the settee, leaning over her and pressing his chest against her heaving bosom, his lips seeking hers. She struggled fiercely and cried out. Impatiently he clapped one hand over her mouth.

"Have done!" he exclaimed angrily. "You have defended your virtue long enough to satisfy the rules of propriety! Save your innocence for your husband!" She twisted wildly against him, but the weight of his body held her down and she was trapped. He took his hand off her mouth and began to grope hurriedly at her skirts. She gasped as his hand slid under her petticoat, searching fingers exploring her bare flesh. Desperately she thrashed about under his grasp, shaking her head from side to side. She could hear the pearls dropping from her coiffure and rattling across the floor. His other hand still held her by the shoulder; she lifted her head slightly and closed her teeth about his wrist, clamping down with such ferocity that he howled loudly and leapt back, releasing her. Before she had the opportunity to move away, he was upon her again, straddling her body and pinning her wrists to the settee. His eyes blazed fire.

"Vixen!" he hissed. "I have waited long enough! I am weary of your games! It is time for you to keep your promises!"

"Let me go!" she panted. "I never gave you cause!"

He sneered. "Bees do not buzz around flowers with no honey! Every man who paid you court gave me cause!" He bent to kiss her, his hungry mouth seeking her bosom. She cringed and shrank away, wishing she could sink into the settee, and closed her eyes tightly as though she could make him vanish. Suddenly he was gone. Her eyes flew open. André stood above her, his face contorted with rage. One hand gripped Saint-Denis by the shoulder; as she watched, the other hand, knotted into a fist, exploded against the Duc's chin with a terrible cracking sound. Saint-Denis crumpled to the floor, moaning, as a thin trickle of blood seeped from his sagging jaw. Narbaux rushed to his side and knelt down, effectively screening him from further violence, and stared fixedly at André's face until some of the anger subsided.

"No need to kill him, my friend. From the look of this rakehell, it will be long before he can again sing his songs of love! Best find him a surgeon!" He helped Saint-Denis to his feet, supporting him with a shoulder, and led him, stumbling, from the room.

André glared down at Marielle. Grabbing her hands, he jerked her roughly to her feet. His eyes, dark with anger and disgust, took in her torn costume, her wild hair tangled about her face. She bit her lip and sniffled, her shaking fingers plucking at bodice and sleeve, assessing the damage.

"You little fool!" His eyes burned into her. "I warned you! Did you not know this would happen? *Nom de Dieu!* Did they keep you hidden in a box at La Forêt?" He stopped abruptly, as she began to tremble violently, her body shaking with great sobs. She turned away and buried her face in her hands, her shoulders drooping forlornly. Relenting, he turned her around in his arms, cradling her tear-stained face against his chest. He sighed deeply, resignedly.

"Tomorrow," he said gruffly, "we return to Vilmorin. I think it is time to go home!"

Chapter Eighteen

THE AIR WAS RICH AND HEAVY WITH THE SCENT OF GRAPES. André breathed deep. He could already smell the tang of fall, the heady mixture of smoke and crackling leaves and grapes so golden and ripe that the perfume of the wine seemed ready to burst from their hazy skins. He guided his horse through the fields, dismounting now and again to check the heavy clusters. If the weather held, they could begin harvesting tomorrow. It would be a good yield—the vines had been fruitful and the grapes were rich and sweet, promising a robust wine.

It felt good to be home again. There was a solidness, a reality about Vilmorin that fed his soul, brought substance to his days. He laughed ruefully to himself. In truth, there seemed less stability at the moment than he would have wished. While he and Marielle had been in Paris, Grisaille and Louise had spent a great deal of time together. Now, cow-eyed and distracted, Grisaille went about the estate in a daze, and Louise, as skittish as a blushing bride, had to be continually reminded of her chores. Clothilde's behavior was even odder. He remembered how warm and friendly she had been, in those days before Paris when he and Marielle had been locked into silent rage against one another. Strange. He almost had the impression that she had expected Paris to produce the final rupture between them, and had been hurt and disappointed when he returned with Marielle. There was a new note in her behavior, a tense brittleness, almost a desperation to win him back that surprised and dismayed him. He did not think he had given her reason for renewed hope—despite the tangle of his relationship with Marielle—but he felt a pang of guilt and responsibility. He would have to ask her to leave after the harvest; it would be best for all of them.

Marielle too was different since Paris. Subdued, shy, she went quietly about Vilmorin in a cloud of embarrassment, as though she still felt the shame of what had happened, upset by her own gullibility. There was a sadness about her—until now he had not thought to wonder if she were happy at Vilmorin. Whenever he looked at her (which was often, lately), he seemed to see a wall between them. He began to feel guilty for wanting her so desperately. *Nom de Dieu!* As though a man had no right to desire his own wife! He should have taken her as soon as he could; the longer they behaved as they did, the harder it became to change the pattern. Coward! He thought of the rainy afternoon, when she had resisted him and he had cursed her, conjuring up Gravillac. There had been a wall between them that day, but now, recalling what Narbaux had said in Paris, he was sorry he had not persisted. Perhaps that wall was more flimsy than he supposed, and he should not have allowed himself to be put off. She melted at his kisses, that was not feigned; if he had insisted on his rights as a husband, he might have been able to break through the wall. Now, after all that had happened, he was no longer sure he was willing to risk his own pride. Curse Gravillac, La Forêt, that betraying moonbeam that had lit up her face and unsettled his life forever! He yearned for bachelorhood again, and noted with a disturbing ache in his loins that it had been two months since he had had a woman. If rumors could be believed, Cardinal Richelieu himself was less celibate than he!

Still, Narbaux said she loved him. Who could tell? Perhaps it was so, and his jealousy of Gravillac had made him blind. He began to feel a surge of hope. Away from Paris and the gallants who might turn her head . . . with the long autumn nights approaching . . . he might still have a wife to warm his bed.

He looked up suddenly. At the edge of the field Clothilde was waiting, a large jug of ale in her hand. He rode slowly toward her, uneasy, guarded, feeling himself besieged. She smiled and handed the jug up to him.

"You rode out early this morning, my lord. Cook said you hardly stopped for breakfast."

He took a large swig of ale, then made a sweeping gesture toward the vines, as if in explanation. "I was restless and could not sleep." He regretted his choice of words at once. She laughed, her voice strange and hard.

"The nights are chill, my lord. Mayhap you find your bed too cold for sleep!" He could hardly mistake her meaning. Disconcerted, he handed back the jug and would have wheeled his horse around, but she put her hand on the bridle and stopped him. Her words tumbled out in a rush, and the smile she turned on him seemed frozen. "If there is some service I might perform . . . something I can do to ease your discomfort, my lord . . . !"

"Yes," he said, annoyed, feeling trapped. "You might run some heated bricks between the sheets before I retire." And turning, he rode away. Her eyes, dark and troubled, followed him.

The following day was clear and sunny, the cloudless sky so blue and pellucid that it seemed likely to remain so all day. For the past week, Vilmorin had had an air of expectancy, of anticipation, like some great army marshalling its forces for a great war. The day of battle had now arrived and Vilmorin exploded with activity. The large fermenting vats were dragged out of the chalk caves and brought to the grove of fruit trees below the bluffs. They were placed beneath two large and leafy elms whose branches would shade them and keep them cool. Men and women with large rush baskets on their backs made their way down the long rows of staked grapes, plucking the golden clusters by hand or cutting them with small scythes. Although some of the fields belonged to André's tenant farmers who paid him rent, and some were cultivated by the sharecroppers who contributed a portion of their yield to their landlord in exchange for the use of the land, at harvest time everyone worked together, the farmers side by side with André's own servants. The grapes would be crushed and processed without regard to ownership; the division of the wine would come later, when each man would be given casks according to the proportion of his own harvest. Since the vats and the wine press belonged to Vilmorin, André would be expected to take the first press of the grapes, the best wine, in lieu of a fee for the use of the equipment.

Marielle worked in the grove, supervising the setting up of tables and benches, for it was traditional at Vilmorin to celebrate the harvest with a party. A large bonfire was built over which the cook placed a spitted lamb which hung between two poles and roasted slowly. There was bread and cheese and large jugs of cool ale to sustain the vintners as they worked during the day; when the last cluster of grapes had been cut the ale would be replaced by pitchers of good Vouvray wine, and the feasting would begin in earnest. Ham and sausages would join the lamb, and succulent vegetables from the Loire valley. Louise, hands on hips, was scowling up at two young boys she had sent into the apple trees to pick the ripe fruit. There would be rich apple tarts, hot and fresh, for those who survived the meats. Clothilde assisted Marielle and obeyed her orders smilingly and without question, knowing André was nearby, but her gray eyes betrayed her ruffled feelings.

By late afternoon, although there were still clusters to be picked, the vats, fed by a steady stream of filled baskets, held a thick layer of fragrant grapes. This was the moment that the children (and not a few of the adults!) had been waiting for. Laughing and giggling, shoes thown aside, they tumbled into the vats, there to stomp and squash the tender grapes, while a young man pounded out a rhythm on a large leather drum. In the fields the cutters lifted their heads and smiled at the steady drumbeat, then hurried to finish the last row, the last field, that they too might join the revelers.

The sky was glowing red as the last baskets were emptied into the vats and the men let out a cheer when the casks of wine were brought out. Tired but content, André smiled warmly at Marielle and was dismayed to see the unhappiness in her eyes. He would have gone to her side, to discover what troubled her, when he was distracted by shouting. Grisaille and Louise were quarreling violently, their voices loud above the happy laughter and the beat of the drum. Louise was determined to take a turn in a vat; Grisaille just as determined she should not. At length, glaring at him, she hitched up her skirts, kicked off her wooden clogs, and marched willfully to the vat, calling on a young farmer to help her up, and stomping triumphantly through the grapes while Grisaille glowered at her. The clusters by now were well-trod and slippery; Louise's feet suddenly slid out from under her. With a surprised whoop, she vanished into the pulpy mass, and reappeared a moment later dripping with juice, her clothing embellished with mashed globules and stems. His anger forgotten, his face filled with concern, Grisaille dived in after her, meaning to rescue her; he succeeded only in upsetting her yet again, and himself in the bargain. When finally they were able to drag themselves out to the merriment of all, Grisaille declared that the grapes had been trampled enough, and while he and Louise went to change their clothes, large wooden lids were placed loosely over the vats.

André had sent for a fiddler from Vouvray who scraped out merry tunes to accompany the feasting; as the wine flowed more freely, it was not enough merely to listen to the music and tap the foot. More and more couples jumped up to join the reel, trampling down the grass with their lively dances. André danced with Marielle for a spell, but she seemed so aloof, so distant and sad, that he felt like an intruder on her thoughts and led her finally to a bench somewhat removed from the dancers, that she might sit alone and at peace.

Though he rejoined the company, his eyes strayed ever to his wife, and he began to drink more than was his wont. When the fiddler struck up a fresh tune, he allowed himself to be dragged among the dancers, then saw with a start that his partner was Clothilde, her eyes bright and shining. He would have turned away, but the other dancers insisted that Monsieur should take a turn. Glancing uneasily at Marielle, he reluctantly put his arms about Clothilde's yielding waist. She seemed to linger in his arms, smiling up at him, and once she tripped, falling heavily against him, her full bosom pressed against his chest. His eyes flew again to Marielle, but in the flickering light of the bonfire he could not read her expression. *Did* she love him, as Narbaux claimed? Then surely she would be upset by Clothilde's advances. Angrily he pushed Clothilde away, and pressed through the dancers, throwing himself on a bench and retrieving his cup of wine. When he looked for Marielle, she was no longer where he had left her. He gulped his wine in one draught, then leaned his arms on the table, laid his head upon them and fell asleep.

When he awoke, the fire was dying, and most of the people had left. His head was still spinning, but it would take a great deal more wine than he had already drunk to still the unrest within him. He reached for a fresh pitcher, then saw that Clothilde was sitting nearby, as though she had been waiting for him to awaken. She smiled hopefully, but the invitation in her eyes repelled him and he snarled at her and told her to leave him alone. The wine made him less diplomatic than he might have wished, and she turned in a huff and flounced away.

The wine was good. It deadened his brain. He looked

around. Most of the peasants were already abed, but here and there a couple locked in tender embrace reminded him of his loneliness. Where was *his* wife? *His* partner? He felt anger, righteous indignation. She did not mind his company when he took her to Paris! She did not object when he rescued her from those leering gallants! His blood boiled again, remembering the costume she had worn in the ballet. How dared she disobey him? How dared she tempt every man with her beauty? He thought suddenly of how she had looked, and his heart began to pound in his chest, desire rising within him. By *le Bon Dieu!* Why not? She was his wife—everything a man would want—and Narbaux said she loved him! He took another swallow of wine and jumped up, full of hope, longing, desire. Then he groaned as an ugly thought, all unbidden, sprang into his head.

Why had she gone to bed with Gravillac? Always Gravillac! He pounded his fist on the table, his brain whirling in torment. Damn her! She knew well enough how to tempt a man—with her low-cut dresses and her perfumed body! It was time to see if she could please a man! Even through the haze of wine, he ached with longing, a hunger that tore at his vitals. He would burn her with his passion, sear out the memory of Gravillac, breach that wall between them once and for all! Staggering slightly, he headed for the chateau and his wife's bed.

Chapter Nineteen

THE CORRIDOR WAS DARK, SAVE FOR A LARGE CANDLE ON A table near the end of the hall. It shone like a beacon in the black night and he stumbled toward it, conscious only of the silence and the darkness around him. He was aware suddenly that his boots clacked noisily on the smooth tile; the sound disturbed him, and he pulled them off, tucking them under one arm. Heart pounding, he reached Marielle's door and tried the knob, feeling suddenly stupid and unsure. More like a prowler than a lover, he thought. Well, perhaps he would just look at her for a moment—he was really feeling too unsteady for anything else. He turned the knob and pushed open the door, then picked up the candle and entered her bedchamber. Dropping his boots softly at the foot of her bed, he crossed over to where she slept and placed the candle on a nearby table.

The sight of her was like a blow to the top of his head, driving out the wine and the drunken haze, causing his knees to near-buckle beneath him. She was so fragile, exquisite. She lay on her back, her arms flung out, her burnished hair so full and loose it almost hid the pillow. Even the coverlet could not conceal the soft roundness of her body. He drew in his breath sharply, the sound rasping in his throat. *Mon Dieu!* How could any woman be so beautiful, so desirable? Her witch-craft drove all reason from his mind. He wanted her. Reaching down, he stripped off the coverlet, noting the nightdress that had ridden up above her knees, thus revealing the creamy smoothness of her thighs. She woke with a start and gasped, her eyes flying open. Something flickered—fear?—in their green depths.

"Nom de Dieu! André! What is it? Has something happened?" There was concern in her voice, but her hands were quick to smooth down the shameless night-dress.

"Nothing has happened," he said, and was surprised to hear how slurred his own voice sounded. "Everyone has gone home. The fiddler has gone home. The farmers. Everyone. To his own mate. But the lord of the manor is lonely and cold! Is that fair . . . wife?" She stirred uneasily, inching her way slowly and care-fully toward the far side of the bed.

"Go away, André," she said firmly, trying to keep the anger out of her voice, lest she provoke him into action. He sat down on the edge of the bed, while she watched him warily.

"Wife!" he said again, his voice husky with desire. Bending down, he kissed her full on the mouth, feeling the familiar warmth of her lips, her melting response, as always. Suddenly she pushed against him, turning away angrily, as though her vulnerability to his kisses was a weakness she could no longer tolerate. She rolled away from him and started to get up, hoping to put the bed between them. He clutched wildly at her and caught his hand on the back of her gown. There was a loud tearing sound as she sprang from the bed, and he had a brief glimpse of her smooth back and the rounded firmness of her buttocks before she whirled to face him, clutching her tattered garment to her, her eyes blazing in fury.

"Drunken sot! How dare you? Get out of my room!" She cursed him with every curse she knew, and then with oaths she had heard and did not even understand. He did not seem to hear; he was conscious only of his hunger, the desire that burned like fire in his veins. He leaped off the bed toward her, and she backed away, her eyes never leaving his face. She watched him like a hunted animal, as though gauging her chances for escape, the seriousness of his purpose. Warily they circled the room. He lunged forward, she shied away, barely avoiding his grasping fingers, but he caught at her gown as she scampered back. There was a final wrenching tear, and she stood naked in front of him. Bosom heaving in anger, she cursed him again, while his eyes raked her body and his passion mounted. Again he lunged and she sidestepped nimbly, heading for the partly-opened door and the safety of Louise's room. With a small shriek, she tripped over his boots and fell heavily, sprawled upon her belly. He stopped his pursuit, eyeing the firm roundness of her bare bottom, then his jaw tightened. Stooping down, he swung his hand in a great circle, the broad flat palm outstretched. There was a satisfying smack. She yelped in indignation, and scrambled to her feet, rubbing her stinging flesh, her eyes on fire.

"That, Madame, is for playing the coquette in Paris!" His voice was thick with wine. "Perhaps you have found it easy ere now to forget you have a husband—but no more! No more, my lovely Marielle! I claim a husband's right to collect what is owed me! You have a wife's duty to obey!"

"Bah!" she spat. "A wife's duty! You call me whore at every turn . . . you behave as though you thought I meant to seduce Saint-Denis and half the Court . . . oh!" She stamped her foot in fury. "You play the jealous lout who thinks his wife sleeps with every man she meets . . . and then you stagger in here like a besotted animal and talk to me of a wife's duty! You who must get drunk just to take me! Damn you for a coward and a villain!"

He growled angrily and leapt at her, his shoulders held low so that he caught her around the middle and, standing upright, was able to sling her across one shoulder. She shrieked in protest, her head hanging down his back, and pounded furiously at him as he carried her across the room and pitched her onto the bed. He fell upon her, covering her with kisses, while she struggled and trembled beneath him. His searching hand found the soft warmth of her thigh and followed its velvet contours to that which waited beyond. She shuddered under his touch and strained against him, but her efforts were feeble. In that moment he knew that he had won. She might struggle, but the wall would crumble, she would be truly his at last. He sat up to rip off his shirt; in that split second she had drawn her knees up to her chest, muscles tensed like a coiled spring.

"NO!" she screeched and kicked violently against his belly, sending him flying backward, caught off guard. As he staggered, his balance precarious, she leapt up in fury and hurled a water jug at him. It narrowly missed his ear, shattering against the far wall, and sent him into retreat, while she looked wildly about the room for something else to throw. His heavy boots were still lying on the floor; the first one glanced off his head and set bells to ringing in his brain. He staggered backward and felt the open door. The second boot came flying out as he beat a hasty retreat to the corridor. She slammed the door. In a moment he heard the key turn.

He leaned against the door while his head cleared, then grinned in triumph. He had won her. He knew it! She was magnificent in her fury, but she would be his despite her protests! There would be a battle royal, ending in happy submission. He felt almost cocky. It was so simple he was astonished he had not thought of it before. He had known other women who gloried in a fight, who begged to be taken by force, why not Marielle? It was only the surprise of discovering that his dainty flower was a delightful briar in the bedroom. His passion flamed anew within him. He briefly contemplated the locked door, then shook his head. If he were sober it would be a foolish assault; in his present condition he would probably break his skull. He smiled, remembering the small door through the sitting room. He could taste victory as he hurried around through the sitting room, his fever mounting. Exultant, he burst through the door.

For a moment, in the flickering candlelight, he could not see her. A soft whimpering drew his eyes to the locked door. She crouched there, trembling violently, her bare shoulders heaving with small breathy sobs. Dazed, he passed a hand over his eyes, hardly believing what he saw, and stepped toward her. At his approach she shrank against the door and threw up an arm as though to ward off a blow. She stared at him, her eyes blank and unseeing. He staggered from the room, fleeing from what he had seen in their depths—naked terror.

Clothilde examined her body in the mirror. She was too plump. Her bare breasts, which once had pleased her, were now too full and had begun to sag slightly. The flesh about her waist and hips was no longer firmly rounded, but puckered here and there, making her body look old and tired. She lifted the candle to the mirror and peered searchingly at her face. Did she imagine the first wispy lines about her eyes, the creases on her forehead? A sob caught in her throat. Old! she thought mournfully. But he did not think her old until he brought that innocent-eyed babe back to Vilmorin. Ah, *Dieu!* She was so tired of searching! She had been so sure that this time she would get to Paris, live the life she was meant to.

Damn him! Damn that cold bitch he was married to! They did not even sleep together! She should have pursued him, wife or no wife. She could have played upon his conscience, tormenting him until he sent her packing to Paris with a fat purse and letters of introduction to the Court. Now it was too late. She would have to find another patron. Desperation clutched at her throat. And who would want a woman who was getting old and fat? She thought suddenly of Perrot, her first love. Ah, Perrot! She had sold her life for him. Now, seeing her reflection, she wondered for the first time if he had been worth it. She saw the long lonely years stretching ahead, and she was filled with panic. She might have been a vicomtesse, she could have remained a rich man's daughter and had a fat legacy to cushion the passing of the years. She wept. The memory of

Perrot could no longer warm her bed at night. It was too long ago and he had left her with nothing.

She heard a sudden noise from the stairs. Blowing out her candle, she opened her door a crack and was surprised to see Monsieur le Comte staggering, bootless, down the hall in the direction of the stables. By the dim light of the *torchère* she could just see his face—disappointed, angry, bewildered. Her eyes traveled the length of his body; it was apparent he had not got what he wanted from his wife this night! She watched him stumble toward the stable, then softly closed her door and smiled to herself. Perhaps it was still not too late—Paris might yet be hers! She splashed on her rose-scented perfume, remembering how it had tempted him once before, and wrapped her coverlet about her naked body. Her heart beat furiously; she felt almost giddy with renewed hope. Crossing the courtyard, she tiptoed into the stable, then stopped, feeling as though she must scream with rage and frustration. He lay sprawled on a pile of straw, fast asleep and snoring loudly.

The sun was too bright. The horse was shod with steel—as thick as a man's arm—that thundered loudly on the turf. Surely the boots he had sent the stableboy to fetch were the wrong ones! Was it only one cuckoo that sang in the woods? No. It must be a whole flock! With a groan of pain, André reined in his horse and threw himself out of the saddle. He flattened himself to the ground, face buried in the cool grass, arms and legs thrown wide as though he would still the whirling of the earth. She had called him a drunken sot. She was right. Never in all his life, even in his wild student days, had he managed to drink so much and feel so terrible. The world had stopped spinning. Carefully he rose to his knees and crawled over to the river bank. Taking a deep breath, he plunged his head into the chilly Loire and emerged sputtering and shaking his golden mane like a soggy lion. The icy water made him feel better, and he sat back against a tree and allowed himself at last to remember the previous night. Never before had he needed the encouragement that the wine had given him. Never had his behavior been so at odds with his feelings. Ah *Dieu!* He must have seemed the animal to her, slapping her, tearing her clothes—a monster filled with lust and wine. No wonder she had been terrified! Whatever had created that wall between them, he had been a drunken fool to think that violence could win her love. And it was her love he wanted. He knew that suddenly, just as he knew he loved her. Not with the hot passion of La Forêt, that instantaneous, blinding flash, that ephemeral flame, that love without substance. Nor even the love he had felt in those weeks when he had thought her dead, and apotheosized her into something unreal, a saint, a creature of perfection. No. What he felt now was much deeper, substantial and real. He wanted to care for her, to make her smile and laugh, to protect her from pain. He cursed silently, filled with remorse at his own part in her unhappiness. But he would change. He would tell her he loved her, he would be her gentle and loving friend, he would put all thoughts of Gravillac out of his mind forever.

But . . . all women are fickle! Hadn't he always known that? Didn't it echo like a litany in his brain every time he looked at her? He groaned and held his head. He could not stop loving her, wanting her, any more than he could drive out the ugly thought that she would betray that love. Heartsick, he mounted his horse again. It was simpler to love a dream—dreams did not trail doubts and uncertainties in their wake.

Jean-Auguste, Baron Narbaux, tethered his horse to a large oak and hurried across the wide lawn of Vilmorin to where Marielle was waiting. He had been reluctant to leave his vineyards—there was still so much to be done—but the urgency of her message ("If you deem that we be friends, I beg you to come at once") had persuaded him. Her face was pale and drawn, the eyes red-rimmed and sad. She smiled wanly and thanked him for coming, making small talk and prattling on about the harvest until he took her hands in his and looked deep into her eyes. Her voice faltered then and she turned away, soft chin quivering. He waited for her to compose herself.

"You are his friend," she began softly. "You can talk to him. Ask him . . . beg him . . . to let me go. I do not belong here—I am not a fit wife for any man!"

"What nonsense is this?"

"He hates me!" she wept. "He cannot forget. He cannot forgive. Gravillac's specter perches on the rooftop and haunts us both! If you talk to him . . . a divorce . . . annulment . . . whatever the grounds. Say that we married under duress at La Forêt . . . that I am a disobedient wife . . . whatever he wishes!"

"But you love him! *N'est-ce pas?*"

"Does it matter? Does it keep me from grief? Oh, Jean-Auguste! I can no longer bear the pain we give to one another!"

"And what of his love for you?" he asked softly. "Do

you know how he suffered when he could not find you at La Forêt?" Her eyes wavered, but she shook her head.

"No. No, it is not love he feels for me. More and more I have seen it in his eyes since Paris. It is not love he wants. He will never think of me as his wife—only a mistress with a wedding ring!"

"I think you make more of this than what is warranted. Be patient. Marriage is strange to him. It may be hard for him to settle down. And his pride was grievously wounded because of Gravillac!"

She frowned. "But there is something deeper," she said slowly. "An undercurrent . . . I cannot explain it . . . a feeling, no more. As though he . . . expects me to disappoint him."

He laughed shortly. "But that is what he thinks of all women! I thought he felt differently about you, at least. My friend André is a fool!"

"Perhaps, growing up without a mother, he never learned to trust a woman's love. Perhaps he felt abandoned when she died." She looked at Narbaux thoughtfully. "What was she like? He never speaks of her."

"She died very suddenly. I was younger than he, but later, when we became friends. . . ." He shook his head, remembering, surprised. "He never talked about her! I do not know if he felt her loss, but his father did. The old man languished for years, bent with grief, before he died."

"Poor André!"

"You see? Could you really leave him?" he asked tenderly. She sniffled and smiled softly, then wiped her eyes and blew her nose with the handkerchief he had proffered. "Stay with him," he continued. "It has not been so very long—how can you judge a marriage that has hardly begun? And then . . . he loves you!"

She sighed. "I find myself unwilling yet to believe that . . . but . . ."

He smiled, his fiery mustaches bobbing. "I expect to be invited to the christening of your first child!"

She threw her arms about his neck, pulled his head down, and kissed him warmly on the cheek. "You are a good and loyal friend, Jean-Auguste!"

"Yes," he said, his voice hoarse in his throat. Something in his tone made her look up suddenly. She searched his face, her own awash with sympathy and understanding. Gently she reached up to touch his cheek.

"I am sorry," she said softly.

He turned away. "Yes," he said with a shaky laugh. "If I were not such a good friend, I would persuade you to leave him this very moment!" He strode quickly to his horse, mounted it and was gone. She watched him gallop out of sight, her heart filled with sadness for him.

"Such a charming scene! I did not wish to interrupt!"

Surprised, she whirled to face André. He looked disheveled, unkempt, his face drawn and haggard, but the icy blue eyes glittered with scorn. When he spoke his voice was heavy with sarcasm.

"I came to apologize for my churlish behavior of last night, but it would seem I returned too soon!"

"Do you see rivals behind every tree?" she said, tears of anger springing to her eyes. She pushed past him and hurried toward the chateau. He watched her for a moment, then impulsively strode toward her, turning her roughly about and pinning her in a fierce embrace. He bent and kissed her hard, bruising her mouth, while she struggled vainly against him. At last, with a great effort she pushed him away, her breath coming in deep gulps, her face a mask of anger and contempt.

"Don't ever touch me again! Not ever!" She glared fiercely at him; he recoiled as though she had struck him across the face. Her glance wavered, the brave show collapsing. With a sob, she ran inside, leaving him to his remorse.

But the imp perched on his shoulder and whispered in his ear: Narbaux. Your friend. It is not just Gravillac. She will betray you with all men! And he hardened his heart against her tears.

Chapter Twenty

GRISAILLE REMOVED A SMALL WOODEN PLUG FROM THE
lid of the fermenting vat, sniffed deeply, and turned to
André.

"A few more days yet, Monsieur!"

It had been nearly a week since the grapes had been
crushed, and in that time the large vats had seethed and
bubbled, giving off strange noises and intoxicating
aromas as the fermentation took place, generating
considerable heat that could be felt even through the
heavy staves. Only the chill of the autumn evenings
kept the wood cool enough to be touched. In a few days
the burbling would slow and then cease, and the juice
would be run off into large barrels. Then the "must,"
the thick, viscous mixture of pulp and juice, would be
transferred to the wine press, where the rest of the
liquid would be extracted. When the barrels were full
and loosely sealed, they would be transferred to the
coolness of the caves, there to rest and age for several
months, while the cloudy sediment sank to the bottom.

The wine would then be racked off into smaller casks and hogsheads and sealed with straw plugs.

André sighed deeply. He should feel contented, but the thoughts that seethed in his brain stirred up more heat than the roiling grapes in the vats. Fall had always been a pleasant time at Vilmorin—the work finished, there was time at last to enjoy the golden days, the long cool nights. When there had been no campaigns to be waged, he and Narbaux had spent many companionable hours, riding and hunting in the leaf-strewn woods. How could they now be friends, when suspicion gnawed at him? And yet to stay at home, to look at Marielle . . . to ache with love for her . . . to doubt her, and loathe himself for his doubting. . . . More and more, he found himself sharp and angry with her, hating her for the dilemma his own uneasy thoughts caused. Perhaps when the last of the wine barrels was stored, he could escape, alone, to Paris for a time.

Marielle arranged the last of the roses, her fingers deft and nimble as she stripped off the superfluous leaves and tucked the fragrant blossoms into the large vase. Her hands had not been so sure at the noon meal. André had been so surly and abrupt that she had felt stupid and awkward, and had tipped over her wineglass and watched in dismay as the stain spread on the linen. She had fled the room at his angry scowl, trying not to see Clothilde's smirk of pleasure at her discomfort. Now, though her fingers were obedient to her will, her thoughts were not on the pink and scarlet clusters she held. It was only something to do to keep from feeling useless, as superfluous to Vilmorin as the leaves she pulled away. Mistress of Vilmorin! What kind of mistress could she be? She was unwomanly, she had failed him in every way. He did not seem to want her friendship any longer, but, God forgive her, she could not be a proper wife. Seeing his anger these last few days, for which she felt such a heavy responsibility, she had even crept to his bedroom door one night and stood there, shuddering in fear, unable to enter, until at last she retreated to the safety of her own bed and the pillow that muffled her heartbroken sobs. There was no need for her anywhere at Vilmorin. The servants took care of the estate, and Clothilde still anticipated most of André's needs and openly resented Marielle's intrusion—except when André was nearby to see her perfect obeisance to her mistress. In agony Marielle wondered what other need the housekeeper might fill for him. With a sigh, she carried the roses into the vestibule and set them down on a small marble table near the staircase. She glanced up. Clothilde was descending the stairs, her face a mask of hostility that made Marielle wince.

"If you please, Clothilde," she said quietly, "while I am aware that you do not hold me in high esteem, I would prefer to see a smile upon your face rather than the sullen frowns to which I am subjected."

"What I think is my own concern, Madame!" said Clothilde insolently. "Can I help it if my face does not hide my thoughts?"

"Then I must insist . . . nay, command . . . that you make an effort to be pleasant. It is the least you owe to the mistress of the house!"

Clothilde took a menacing step forward. "And how long do you think you will be mistress here if you cannot keep him in your bed?" Marielle gaped, speechless at this effrontery, stricken to the core by the woman's brazen cruelty. Clothilde purred, seeing her arrow draw blood. She smiled wickedly and lowered her voice. "Who do you think shared his bed the night of the harvest—when you turned him out?"

It was too much. With a despairing cry, Marielle lashed out at her, striking the insolent mouth and catching Clothilde unawares so that she stumbled back and fell heavily upon a small bench, where she sat stunned, her cheek glowing crimson, hatred burning in her eyes. Suddenly she drooped and began to wail pitifully. The transformation was so surprising that Marielle would have gone to her and offered comfort, but a noise behind her caused her to turn and see the reason for the unexpected change. André had come storming into the vestibule and he took in the scene at a glance: the weeping Clothilde, red-faced, and Marielle, fury in her eyes, her hand still raised against the poor girl. He advanced upon Marielle, his rage kept in check by the strongest effort of his will.

"Now Madame," he said coldly, his jaw rigid. "God knows you are hardly chaste enough to call yourself a lady, but you might at least behave like one!"

She gasped, a long, slow intake of breath that seemed to linger deep within her for a moment, then emerged from her throat as a low moan that ended in a choking sob. She ran up the stairs, pushing aside Louise who had come down the stairs in time to see the whole distressing scene, and who now pursued Marielle to her room, vainly trying to comfort her.

André bent to Clothilde, drying her tears sympathetically and sending her off to her room to rest, but his thoughts were on the grief he had seen in Marielle's face. Distracted, he wandered into his small library and sat down, cursing himself for a blackguard. What had possessed him to say such a terrible thing to her?

Restless, guilt-ridden, he jumped up and began to pace the small room, wondering if he ought to go and apologize to Marielle. Suddenly the door flew open and Louise burst into the room—the avenging angel, the she-wolf come to defend her young. Fists upraised, she stalked to him and pounded on his chest with all her might until, gasping for breath, he was able at last to push her to arms' length, holding her at bay while he recovered himself.

"Damn you!" she cursed. "You pig! You stupid fool! She will not let me in . . . she will not let me help her! If I were a man I would run you through! I would tear out your heart with my bare hands the way you have done to her! Damn you to Hell. *His* cruelty left wounds you could see! *He* only broke her spirit—you break her heart! And that conniving witch Clothilde . . . are all men as blind and stupid as you?"

"His cruelty?" said André in disbelief. "But at Quiot I saw—"

"Pah! You saw what you wished to see! It pleased you to think her unfaithful!" She took a deep breath, forcing her anger to drain away, then curtsied quickly, her eyes on the floor. "I beg your pardon, Monsieur le Comte. I have said more than I should have." She curtsied again and headed for the door. On the threshold she stopped and turned, her voice low, her eyes filled with remembrance and regret. "I saw him grow from a boy . . . there was always something dark and evil in him . . . you could see it in his eyes, even when he was a child. But you . . . innocent face . . . break a girl's heart . . . what demons hide behind your mask?" Then she was gone.

What demons indeed? Brooding, he sat down heavily, his head dropping forward into his hands. Why did he find it so difficult to believe a woman could be faithful? Was it because of all the women he had known, the husbands so easily betrayed, the easy coquettes who played at love? From the first, he had been unfair and suspicious of Marielle. But why? She had never claimed to be a saint, and certainly not a virgin after Quiot. It was he . . . in all the weeks he thought her dead . . . who had created this perfect creature in his mind. After that, the reality of her could never match the dream, and she suffered in comparison with the woman she had never been, but he insisted upon recalling. No wonder she had been so unhappy—she could not have pleased him, no matter what. As for himself, finding her only human, he had no longer expected her to be faithful—and had treated her shabbily, with suspicion and ugliness. Why should he have been surprised when she turned to Narbaux for warmth and love and comfort? It was the very comfort that he had given her at La Forêt that had won her love. He sighed deeply. He owed her the opportunity to be herself, to be judged, seen, accepted for what she was. As for Clothilde, she had been there when he needed a woman—had his gratitude and guilt blinded him to her real nature?

He started at the sound of tapping on the paneled door. At his command, the door was opened and Clothilde came timidly into the room, carrying a small tray with a cup of wine. She smiled shyly as she handed him the cup, and he realized with a start that she was playing the same innocent maiden who had beguiled him into her bed. What new game was this? Fascinated, wary, he waited for her to speak.

"Thank you for your kindness this afternoon, my lord. I do not know why Madame hates me so!" He did not reply. She edged closer to him, her eyes cast down, her voice so soft he could barely hear her. "I have missed you from my bed." *Mon Dieu!* Was she going to manage to blush? He felt like a fool. What would they say in Paris? The great lover! After all the women he had known! And until this moment, he had thought Clothilde straightforward and honest! Emboldened by his silence, she leaned over suddenly and kissed him on the lips. He allowed himself a moment's response, his lips remembering a simpler time when he had needed her comfort and nothing more. Clothilde, thinking only of his anger at Marielle, and desperate at the thought of losing him, read into his response that answer she was seeking. She smiled in triumph, careless in her victory.

"As though *she* could ever really be mistress here!" she sneered.

She did not see the coldness in his eyes, the subtle net he had begun to weave. "But she is—under God—my wife," he said mildly.

"Not even the Church could object to the dissolution of a marriage that never was."

"What makes you so sure of that?"

She laughed. "Women know these things instinctively."

"Just as she . . . no doubt instinctively . . . knew what had transpired between you and me?" She smiled like a cat, but said nothing. "Or did you suggest as much at every opportunity?" His voice was sharp-edged. She stirred uneasily and would have kissed him again to placate him, but he pushed her roughly away and stood up, facing her. "What did you say to my wife this afternoon?" She stammered, then was silent. He went on, his voice deepening with anger until it rumbled in his chest. "Did you boast of our intimacy? Did you gloat over her unimportance in this household? Did you finally drive her to the edge of that abyss of despair that I have managed to create?"

She began to blubber then, her voice shrill and ugly, reminding him of all that she had done for him, of how she had loved him, until he was filled with remorse at his own thoughtlessness.

"I am most truly sorry, Clothilde, for what has happened," he said gently. "But I never gave you cause to believe I was in love with you. And from the moment I brought my wife to Vilmorin, I gave you no reason to think that I would be unfaithful to her . . . nor have I. It would be best for you to leave. I'm sorry."

"Five hundred *livres!*"

"What?"

"Five hundred *livres!*" she repeated coldly. "A good year's wage! That is what I want from you!"

He laughed sardonically. "So much for love! Poor Clothilde. You must have thought I would be a perfect catch. How were you to know I had a wife?" He crossed the room and opened a large armoire, removing a small brassbound casket that he unlocked with a key from his pocket. "Here you are," he said, handing her a small sack that clanked metallically. "Two hundred crowns. More than you asked for. More than you are worth. As a housekeeper, or . . . anything else! But perhaps you will find a nobleman more gullible or foolish than I! I expect you to leave Vilmorin at once." And he turned his back on her until she had left the room.

He was impatient suddenly to be with Marielle, to beg her forgiveness, to cover her with kisses. He took the stairs two at a time, remembering with shame the last time he had hurried to her room. Louise had said she had locked the doors, but that was over an hour ago. Perhaps by now she would not be so upset and he could speak to her softly through the sitting room door. He was surprised to find it unlocked and slightly ajar, and her bedchamber empty. He bellowed loudly for Louise and paced the floor until she came puffing up the stairs.

"Where is she?"

Louise shook her head. "I know not, Monsieur! I did not see her leave!" Louise prowled the bedchamber, poking into oaken chests, searching armoires. "Her riding cloak is gone. Nothing more."

André muttered an oath. "Tell Yves to saddle my horse, and then return to me here. I may have need of you."

He was in his bedchamber when she bustled back, flushed with news. Yves had saddled Madame's horse and had seen her off less than an hour ago, heading east.

Busy pulling on his riding boots, André stopped, wondering. "Narbaux?" Louise shrugged. André stripped off his linen doublet and replaced it with a warm velvet one; evening was coming on and it would be a chill ride. He opened a large chest and removed his sword and its broad leather harness, buckling it on and wondering as he did so what was amiss in the contents of the chest. Of course. The small black box, normally fastened with a silver latch, was lying on its side, its lid askew. He lifted it carefully and raised the lid. Where there was usually a brace of pistols, nestling in their velvet beds, there was now but one. Wordlessly he held it out to Louise. She gasped, her hands flying to her mouth, her eyes filled with apprehension.

"What is it?" he asked, surprised.

"*Mon Dieu!* She has gone to Quiot! I know it!"

"To Quiot? Why?"

"To kill him," she said scarcely above a whisper. She began to weep, large tears coursing down her round cheeks. "She said it only this week. I should have known. 'Louise,' she said to me, 'I shall never be at peace while that man lives.' I thought it was only talk."

"What happened at Quiot?" he said quietly. She shook her head stubbornly. He repeated the question, his eyes boring into her.

"No! She did not want you to know. She begged me not to tell. I think she hoped that you would see into her heart, and find the love there, and all the ugliness would be washed away." She lashed at him in sudden anger. "As though a thick-headed clod could begin to understand a woman's love!" The lash bit deep and he flinched.

"What happened at Quiot?" he said, impatient now.

Hesitantly at first, she began to tell him what she knew, of Gravillac's cruelty, Marielle's pain and grief and shame. She wept afresh, remembering the nights she had listened outside of Marielle's locked door, hearing her sobbing, or crying out or begging Gravillac to leave her in peace. André groaned and turned away, unwilling to expose his own naked pain.

"I know he hurt her often," she said. "There were bruises sometimes . . . but the worst pain, I think, was in her heart. She thought that you were dead, you see.

She spoke often of you . . . and her brother and her father. She had lost so much—mayhap her grief was so strong it blotted out the pain of his abuse."

"And could she not escape?" asked André, his voice hoarse and choked.

"She tried once, but I think Molbert betrayed her. I do not know what she used to bribe him; that animal would do nothing without pay."

"Oh, God! The ring! And I called her careless for losing it!" His voice was filled with the agony of remorse, pity for Marielle.

"It was worse when she knew about the baby. She was terrified that he would find out and kill her. And yet . . . sometimes . . . I would see it in her face . . . a kind of madness . . . and I was afraid. I think at times she wanted to goad him into a rage, hoping that he would kill her, and end her misery."

"Gravillac! With my bare hands . . . !" He choked on his own fury and could not finish.

"I saw him grow from a child—he was cruel and spoiled and selfish. He whipped a stableboy once and nearly killed him—because the boy had beaten him in some child's game! He could not bear to lose—he took cruel revenge on his rivals!"

"What a blind fool I was! I knew him at the Academy—he was the same. I should have guessed he would not forgive La Forêt! Was I so stupidly jealous that I could not see the obvious—that she had no choice?" He covered his eyes and turned away, feeling suddenly unmanned by his grief and self-reproach. Louise clapped her large hand on his bent shoulders.

"Go and find your wife!" she commanded. "There will be time later to weep over the past!" She helped him on with his heavy cloak while he pulled on a pair of soft leather gauntlets, feeling cheered by her earthy warmth.

"It will be chilly tonight," he said. "If she has no other clothes but what she was wearing, she will be cold. Make me up a packet of some of her things. And food. I would wager she did not think to bring that either."

"You are in charge here, Louise," he said as he rode out. "If Clothilde is still about, see that she leaves at once." And he galloped off into the twilight.

Chapter Twenty-one

HE RODE LIKE A MADMAN PURSUED BY DEMONS, AFRAID TO slow his pace. She was a good horsewoman, and if indeed she meant to kill Gravillac, she would not spare her horse or herself. She was a good hour ahead of him, with the advantage of daylight, when the narrow road would have been visible and easy to follow. He shivered. The night was cold, with a crispness that warned of winter. From afar he heard the hoot of an owl, and once there was a loud rustling in the underbrush as the thundering hooves disturbed some small creature of the night. At length, and far off, he discerned a pinpoint of light that he soon saw to be a small fire, set at some distance from the road. Cautiously he guided his horse toward it, concerned lest the animal stumble in the dark, conscious as well of the danger of bandits. If these were simple travelers they might have seen Marielle; still, it did no harm to be careful. He sniffed, the smell of roasting meat filling his nostrils. Poachers. Honest folk did not feast in the woods—a rich man would want the comfort of his chateau, a poor man the benediction of his family. Quietly he dismounted, tying his horse to a small tree and drawing his sword. He dropped his cloak, that he might be free to maneuver, then crept slowly forward, muscles tense, ever the trained soldier.

He saw Marielle first. She sat at some distance from the fire, her back against a tree, her arms stretched cruelly around its trunk and tied with a stout rope. Her jacket had been torn away at the neck, her shoulders bare, bosom covered only by her tattered chemise. She was too far from the fire to enjoy its warmth, and she shivered with cold, ignored by the three men who sat close to the blaze, feeding on what appeared to be the carcass of a small rabbit spitted and crackling over the flames. Two gray asses, burdened with large bundles of kindling, grazed nearby. André judged the men to be farmers or woodcutters, one of them no more than a lad of fifteen or so. It was impossible to guess the ages of the other two; their faces and bodies were so stooped and worn with work and hardship and disease that they might have been twenty-five or fifty. In his hand the boy held André's two-shot pistol, and he began to argue with the men, brandishing the weapon all the while.

"It is not fair!" he said petulantly. "Why can I not have her? What harm? All she had in her pocket was ten *sous!* Ten miserable *sous!* She is nobody! Nothing! Who will care?"

"Shut up, Michel!" barked one of the men. "I will tell you yet again! She may be nobody, but she rode a horse with a crest on its saddle! Do you want to hang for raping a nobleman's lady?"

"I do not care! Who would know?" he asked sullenly. He turned to the other man. "Isn't it all right, Charles? Isn't it?"

Charles looked at Marielle, and ran his tongue across his lips, his eyes glittering. "I never had such a pretty one myself!" Then he sighed in resignation. "No. Emile is right. Better just to hold her for ransom. Her horse won't get far with that thrown shoe. In the morning we can find out whose crest is on the saddle—he'll pay a pretty penny to get his lady back!"

The boy Michel smiled and turned toward Marielle, pointing the pistol at her bosom. "Mayhap we do not have to wait till morning! Mayhap she will tell us who she is tonight!" André stiffened, measuring the distance between himself and the lad. But the man called Emile jumped up and snatched the pistol from the boy's hand, giving him a cuff across the ear that sent him sprawling. Michel glared at him, but contented himself with rubbing the side of his head and wolfing down another piece of meat.

Emile scratched at his groin and, handing the pistol to Charles, unfastened his breeches and headed for a dark patch of trees beyond the fire's light. Carefully André circled around and came up behind him as he was straightening up, his breeches still drooping about his ankles. One powerful arm went swiftly around Emile's neck, the hand clapped firmly against his mouth; with the other hand, André rested his sword lightly at the base of Emile's throat, its edge just grazing the vulnerable flesh. Prodded by André's knee in his back, the terrified farmer minced and hopped his way to the firelight, his feet hobbled by the encumbering breeches. Michel gaped and started to laugh at the sight of his friend, half-naked, his knees knocking in fright; then he saw the yellow-haired giant behind him, who stood a full head taller than Emile, and he gulped and kept still. André shifted his arm, that he might get a firmer grip on the man's neck; Emile, his mouth freed, began to babble like a madman. Charles, realizing that he held a pistol against the stranger's sword, lifted it in his shaking hands and pointed it toward André and Emile; the latter, fearful suddenly that he would lose his manhood to a pistol ball, screamed in terror and clutched his hands protectively against his groin.

With a sudden movement André flung Emile away from him, propelling him with such force that he crashed into the other man, knocking the pistol in his hand so it discharged with a roar, sending the shot through Charles' foot. The two men fell heavily to the ground, Charles moaning and writhing in pain. In one long stride André reached Emile and lifted him by the scruff of his neck. He turned his sword backward in his hand and, with the heavy pommel, gave the man a rap on the head that toppled him once again. Emile had had enough. Scrambling to his feet, he pulled his breeches about him as best he could and ran for one of the donkeys, mounting it in one leap; he fled toward the road, his feet furiously kicking the poor animal's flanks, and was soon lost from view. André turned his attention to the other two. Charles, crying in pain, was slowly limping toward the other donkey, leaving a bloody path behind him. The boy Michel, with the foolhardy arrogance of youth, had retrieved the pistol, one shot still in it, and was now pointing it defiantly at André, who advanced on him, sword in hand, his eyes cold and hard. Under that withering stare, the pistol wavered, then swung to Marielle, then back again to André. Still the blue eyes held him, the inexorable figure advanced. With a sob Michel flung down the pistol and would have fled, but a strong arm grabbed him, held him fast. Bending the boy over one outthrust knee, André beat him soundly with the flat of his blade until Michel howled in pain. Then, with a kick, he sent him on his way after Charles who, already mounted, was crashing through the underbrush, whimpering in fear and distress.

Swiftly André untied Marielle and led her to the warmth of the fire, noticing for the first time how tired she looked, her face drawn, shoulders drooping with exhaustion. He smiled gently. "I seem always to be rescuing you from evil men." Embarrassed, unwilling to look at him, she concentrated on the fire, hugging her body for warmth. "Where is your cloak?" His eyes were filled with concern.

"I . . . I lost it . . . I know not where . . . the horse stumbled, cast his shoe . . . I thought . . . they would help me. . . ." Her voice trailed off and she bit her lip, trembling on the brink of tears. He had never loved her more, never felt such a need to shield her and protect her from harm, never been more aware of his own lack of courage to say what was in his heart.

"Have you eaten at all?" She shook her head. Gingerly he plucked the remains of the rabbit from the fire, dropping it onto a flat rock in front of her until it should cool. He laughed ruefully. "I trust the Seigneur of this district will not look with the same disfavor upon scavengers as he does upon poachers." He left her to her food and went to fetch his horse, leading the animal into the circle of firelight, and he unwrapped the packet

Louise had given him. He retrieved the pistol and tucked it into his sash. Then he sat beside Marielle and watched her in silence, his eyes filled with tenderness, until she stirred uneasily, conscious suddenly of their isolation, the temptation of her torn garments.

He hesitated, finding words difficult. "I . . . have been less than kind to you, I think. Crueler even than Gravillac." She gasped, her eyes flying to his face, wondering and fearing at the same time. "Why could you not tell me?" he asked gently. Now the tears fell unchecked, great sparkling drops that welled up in her eyes and coursed softly down her cheeks.

"I could not bear for you to know my shame," she said, her voice so low he had to strain to hear. She turned away, as though even his glance brought a humiliation she could not endure.

"Shame?" he said angrily, and turned her roughly to face him. "The shame is mine for ever having believed aught but good of you!" His breath caught. He was aware suddenly of her bare shoulders under his hands, the heaving bosom, the ripe mouth wet with her tears. He dropped his hands and rose unsteadily, putting some distance between them. "Louise sent along warm clothing." His voice was gruff in his throat, and he indicated the packet with a jerk of his chin, his eyes reluctant to meet Marielle's.

She stood up and began to remove her tattered jacket, then waited modestly until he had turned his back. He could hear her small movements behind him, picture in his mind's eye the jacket dropping, then the chemise—the rosy glory of her full breasts; he shut his eyes tight, trying to drive out the tantalizing images. It suddenly seemed important to speak, to say anything that would help him forget the desirable woman but an arm's length away.

"You are tired," he said. "We will rest here until morning. It will be time enough to see if we can get you a horse for the ride back to Vilmorin."

"Why should I return?" she said tiredly.

He stared into the darkness of the trees. "Because you are my wife, and I want you there. Because I love you," he said simply, and ached to turn around to read her face. There was silence. But when at last she indicated that she was dressed again, he saw that she was trembling, and his heart flared with renewed hope. Louise had sent along a warm mantle. Marielle wrapped herself in it and lay down close to the fire, closing her eyes in exhaustion. André fetched extra logs for the fire and banked it carefully that it might burn throughout the night; then, pulling his own cloak about him, he lay down opposite her and dozed fitfully, his mind a whirl of desire and unrest.

He woke again at dawn, feeling chilled. Beyond the clearing where they lay, the damp mists rose between the trees. The sky was a silver gray, pale and luminous, awaiting the first kiss of the sun. The fire had nearly gone out, despite his precautions of the night before; he built it up again and huddled close to its warmth, his chin on his knees, lost in his thoughts. Beyond the fire Marielle stirred in her sleep and shivered, tugging at the mantle on her shoulders. He took his own cloak and, crossing to her side, knelt down and tucked its warm folds gently about her sleeping form. She sighed softly and opened her eyes. For long moments their glances held, hazy green eyes searching clear blue ones, questioning, hoping; at length he smiled, a tentative, shy smile born of his uncertainty. One long slim finger traced the delicate curve of her chin, the ripe fullness of her lips. A morning lark sang in the distance.

"My love," he said gently, his eyes enveloping her in their warmth.

A look of pain crossed her face, her eyes filled with tears. "I cannot . . ." she began softly, then stumbled and stopped.

"Do you remember how you slept in my arms at La Forêt?"

"The maid from La Forêt is dead!" she said desolately, turning her face away. He cupped her chin gently in his hand and smiled into her eyes.

"Nay! I have seen her often these past months, sweet and good and kind—though my stupid pride and jealousy near drove her away! Can you forgive the pain I caused you? The ugly words I have spoken?"

She shook her head. "And have I not made you suffer in the cruelest way? What kind of wife have I been to you?"

He laughed ruefully. "More than I deserved. Ah, Marielle!" he burst out. "How could I have forgotten that I loved you—that you were my friend?"

"And Clothilde?" she asked softly, biting her lip.

"I have sent her away. She means nothing to me, nor did she ever."

"But I thought . . . she said . . ."

"It matters not what she said! I swear to you, my love, as *le Bon Dieu* is my witness, I have not been unfaithful to you since first I brought you to Vilmorin . . . though it has not been easy!"

"Poor André!"

He grinned. "I am a soldier. I have survived worse campaigns!" They laughed together at that, with a lightness that neither had felt for weeks.

"And will you besiege me, Monsieur Soldier, until my defenses crumble?"

"Nay, for I have conceded defeat. It is you who must dictate the terms of peace!"

For answer, she reached up and pulled his face down to hers, parting her lips in sweet surrender to his gentle kiss. "Marielle," he breathed, his heart filled with the wonder of her love. Her lips awoke the raging passion that burned within him and he clasped her fiercely to his breast, his mouth hungry and insistent.

"No!" she cried, pushing him away. She sat up, her shoulders shaking violently. "Oh God," she whispered in agony. She turned away from him, sobbing as though her heart were broken. "Help me, André," she moaned, "for I am a cripple haunted by memories that will not be stilled!"

He folded her tenderly in his arms and stroked her hair and murmured tender words of love until her weeping ceased; then he held her apart and smiled into her eyes. "Come, wife. Let us go home. We have a lifetime to exorcise those ghosts!" He stood up quickly and crossed to his horse, busying himself with saddle and harness, glad of the distraction, the opportunity to quell the raging fires that consumed him, knowing he could not take her unwillingly, despite his hunger. He remembered the terror in her eyes, and prayed that when the moment came, he could love her gently and with tenderness, making up in part for all the unhappiness he had caused her.

"André."

He turned, then drew in his breath sharply, his heart

beating wildly. She was standing where he had left her, her chin proud and determined, a small defiant smile upon her lips. At her feet lay the jumble of her garments, cast off with uncertainty and fear; she shivered slightly, despite the brave smile. He gaped in wonder and awe. The sun had begun to rise, the sky a rosy pink that suffused the air and reflected on the creamy perfection of her beautiful body until she glowed like the incarnation of Dawn itself. In two strides he was before her, searching her face as though he would probe her very soul.

"Are you sure?" he said at last.

She shook her head, her voice trembling as she spoke. "No. But how will I ever know, if I let my fear rule me?"

He lifted her gently in his arms and laid her down upon the outspread mantle, and there, in the glory of the morning, she became at last truly his wife.

Marielle smiled at André across the clearing. He grinned back, his white teeth dazzling against his burnished skin. In truth, they hardly seemed capable of anything but smiles, tender, radiant, beaming. They had dressed with smiles, breakfasted with smiles; when they stopped occasionally to kiss, their lips would hardly be parted before they curved upward into smiles again. Now Marielle watched him, her face mirroring the joy in her heart, filled with a gladness she had not thought possible. She regarded him as he busied himself with the horses—her own mount having reappeared—and trembling a little, smiling a little, she relived the morning.

She had marveled at his gentleness and sweetness, all the more touching because she was aware of how he burned for her, and kept his passion in check to still her fears. He had lain beside her for a very long time, kissing, caressing, his hands gentle and tender as they roamed her body. Sometimes she would stiffen in his embrace, filled with the familiar terror and loathing; he would stop, and soothe her with words of love and the soft kisses he knew pleased her. At length, his ardor beyond containing, he possessed her, swept away on a tide of mounting ecstasy he could no longer control. Open-eyed, she watched his face, the sight of him a reassurance. André. Her André. No other. When at last his body had stilled, she closed her eyes, content. He would have withdrawn, but she held him fiercely and would not let go, feeling him within her, the warmth of his body upon hers, the sense of fitness in the act itself. Because of Gravillac, she had found it ugly, distasteful, cruel; now, with André's strong arms about her, she knew that it was for him as much a part of love as his kisses, his tender solicitude—an act of giving, not taking. Her heart was filled with gratitude and love, a tide of emotion that welled up within her; warm tears seeped out from beneath her closed eyelids.

"Marielle. Love," he had said, his voice warm with concern, "are you yet afraid?" Wordlessly she had shaken her head, and smiled at him with a look of such radiant happiness that his own eyes had filled with tears and he had kissed her almost reverently, his lips doing honor to her sweet face.

Chapter Twenty-two

THE WHIP ROSE AND FELL. THE BLACK STALLION REARED
up on its hind legs, eyes rolling wildly in its head, and
slashed the air with its front hooves. Again the whip fell
and the great horse snorted and bared its teeth.

"*Nom de Dieu,* Renard! I vow that brute will kill
someone one of these days, the way you treat him!"

The Marquis de Gravillac whirled, his eyes as black
as the horse. "I scarcely need your advice, Barrault!
Only with God's help will that bay you are riding get
you to Spain!"

The Comte de Barrault looked mournful. "I would
have no worry at all if you would abandon your wild
scheme! The die has been cast. Why delay our depar-
ture from France longer than we must?" He turned for
affirmation to the Duc de Tapié, who was giving orders
to his lieutenant.

"It is true enough, Gravillac," said Tapié. "You
know the wisdom of riding south through Languedoc—
there are still loyal Huguenots who would see us safely

to Spain, in shorter time and with less risk of word getting back to Richelieu's spies!"

"Bah!" spat Gravillac. "Think you there is safety in the Languedoc? Since the Peace of Alès every governor in the region has been handpicked by Louis. And every Huguenot prince seeking to wheedle his way back into the King's favor would be happy to betray us. I for one have not pledged my sword to Philip of Spain only to be dragged back to Paris in chains because some provincial fool grows suspicious of our journey. Far better to make for the seaboard and La Rochelle, and from thence down the coast to Bearn and Spain. There are Huguenot loyalists there as well, but the memory of war has dimmed and life is more normal. Who would question three noblemen and their servants on a visit to some Bearnais lord? It may be a longer journey, but far safer!"

"And Touraine Province?" asked Barrault sourly. "Where is the safety—or the sense—in going first to Vilmorin? It is not that near to La Rochelle. And for what? For honor?"

Gravillac's eyes flashed dangerously. "It is *my* honor we talk of! Do you think I can leave France knowing du Crillon lives?" He swept his arm around the courtyard, taking in the fields of Quiot. "Look you! Was your harvest like this? Your fields so empty of men? Will you soon see the wooden bottoms of empty coffers, your fortunes wasting away like mine? 'Twere his lies that cost us La Forêt, and I mean to challenge him for the lying scoundrel he is!"

Barrault shook his head. "I doubt we would have prevailed at La Forêt, du Crillon notwithstanding. Privas fell and was put to the sword, and Nîmes and Alès—none of the towns could have held out against the Royal army. Why seek revenge against one man?"

"Because he lied to me! To me!" Gravillac almost shrieked in his fury.

"And if you challenge him to a duel, and kill him . . . what then? Richelieu has forbidden dueling on pain of death! How will we get out of France then?"

Gravillac shrugged. "There are still many who look upon dueling as a gentleman's right, and would hardly be anxious to turn informer—we would be in the Court of Philip before word reached Paris!"

"But why should du Crillon accept your challenge? It is he, after all, who is in the King's favor at the moment. Why should he take the risk?"

"Because he is a gentleman of the old school, trained in honor and chivalry," sneered Gravillac. "And because"—he gave a malicious chuckle—"mayhap he feels he has an old score to settle!" He swung his lean body into the saddle. "Molbert!" he barked. "Does everyone at Quiot know what he is to do whilst I am away? I expect Marcel to oversee my estates well—tell him I shall send you back from time to time . . . and warn him how I reward stupidity or incompetence!"

They rode out from Quiot, taking the path that led northwest toward Touraine and Vilmorin, each noble accompanied by his trusted lieutenant. Barrault and Tapié eyed each other nervously—it still seemed a foolish undertaking—but neither man was willing to risk the fury of Gravillac, and they depended on his connections in the Spanish Court. As for Gravillac, he felt an exultation that threatened to burst through his chest. He grinned jubilantly. At last! He would have it all! He saw André du Crillon dead before him, those challenging blue eyes closed in defeat once and for all, the threat of him gone forever! And she would be his, with no one to take her away, to claim her; she would be his! There was no need to resurrect her memory; she had never left his thoughts—the glowing hair, those soft green eyes, the body that promised a thousand delights. He no longer knew or cared if what he felt for her was love . . . or lust. She would be his. Nothing else mattered.

"Two hours, my lord. I promise it! The horse will be ready." The blacksmith straightened up and patted Marielle's horse.

"But be quick about it, man," said André. "It is nigh on to the noon hour, and we have more than a few hours' ride ahead. I would reach home before dark."

The blacksmith bobbed respectfully. "Begging your pardon, my lord. I must make a new shoe. I am a poor man, Monsieur, and with no one but Achille here to help me. . . ." He took a swipe at his apprentice, a runny-nosed urchin of eleven or twelve, who scraped off his cap and bent a leg to the Gentleman, though his large eyes never left the Gentleman's Lady. Marielle smiled, her face dazzling; the poor lad gulped and turned red, twisting his cap in his hands and backing up until he tripped upon a bucket and fell sprawling. He scrambled to his feet and fled to the dark interior of the smithy. Laughing, André tucked his hand firmly under Marielle's elbow and guided her away.

"Sorceress," he said, "will you enchant us all? I think I shall keep you locked up in Vilmorin, away from the company of all men!" She did not laugh, but turned to face him, her eyes solemn, almost sad.

"And do you trust me so little, André?"

Flustered, he made no reply, but lifted her onto his

horse and swung up behind her, guiding the steed through the little village toward a small copse that they had passed that morning. They rode in uneasy silence, Marielle leaning her head against André's chest; he, chin down, face buried in her fragrant hair. Did he trust her? He thought again of the morning—she had come to him willingly, despite her fears; she had held out her hands and given him all her faith and trust and love. She had set him to be the guardian of her heart, without reservations—he had never known love like that, so awesomely pure and complete. He felt overwhelmed by the wonder of it. What folly! How could he doubt her faithfulness, when she trusted him with her very soul? He dropped the reins and enfolded her in his arms, kissing the top of her head and murmuring her name; she twisted around and peeped shyly at him over her shoulder, surprised by the sudden intensity of his feeling. And so, smiling a little, and sighing and kissing, they made their way through the bright blue October day. The narrow path they followed wove in and out of the trees—scarlet and orange and gold, scented with the tang of autumn—and came at length to a gurgling stream crossed by a small wooden bridge. Here André stopped and dismounted, and lifted Marielle down. With a flourish he swept his mantle from his shoulders and spread it over a patch of bare ground; he bowed elaborately to Marielle, catching her fingertips to his lips.

"It is not the Bois de Boulogne, I warrant, but would Madame care to join me in a picnic?" Marielle laughed and spread her skirts daintily upon the cloak while André took from his saddlebag a small joint of meat and a chunk of bread. While Marielle sliced the meat with the knife he handed her and laid the slabs on

pieces of bread, he removed the pistol from his sash
and stowed it in the saddlebag, then he unbuckled his
sword and laid it on the grass; finally he unwrapped the
sash and removed his doublet, flinging his arms wide as
though he would embrace the glorious day. He felt
new-born, coltish and giddy, and he flung himself down
upon the mantle and sprawled there, grinning up at
Marielle like a callow youth in the throes of first love.
She shook her head at his antics and bent away to fetch
his food; he could not resist her vulnerability, and took
the opportunity to pinch the target she had so tempt-
ingly (though unwittingly) presented. She shrieked and
fell upon him, tickling him unmercifully, while he
writhed and roared and begged for quarter. Still taunting, she jumped up and fled to the stream, bending low
and scooping up a handful of water, threatening him if
he should come near. Ignoring the icy water that she
splashed on his face and hair, he swooped down and
swept her into his arms, swinging her menacingly over
the crystal stream while she squealed and clung fiercely
to his neck.

"Now, Madame," he laughed, "will you yield?"

"Always, my lord," she whispered, her eyes suddenly misty and filled with love. He set her gently on the
bank and drew her close in his embrace; she tipped up
her chin and closed her eyes, waiting for his kiss. He did
not move. Surprised, she opened her eyes to see him
peering over her shoulder, a bemused smile on his face.
Turning in his arms, she followed his glance. From
beneath a bush, hard by the stream, she spied two pairs
of dark eyes, wide and serious, set in two tiny faces.
With a little cry of delight, Marielle sank to her knees,
motioning the children to come to her; after a moment's hesitation, during which they seemed to com-

mune silently with their eyes, they emerged from the underbrush. They were not very old, the boy perhaps seven, the girl five, but hunger had made them thin and gaunt, their faces pinched like old men, their eyes filled with pain beyond their years. Marielle bit her lip and looked helplessly to André. At La Forêt she had seen poverty and its effects on the people, but within its thriving walls there was always someone to distribute alms, a warm church for shelter, a generous farmer or shopkeeper to look the other way when a hungry child filched an apple or a piece of bread.

"Times are hardest in the small villages," said André heavily. "If the crop fails, the peasants have nowhere to turn. God knows their taxes are already oppressive—if Richelieu pulls France into the war with the German princes, we shall see rioting in every provincial capital!"

"How can such inequities be?" cried Marielle. "As a nobleman you pay no taxes at all! Why must these people bear the burden? Can nothing be done?"

André shook his head. "I think that the Cardinal has tried. But too many years have gone into the building of France—the ship of state is burdened with too many bureaucrats, too many government functionaries, too many regulations. As long as a man can buy an office, or secure a pardon with a bribe or cheat with impunity, people like this will suffer. God alone knows where it will all end!"

Marielle sighed, her eyes filled with pity—for the peasants, for the children, for France. She gathered the children to her and brought them to the outspread cloak, seating them gently and pressing food into their hands, talking softly to them as they wolfed down the bread and meat, smoothing an unruly curl on a tiny head. André stood apart, watching Marielle, his heart filled with love and pride: how natural she looked with children at her side. When the poor urchins had eaten their fill, Marielle pulled a handkerchief from her pocket and wrapped up the remains of the food, tying the cloth securely in the corners, and handing it to the little boy. The children, still disbelieving their good fortune, could only smile shyly before they scampered across the bridge and vanished among the trees.

"I fear we must do without our picnic, André."

"I have feasted already, my love," he said, his eyes so warm and enveloping that she felt a glow down to her toes. "You will prove a loving mother, I'll wager!" He sat beside her and kissed her gently—then not so gently. "Wench!" he said hoarsely. "Will you give me sons?" He pressed her down upon the mantle, his lips finding the hollow of her throat. She giggled and squirmed under his kisses.

"Wicked man!" she teased. "When we are back home at Vilmorin!"

He sat up, disappointed. "Then it must be before I go. . . ." He stopped abruptly, his eyes refusing to meet hers.

Now it was she who struggled upright. "Go where? André?"

He rose to his feet, his back to her. "I shall see you safely to Vilmorin, and then . . . I shall ride . . . to Quiot!"

"No! I will not have it, André!"

He whirled to her, his eyes stormy. "Do you think, after what Louise has told me, I can let him live?"

She rose to him and put her hand softly upon his arm. "If I can let him live . . . can you not do the same?"

He frowned. "But you yourself would have killed him!"

"Only when I thought that his specter came between us. Ah, André! What does his life matter to us now? Shall I lose you because of vengeful pride?"

"Your confidence in my sword arm is touching, Madame," he said dryly.

She stamped her foot in impatience. "If you kill him, you yet risk the headsman's axe!" Eyes flashing in anger, she would have turned away from him, but he held her fast and smiled into her scowling face.

"Come, my love," he said gently. "I have no wish to quarrel on this lovely day." He laughed as she began to melt. *"Mon Dieu!* I forget at my peril the tiger that lurks behind your eyes. My head ached for days from that boot you threw!"

"Pah!" she scoffed. "Your head ached from too much wine." But she smiled and threw her arms around his neck, kissing him firmly on the mouth. He held her tightly, lips pressed against hers, his body on fire from the touch of her hips and thighs and firm breasts, and wondered how he could wait until nightfall. "André," she whispered against his ear, "promise me you will not try to kill Gravillac." He felt his passion die, and he held her roughly away from him; her luminous eyes gazed at him tearfully. "I love you. Would you stain that love with ugliness and revenge? Give me your promise. I beg it of you!"

"I cannot!" he said, anguished. "Gravillac haunts me as well! I know not if I must kill him, but I shall not swear to you what promise I may not keep! Ask me no more." Without another word, he donned doublet and sword and cloak, and set Marielle upon his horse, while he walked on ahead and led the steed through the woods. The sky was no longer blue: large clouds had begun to gather, white and billowy, but here and there was a darker hue, a stormy gray that threatened rain from far off. It seemed to Marielle that a cloud hung between her and André as well, and she sighed for the loss of their sunny day.

Marielle's horse was ready and waiting when they returned to the village. The blacksmith's apprentice, seeing the frown on the Gentleman's face, took care to stay well clear of André, but he peeped surreptitiously at the beautiful Lady with the bright hair—there would be much to tell his family at supper this night! André lifted Marielle to her saddle, paid the blacksmith and mounted his own horse; then, spying the boy at the door, he tossed him a coin and grinned as the lad caught it nimbly in mid-air. Marielle moved her horse close to André's and held out her hand in conciliation; he pressed her fingers to his lips, his eyes filled with love. There would be time later to settle their disagreement; for now, it was enough that their sun shone brightly again, though the October sky lowered threateningly.

"André, I shall not go one more league unless you promise me that we shall eat!" Marielle reined in her horse abruptly. They had ridden hard for several hours, anxious to reach Vilmorin, to avoid the rain that now seemed imminent. André knew that they had more than an hour's ride yet, and night would soon be upon them, but Marielle looked so determined—and so hungry!—that he was reluctant to refuse her. He was close enough to home to recognize his surroundings; there was a cozy inn, he knew, but a few leagues further on where they could get a hearty meal.

"Ah," he said with mock seriousness, "is this what it means to be married? Petticoat tyranny? Very well, wife! Come along. There is an inn not far; I shall see that you are fed." The devil glinted in his eye. "But it will cost you dear, for I too have an appetite!"

Marielle wrinkled her nose at him, then smiled demurely. "Ah, Monsieur—alas!" she said, her eyes wide and innocent. "Is this to be my lot henceforth? That I must buy my supper with favors?" She dimpled mischievously at him and galloped off toward the inn, André in close pursuit.

The inn was set just back from the road, a small thatch-roofed cottage with shuttered gables and overhanging eaves. In front was a dusty courtyard, well-trampled by countless horses and travelers; to the left, a large stable with wide doors, and an ancient water trough, its oaken planks bleached silver by the elements. Situated as it was on a well-traveled highway, the inn never lacked patrons for food or lodging. The proprietor, with the help of his son, managed the stable and saw to the horses and occasional carriages that came to his door; the innkeeper's wife set a fine table both for the hungry wayfarer and those who chose to spend the night in one of the rooms beneath the eaves.

The first large drops of rain had begun to fall as André and Marielle rode up before the inn. Each heavy raindrop sent up a little puff of dust as it landed on the dry courtyard—in a moment the ground was pockmarked; in another moment the pale dust became dark earth as the heavens opened up and the rain began to soak in. Dismounting quickly, André reached for Marielle and together they raced for the shelter of the inn, gratified to find a hearty fire blazing on the wide hearth. The innkeeper, who had served the Comte du

Crillon in the past, bowed low in welcome before sending his son out to stable and feed the Comte's horses. In a twinkling, steaming food appeared and, shaking off their wet garments, Marielle and André set to with relish.

At length, sighing with contentment, André leaned back in his chair and looked at Marielle. She was in the act of raising her winecup to her lips but, at his piercing stare, she stopped and lowered her eyelids, the dark lashes brushing modestly against her cheeks. Damn, he thought. In spite of the morning, he still felt awkward and nervous. They had spoken gaily and frivolously of love all the day, but he was far from certain that their lovemaking of the morning heralded a permanent change. She had been willing to please him, and he knew he had her love, but he could not forget her tension, the panic that she suppressed with difficulty. There had been magic in the silvery mists, the quiet woods; in the reality of this room, warm and cheery and ordinary, he was assailed by doubts. It seemed ironic to find himself in such a dilemma. He had wooed and seduced and persuaded countless women, never fearing or doubting the outcome; now he felt tongue-tied. Was it because she was his wife? Or because he loved her so deeply that he feared her refusal? Damn! he thought again. How does a man woo his own wife?

She finished her wine and smiled gently at him. "Think you the rain will end soon?" He shrugged but said nothing. "It has already grown dark." He nodded, lost still in his own thoughts, averse to idle chatter. Did he imagine an edge of impatience in her voice when next she spoke? "Must we return to Vilmorin tonight?" His head snapped up and he searched her face. Her eyes smoldered with green fire, a warmth that stilled his fears and made him chuckle aloud. It always surprised him, the way she seemed to read his mind, plumb his thoughts—he should have guessed that she would sense his uneasiness. He put his hands over hers.

"Do you want to return tonight?" She shook her head, and her eyes turned to the staircase.

It seemed an eternity while he arranged for a room, and left instructions that their horses should be waiting in the courtyard an hour after sun-up, but at length, hand in hand, they made their way up the stairs, eyes only for one another, while the innkeeper and his wife beamed their approval and wished Monsieur le Comte and his Comtesse a good night.

Clothilde sniffled noisily and wiped her nose with the back of her hand, leaving a dusty streak across her face. She winced as her fingers touched the sore spot just under her right eye; hiking up her skirts, she saw that large dark bruises had already formed on her hips and thighs.

What shall I do? she thought. "What shall I do?" she wailed aloud to the dusty road, the silent trees. She sniffed again, and took a deep breath. Be not foolish, she thought. You know very well what you must do. No need to be upset. All will be well. She shifted her heavy bundle and felt a fresh twinge in her ribs; the bastard could have broken them, she thought, and wept anew. Damn the silk merchant! Who would have thought he was capable of jealousy! She had slept in a cave near Vilmorin last night, her heavy bundles clutched tightly to her: one held her clothes and the lengths of silk she meant to sew into a gown that would rival anything Paris had ever seen; the other contained a little food and the sack of gold coins wrapped tightly in an old petticoat so they would not jingle. In the morning she had come to Vouvray and knocked timidly at the door of the silk merchant. She had always known how to please him, and she meant to have a place to stay while she made her gown, gathered together what she might need for Paris and decided on the best way her money would buy her entrée to the Court. Two hundred crowns. It was a great deal of money. Far more than a simple housekeeper would be expected to have, and it made her an easy prey for thieves and cutpurses. Even one crown would arouse suspicion. She was sure that, for a small compensation, the silk merchant would be willing to hold her money and exchange it for smaller coins when she had a purchase to make.

He had greeted her coldly at the door, but she had smiled and pushed her way in, dropping her heavy bundles and rushing to throw her arms about his neck as though she had been longing to see him. To her surprise and dismay, he had slapped her face and exploded in fury, cursing her for a whore, condemning her for abandoning him after all his kindness—and bringing grief and shame to him. All Vouvray knew she had been the Comte du Crillon's mistress—how dare she return as though nothing had happened! He had struck her again, his fist finding her eye; when she would have fallen, he had tangled his fingers in the hair atop her head, hauling her upright with such force that her feet barely touched the floor. Her hands had shot up to her head, trying to dislodge his hurtful fingers, but he had held her fast, at arm's length, and, grasping the stout measuring stick he used for his bolts of fabric, had beaten her about the legs and thighs and buttocks while she shrieked in pain. At length he had released her, and she had dropped to the floor, sobbing. Her body ached and she despised him, but her mind was as shrewd as ever. She needed him. It was worth the price of a beating if she could stay with him for a little. Dragging herself across the floor, she had thrown her arms about his legs, promising to make amends, begging him to forgive her. She had misjudged the depth of his feelings; his towering anger was not yet spent. With an angry roar, he had kicked viciously at her, his heavy shoe finding the edge of her ribs and forcing a gasp from her lips. Then, still furious, he had cast wildly about the room until his eyes had lighted on her belongings. Hoisting one of the bundles, he had hurled it violently to the floor, spilling out bodices and skirts and her lovingly-folded lengths of silk; seizing a pair of shears that hung on the wall, he had ripped and torn and slashed all her precious things while she gaped in horror. She had lost all control then, and had snatched up another pair of shears that lay on a cutting table, cursing and screaming while she hacked at him with the sharp tool, gashing him about the arms and shoulders until he fell and lay gasping, reviling her for a madwoman. Panic-stricken, she had picked up her other bundle and fled, still clutching the bloody shears in her hand.

She sighed and sat down heavily on a tree stump. She had walked all day. Her body was sore, her feet were tired and sometimes she could not remember where she was going. She rubbed her eyes. Think. Think! Of course. Bourges. She shook her head and smiled at her own forgetfulness. That handsome Marquis from Bourges. She had met him in the spring; he had kissed her secretively in the back of the silk merchant's shop, going so far as to invite her to stay with him at his chateau—but it was obvious from his worn doublet and cloak that he was far from a worthwhile catch. In the spring she had needed money as well as connections; now, with two hundred crowns as enticement, she might even be able to persuade the penniless Marquis to marry her!

Heartened, she set off down the road once again. It was only a few days' journey and she probably had enough bread and cheese to see her to Bourges. Still, she was glad she yet had the silk merchant's shears tucked safely into her waistband under her jacket. She had not liked the way the peasants had looked at her in the last village she had passed. She had tried to cover the bruise under her eye, and hurried quickly to the edge of town, but she had the uneasy suspicion that they knew what was in the bundle and would try to rob her if she stopped for a moment. To take out a whole crown in payment for anything would surely proclaim her newfound wealth to all who might do her ill. No. It would be best to make do with the food she had brought, and sleep in the woods on the side of the road.

It was growing dark. She was weary. Curse du Crillon and his wife. And her father. And the silk merchant. And Perrot. She felt weighted down by her troubles; they made her head hurt and her thoughts wander.

"Perrot!" she cried aloud, her voice tinged with hysteria. Don't cry, she thought. Don't cry. All will be well. In two days' time she would be in Bourges—she would be safe. She would be cared for, and protected and loved. Perrot would take care of her. Perrot would be waiting in Bourges. No. No! She shook her head. Where was her mind today? What nonsense! The Marquis would be waiting, of course! She laughed aloud, a shaky giggle that hung in the still air. Why had she thought of Perrot again? It was simply that all her disappointments had made her forgetful. That was all.

It had begun to rain. Through the trees she could see a small wisp of smoke that curled up and hung against the cloud-darkened sky. She began to run, as fast as her bruises and heavy bundle would allow her; surely she could find shelter ahead. It was a small inn, just off the road; the smoke came from a stone chimney, promising a warm bed for the night. She stopped for a moment next to an ancient water trough and put down her bundle, that she might catch her breath. She glanced into the water, stirred up by the rain; the quivering reflection that stared back at her gave her pause: her hair was tangled and disheveled, her eyes swollen from weeping and there was a large purple bruise under her right eye. She looked nervously about her. How could she go into the inn? They would ask questions. They would want to know all about her. In all likelihood, they were expecting her! They were waiting for her— and the gold! No, no! She would not be safe in the inn. She cast her eyes wildly about. The stable. There was a loft, she could see. No one would think to look for her there, buried among the mounds of hay. She scurried inside, her precious bundle held tight, and climbing the small ladder to the loft she was soon enveloped by the sweet grass. Sighing, she closed her eyes and slept, seeing Perrot even in her dreams.

Chapter Twenty-three

THE ROOM WAS SMALL AND COZY, ITS LOW CEILING AND heavy beams lit by the cheerful fire that burned in the hearth; the large bed, piled high with downy pallets, crowded the tiny chamber until there was scarcely room for more than the wooden stool drawn up to the fireplace. The two gabled windows, their mullioned panes closed to the driving rain, were set into shallow recesses with small cushioned windowseats beneath. On the floor, woven rush mats scented the chamber with their sweet freshness and whispered silkily as Marielle crossed the room and placed her candle on the mantel. Ducking through the low doorway, André closed the door softly behind him, then turned to watch as Marielle perched on the stool and stripped off her shoes and stockings still damp from the rain, placing them neatly on the hearth. She smiled shyly at him. Dear André, she thought. How much she loved him. Ah *Dieu!* Let him be pleased with her tonight, let him find satisfaction with her body. She was not afraid of his lovemaking, for truly it was love he gave to her, but she wanted above all to make him happy, and she was not at all sure how. She had only her experiences with Gravillac to guide her, and remembering how he had chafed at her coldness, she knew suddenly that the greatest gift she could bring to André would be her warmth and compliance, her willingness to yield to his needs as a man.

She stood up and waited, passive, willing, as he crossed the room and drew her into the circle of his arms. His mouth found hers and he kissed her with an intensity that was new to her, his lips and tongue moving and tasting and exploring, sending ripples of feeling through her body, a strange flame that flickered deep within her. Breathless, she clung to him, wanting the flame never to die; but he held her away from him and stepped back, smiling at her with eyes that smoldered and glowed black in the dim light. Slowly he began to undress her, his hands so soft and gentle that she shivered at his touch and the flame within her flared anew. His fingers lingered on every button, traced the line of her collarbone, brushed the velvet curves of her shoulders. Trembling, she closed her eyes and let her head fall back, filled with strange sensations, a kind of impatience she could hardly fathom; his deliberate slowness was an exquisite torture, every inch of her body awakening to new and astonishing feelings. When at last she stood naked before him, her skin glowing in the firelight, he bent his head to her breasts, his lips caressing their soft roundness; she swayed against him, the breath catching in her throat, and gave herself over to the flames that rose and surged within her, racing through her body like tongues of fire.

She moaned softly. She wanted suddenly to hold him

fast, to feel the length of her body pressed against his, and she raised his head from her bosom, needing his mouth on hers, his arms twined tightly about her. Instead, he lifted her gently and deposited her on the bed, stepping back to the fireplace where he began to remove his boots. She felt an odd pang of disappointment, an impatience to have him near her again. She watched as he stripped off his garments and marveled anew at how beautiful his body was: narrowed-hipped, broad-shouldered, his chest and arms browned by the sun, the spun-gold hairs shimmering on his limbs and back; it was incredible that the very sight of him could make her heart pound so. His muscles rippled under the firm flesh; she was overwhelmed by a desire to touch him, and she reached out her yearning arms. He hesitated for a moment, then came to her, meaning to lie down at her side, but she opened wide her arms and drew him down on top of her, holding him tightly as though she would absorb his body into her own. Surprised at the fierceness of her embrace, and swept away by his own passion, he entered her quickly, still half-expecting the tension, the moment of panic. Instead, she clung to him, her body seeming to have a will of its own, writhing in ecstasy, rising to meet his with an eagerness she could not control, filled with an unbearable excitement that was almost too beautiful, too painful to endure. Suddenly she arched her back and gasped, her eyes wide with astonishment, as waves of feeling exploded within her, a searing warmth that filled her being and subsided at last into gentle spasms; then she lay quietly, her eyes closed, filled with a contentment, a completeness she had never known before. At length she opened her eyes to see André smiling down at her, his face filled with wonder and surprise and pleasure.

"I . . . had not dreamed! . . ." she marveled, her voice soft and shaky. He chuckled, his eyes warm with love and pride. In truth, he had only expected her to be a compliant wife, responding to him because she loved him; he had been as totally unprepared as she for the passion his lovemaking had aroused in her. In spite of his skill as a lover, the number of women he had known, he had never felt such satisfaction, such joy; Marielle had responded to him totally—heart, soul, body—all the more touching because her innocence had led her to expect nothing from their encounter but the dutiful willingness she had given him that morning. He kissed her gently, hardly trusting the stability of his own voice, then rolled over and sat up, pulling down the coverlet and helping her into its warm folds. Tucked contentedly in the crook of his arm, her face snuggled against his chest, she let the soft sounds of the rain outside lull her into contented sleep. The last thing she remembered as she drifted off was André, watching her lovingly, and grinning like a jackanapes.

Something had wakened her. Some small sound or movement—or intuition—had penetrated her brain as she slept and she woke, curious, surprised, half-alarmed. The rain had stopped and the skies were already clear, for the bright silver of the full moon flooded the chamber, illuminating all it touched with shining clarity. The candle had burnt out, and the hearth glowed red with the last dying coals. At the same time her hand reached out for the spot where André should have been, Marielle saw him at one of the windows, one knee leaning on the window seat, his shoulders hunched forward until his arms rested on the sill and cradled his chin. He looked lonely, forlorn, his whole attitude suggestive of some deep grief. Swiftly she rose from the bed and wrapped the coverlet about her. She crossed silently to him, feeling somehow excluded from his unhappy world.

"André. André, what is it?" He straightened up, his hands on the windowsill, his back still toward her; when he spoke, his voice was muffled and low.

"It is nothing. A bad dream. Nothing more. Go back to bed."

There was an odd note in his voice; with a sudden flash of insight Marielle remembered when she had heard it before.

"It was about your mother," she said. It was a statement, not a question. He laughed raggedly, surprised as always by her perception.

"Witch!" he said. "How do you do that?" She touched him tenderly on the shoulder.

"Tell me about her." He hesitated, then turned and sat sideways on the window cushion, his head against the side wall of the enclosure. The moon shone full upon his face, but he might have been in darkness for all his expression told Marielle, as though he felt his look would betray him, even to her.

"It is so long ago," he said disconsolately. "You would think I should have forgot by now."

"Tell me," she urged.

"She came from Normandy," he began. "A good family, titled, respected, wealthy. She was very beautiful, and did not want for suitors. Then her father quarreled with King Henry. . . . I never knew what the dispute had been about . . . and his land and holdings and title were forfeited to the Crown. The suitors vanished like the winter snows—save one. My father, for all the wealth and splendors of Vilmorin, was a simple country farmer, but he loved her. I doubt if she had even noticed him until then, but his loyalty and persistence eventually won her over. My sister was born in the first year of their marriage; I did not arrive until eleven years later."

He paused and stared blankly out the window. "I remember how she laughed. All the time. My father and I were good friends—we rode together and hunted and worked the fields—but I think that all the gaiety at Vilmorin, all the happiness of those years, was because of her. The eyes of a child. . . ." He laughed bleakly.

"They did not go often to Court, but my mother returned occasionally to Normandy, where my grandfather had a small cottage, and after he died she still returned to see old friends. It seemed natural enough. She took my sister with her sometimes, which always pleased me—I missed my mother, but I was glad to be quit of my sister, if only briefly. And since my father seldom joined her, there was the added joy of the time we spent together." He paused and rubbed his eyes wearily. "I was twelve. . . ."

"And then . . . she died?"

"I was twelve. I had not been to Normandy since my grandfather had died. She was planning a journey. At the last moment, it seemed, my father decided that he and I should accompany her; I think she was annoyed, for the ride was tiresome and somber, with none of her usual laughter to lighten the way. Desmarches, the caretaker my father had employed to keep the cottage in order—for it was Vilmorin money that had sustained my grandfather after his ruin—Desmarches was surprised to see us all, but he was quick to get our rooms in order, and brought his sister from the village to work in the kitchen. My mother spent the rest of the day with me. She was very proud of her village and its history, and insisted on showing me where William the Conqueror had stayed and where battles had been fought. I remember we laughed about everything that day. How we laughed together! We had never been closer." André sighed, then shook his head as though he would clear it of agonizing memories. "The next day my father and I went out riding—we were to be gone all day—it was to be an adventure. An adventure! But my horse went lame after scarcely an hour. He let me ride his horse back, while he led mine. My father's horse! I was so proud. When we reached the cottage I raced ahead. I could hardly wait to tell her of my ride home. I flew up the stairs and burst into her room." He paused and tapped his clenched fist against his mouth, as if to block the ugly words that formed.

"I remember first a lavender cloud upon the floor, and thought that she was huddled there, buried somewhere in the folds of her gown. Then I saw them on the bed. Desmarches was dark and swarthy . . . she . . . she looked so pale and . . . white beneath him. I could not imagine how she could bear to . . . touch . . . him. . . ."

"Oh, André!"

"Then my father was there. It was like a scene from a bad comedy. He drew his sword—I had never seen him so angry. Desmarches, naked as a snake, leapt from the bed and snatched up a poker from the hearth to defend himself. It was a ludicrous duel—I might have laughed about it . . . in another life. I remember my father slashed at him and there was blood and my mother

screamed—I ran from the room and crouched outside
the door. I could hear the sounds of struggling, and
then my mother's voice. 'Even though you kill him,'
she said, 'I shall not return to Vilmorin! I shall never!
There will be another to take his place.' That is what
she said—'never return!' I thought to myself . . . she
does not want us anymore . . . what have we done to
make her so unhappy? I could not listen to another
word. I fled the cottage and hid myself—God knows
where, or for how long—I could only hear her words
. . . 'never return.' It was night when he came searching for me with a lantern . . . no one was in the
cottage, and all her things were gone. He would not
talk to me or speak of her, but he gave me supper and
put me to bed. In the morning we returned to Vilmorin.
I was afraid to talk to him, or question him, but when
we arrived home he gathered us all in the salon, my
sister, the servants, and told us that the Comtesse du
Crillon had died suddenly of a fever, and had been
buried in Normandy next to her parents."

"Mon Dieu!" Marielle would have touched him, but
he seemed so remote that she feared she could not
reach him.

"After that, he was never the same. My sister
escaped into marriage the following year—a nobleman
from Strasbourg—and I was left to ease his misery. He
began to tell me what their life had been like. She was a
restless spirit—she had betrayed him countless times—
that was why they had stopped going to Court. She was
always sorry, and he always forgave her. . . . I think in
some ways he felt pity for her. That was why he had let
her go alone to Normandy so often—he had not wanted
Vilmorin to seem a prison. But as the years went on, his
bitterness deepened, and he would sit with me, drink-

ing himself senseless, and describe her succession of lovers, humiliating himself afresh with each retelling. God!" He groaned aloud. "I had not even known . . . all those years . . . I thought they were happy!"

Marielle threw her arms about him, cradling his head against her breast; she could feel the wetness of his tears on her bosom, and her heart ached. "But what . . . happened to her?" she asked.

His voice, muffled against her, was filled with agony. "I thought he had killed her. Killed them both. Long after he died, I still thought it."

"Oh, André, alas!"

"Then I found some papers of his. There was a letter. From her. In Paris. It was written only a few weeks before he died. She was not asking for forgiveness, but she was desperate. Sick, abandoned—God knows what ever happened to Desmarches—she needed money. There was another letter as well, written the following week, from a woman in Paris—she was returning only a part of the money he had sent, but times were hard and she begged the Comte du Crillon to forgive her. The lady to whom he had sent the gold . . . she was using the name Desmarches . . . can you imagine?" André stared at her with stricken eyes. "Desmarches!"

"But your mother? . . ."

"She was dead, the letter said. A fire in her *pension*. It was God's blessing, the woman said. Her illness and suffering had been beyond bearing. My father died less than a week later."

They were silent for a very long time. At length Marielle took him gently by the hand and urged him back to bed. He lay down, and would have turned away from her, but she pushed him down upon his back and perched over him, her soft breasts lightly touching his chest, and she kissed his mouth and eyes, caressed his face and stroked his forehead gently until the haunted look faded from his eyes and his arms closed possessively around her. Then she lay down full-length upon him; their two bodies seemed to touch in a thousand places, and every spot a flame that fired his passion. With a groan, he rolled over and pressed her down upon the pillows, feeling again her eager response, the quickening of her hips against his burning loins, her breathless hunger that told him she felt the full wide measure of love. He knew, in that moment before his senses lifted him beyond his body to soar in a firmament of shooting stars—lips pressed to lips, bodies fused as one—he knew with certainty that he would never be tormented by his dreams again.

She woke to the sound of doves cooing under the eaves. The room was filled with the first rays of the sun. Beside her, André still slept, curled up on his side like a little boy, his face in repose strong, yet soft and vulnerable at the same time. How could she have hurt him so, that lady of long-ago who had abandoned him, who had made him feel responsible for her going? And what of his father, who had poisoned his mind, shared burdens a son should not have had to hear? Small wonder he had been so jealous, not only of Gravillac, but of Jean-Auguste, and every other man who looked at her. He had held back love and tender feelings, not out of hatred, as she had thought and feared, but out of dread that she would break his heart the way his mother had. How foolish. She was bound to him by a love so strong that nothing could touch it; it was a needing, a caring that could only deepen with time. She saw their lives together as one silken ribbon stretching into tomorrow as far as the eye could see, smooth and beautiful and unbroken. And there was something more. She smiled to herself, reliving those moments of ecstasy they had shared. Without her quite knowing how or why, André had unlocked a door deep within her—a door that could never be locked again. She marveled at the forces that stirred within her; even now, just thinking of him was enough to start a strange and wonderful tingling sensation deep within her vitals. She closed her eyes and stretched luxuriantly, spreading her limbs wide and feeling a warm glow from her fingers to the tips of her toes. She gasped suddenly, her eyes flying open, as a strong hand gripped her outflung leg; André's merry blue eyes stared down at her.

"Good morrow, my love," he said mildly, and kissed her gently, but the grasping hand, with an independence of its own, was creeping slowly upward from her knee, far less innocent than his smiling face.

"Should we not be returning to Vilmorin?" she asked artlessly, but wriggling under that searching hand.

"I think Louise and Grisaille can manage yet awhile longer without us!"

"Think you there will be a wedding?" Only the twinkle in her eye betrayed the battle that was being waged beneath the coverlet, as she twisted and turned to elude his teasing fingers. With a mischievous giggle, she suddenly pulled free and rolled over on her belly, smiling at her cleverness in leaving him no access to those regions that aroused her so.

"Devil!" he said, and whipped off the coverlet. He kissed the hollow of her back, laughing as she gasped at the sensations his lips awakened; his hands moved gently upon her, touching little secret places that made her jump and set her heart to pounding. Squirming free, she leapt off the bed and danced into a corner, André in hot pursuit.

"I truly think we should return at once to Vilmorin, my lord," she said innocently. "The sun will soon be high in the heavens—Louise will worry!" Her eyes swept his body, noting with a wicked gleam that his passion had not abated. "Think you there will be trouble with your breeches, my lord?" She laughed gaily, but her steps were wary and cautious, expecting the sudden onslaught; instead he stopped his advance and nodded his head.

"You are right, wife. Grisaille might do something foolish. I must warn him against marriage and cruel women!" He allowed himself to pout a little.

"Poor André!" she said with mock-seriousness. "What may I do to make amends?"

"One kiss," he sighed. "One kiss is all I ask!" She hesitated, eyeing him with suspicion. "Look," he said. "I shall put my hands behind my back," and he followed the words with the action.

She curtsied demurely. "Will I be safe from the wicked dragon then, my liege?"

"I give you my word, fair damsel!"

She put her hands softly on his shoulders, and stood on tiptoe as he pressed his lips gently upon hers; then she squealed in surprise as his strong arms caught her in a fierce embrace—lifting and flinging her swiftly upon the bed—and he leapt triumphantly atop her. There was a sudden flicker of fear in her eyes, and he sat up, filled with contrition.

"Marielle! Love! Forgive me. I had not meant to. . . ." Her fingers, pressed against his lips, would not let him continue. She smiled. The moment of terror had passed.

"André. *Mon cher.* I am not so very fragile as you might suppose. I have but to see your face, and my fears vanish. You must not be afraid when I am not!" She pulled his mouth down to hers in a kiss that set his head to spinning, but when at last he opened his eyes he saw that the devil had returned and was grinning wickedly up at him. Laughing, she would have wriggled away, but he caught her and pinned her wrists to the bed, covering her sweet face and tumultuous bosom with his burning kisses, while she struggled half-heartedly against him.

"Ah, no, my lord," she gasped, panting and laughing in the same breath. "Kiss me as you will—I shall not submit so willingly this time!" In a little while, of course, she did.

Chapter Twenty-four

THE MORNING WAS WELL-ADVANCED BEFORE ANDRÉ AND Marielle, laughing gaily, descended from their little room beneath the eaves. They stopped halfway down the stairs: it was André who first saw the pistol pointing at them; Marielle, her heart thudding in terror, saw that the face behind the pistol belonged to Renard de Gravillac.

He sat lolling at the table, a catlike smile on his handsome features, his body seeming relaxed and at ease, but the hand that held the weapon gleamed white from the fierceness of his grip. Molbert, likewise armed, moved out of the shadows and came to stand at the foot of the staircase, pointing his pistol upward toward André's breast. André recognized Tapié and Barrault, who stood somewhat apart, swords at the ready, their faces mirroring their uncertainty at this dubious venture. In a corner huddled the innkeeper and his family, kept to obedience by the nobles' men-at-arms. Gravillac laughed softly, his eyes glittering with malice; he inclined his head politely in André's direction.

"Monsieur le Comte. And his fair Comtesse! You are late abed this day, although"—and here his lascivious eyes swept Marielle—"one can hardly reproach you for that! No, Monsieur," he added, as André, his face contorted, reached for his sword, "I should not move were I in your boots. Molbert would like nothing better than to put a pistol ball through you." André cursed silently, remembering his own pistol, useless to him now, still in his saddlebag.

"How fortunate we were," continued Gravillac, "to have chosen this very place to feed and water our horses." He nodded toward the courtyard through the open door. "Had we not seen the crest upon your saddles, we should have wasted half the day riding to Vilmorin! You have saved us a tedious journey." He smiled again, fully in command, enjoying the look of consternation on André's face. Rising languidly to his feet, he brandished the pistol. "Now, Madame," he said to Marielle, "bearing in mind that if Molbert does not shoot your husband, I am prepared to do so, please be so good as to come down the stairs to me!" Trembling, Marielle hesitated, her hand plucking at André's sleeve; Molbert took a menacing step forward and raised his pistol.

"Wait!" cried Marielle. Reluctantly she left André's side and made her way down the rest of the stairs, stopping at the bottom to look back at him, taking courage from his fearless gaze. She crossed to Gravillac and cringed as he slipped his arm smoothly about her supple waist, drawing her toward him. The pistol in his other hand was pointed squarely at André, who stood rigid, one hand still on the pommel of his sword, the other clenched tight in fury.

"My dear Comtesse, I have missed you," said Gravillac silkily. "Can it be possible that you have grown lovelier yet since last I saw you? Ah, Crillon, I envy the pleasures you have stolen from me! But we shall make things right again. Yes," he said, pulling Marielle closer until she stood in front of him, her back held firmly against his chest by the strong arm about her waist. "We shall make things right!"

"Hold!" cried Tapié, looking wildly from Gravillac to Barrault. "There were rumors . . . stories from Paris . . . a wife abducted . . . *ma foi!* She was the woman, wasn't she? Wasn't she, Renard?"

Gravillac laughed dryly. "I am surprised it took you so long to remember that!"

Barrault's face darkened. "Curse you, Gravillac! You meant only to have the woman! All that talk about revenge and duels—a lie, merely to mollify us!"

"*Au contraire,* my good friends! While it is true that I intended the lovely lady to comfort me in my exile, it is equally true that—as a grieving widow—she will need my comfort likewise!" Almost casually he slid his hand upward until he grasped the firm roundness of Marielle's breast; she flinched, feeling panic rising within her, and looked desperately to André. His face was cold and hard, but a muscle worked fiercely in his cheek; he kept his rage in check by the greatest effort of will. She realized suddenly that Gravillac was deliberately trying to goad André, to force him into some foolish action that would justify his shooting him. Fighting back her tears, she smiled bravely at her husband; she held the smile even while Gravillac, his eyes glittering wickedly, leaned down and kissed her on the neck. André's face betrayed not a flicker of emotion, and his voice, when he spoke, was calm and controlled.

"Are we to duel at last, then, Gravillac? Shall I have the pleasure of skewering you like the pig you are, and leaving you for the jackals?"

"A pistol ball will do just as well, I think. I would not wish any trifling scratches to disturb me when I take your wife to bed!"

"No!" cried Barrault angrily. "To shoot him would be murder! I must insist upon a duel!"

Gravillac jerked his head toward Molbert, who immediately turned his pistol upon Barrault and Tapié. He laughed maliciously. "I think you will find it easier to agree to my plans now, gentlemen. There are two balls in that pistol, and Molbert is a good shot. And when all is said and done, what does it matter? Whether I shoot Monsieur le Comte or run him through with my rapier—in half an hour, we shall be on our way to Spain, having accomplished that for which we came to Touraine." His left arm clasped Marielle more firmly, and he slowly raised the pistol in his other hand. "And I shall have this lovely creature as my reward and comfort."

"Are you a coward as well as a villain?" said André with contempt. "Or are you so enamoured of winning that you dare not risk failure?" He laughed shortly as Gravillac reddened in anger, and pressed his advantage. "But you have failed already, for you could not keep my wife save under lock and key! 'Tis a pity you can not hear the things she has told me of you—when we laugh together!" André's piercing glance caught and held Marielle's eye, as Gravillac shook with fury and the pistol wavered in his hand. With a sudden movement Marielle stamped her heel down heavily upon Gravillac's foot and smashed her right elbow into the hand that held the pistol; he grunted in pain and surprise, his hand flying upward. The weapon discharged, sending the shot thudding into a ceiling beam. At the same moment André vaulted over the bannister, his heavy boots crashing violently into Molbert's head and shoulders, knocking the pistol from his grasp and sending the man flying. Barrault leaped toward Gravillac and wrested the pistol out of his hand before he had the chance to fire the second shot; Tapié had already recovered Molbert's weapon and tucked it into his sash. Marielle fled to André's side; he smiled at her briefly, then pushed her gently behind him and, drawing his sword, saluted Gravillac.

"And now, my dear Marquis, shall we proceed?"

"André, no!" cried Marielle. "Not for vengeance! I would not have his blood on your hands—and you in exile—or worse! He is not worth it!" He scowled angrily at her and motioned her away; Gravillac, confronted by the persuasion of his own friends, armed and insistent, shrugged and drew his own sword from its scabbard.

It was Gravillac who attacked first, his rapier blade flashing. André parried neatly, taking his time, gauging the degree of his opponent's skill. He was content to let Gravillac take the initiative, blocking the murderous thrusts, countering each flash of the sword with a deft parry, holding his ground against each new stratagem. Damn! Gravillac was good in the attack. But could he defend?

With a sudden lunge, André thrust forward, arm and wrist and blade as one; Gravillac fell back for an instant, then recovered himself and countered the swift attack, smiling as his sword turned aside André's rapier thrust.

"If you are to keep your wife, Crillon, you shall have to do better than that!" His black eyes shone with malice. André increased the speed of his sword; the smile faded from Gravillac's face, but still he blocked that lightning blade. André pressed forward with nimble strokes, seeking the advantage; each time Gravillac was able to anticipate his moves and fend off the murderous steel. They were too well-matched. Marielle leaned against the staircase, her hand to her bosom, as the minutes ticked by. The room was deathly still save for the sounds of steel clashing against steel, and the rasping intake of breath as the struggle dragged on and on. André measured his adversary—there had to be another way. Gravillac fought fiercely, his eyes burning with intensity, his emotions precariously close to the surface; by contrast, he, André, was cool and calculating, even when death awaited a misstep. Perhaps he could use Gravillac's weakness against him. He launched a fresh attack, driving Gravillac back toward the open door, his advance sure, his blade dazzling in its thrusts. A sudden flash and a line of crimson appeared on Gravillac's cheek; another flash and Gravillac stumbled backwards into the courtyard, André in close pursuit. He saluted Gravillac with his sword, giving him a moment to recover his footing; the Marquis was purple with rage at such condescension. To André's surprise, however, the man's anger, rather than blunting his skills, seemed to focus his energies, his wrath fueling a renewed onslaught withstood only by all of André's adroitness.

Barrault and the others had followed them out into the sunny courtyard. André regretted that Marielle had not remained within; it would be far easier to do that which he had in mind without her worried eyes upon him. And he knew exactly what must be done. Gravillac was a man who needed to win; ferocious in defeat, he might be careless in victory. André lunged. Gravillac's return thrust, a finely executed parry and riposte, was low and aimed straight for the armpit; André saw it coming and sidestepped, warding off the blow with his rapier, his movements a fraction of a second slower than they might have been. Deflected from the vulnerable ribcage, the tip of Gravillac's blade pierced the soft flesh of André's upper arm; he gasped audibly, his face showing the pain. Marielle stifled a cry, her hand to her mouth. Damn! he thought. It was far more difficult to play the role with her watching and suffering. Gravillac had begun to smile again, and pressed the attack, glad to see André's implacable gaze replaced by a worried frown. Though he still seemed to fight with the same intensity and skill, André was now being slowly driven back, retreating with every fresh offensive, back and back, his sword repelling Gravillac's with greater and greater difficulty.

The Marquis laughed exultantly, tasting victory. "You should have let me shoot him, Madame!" he cried to Marielle. "It would have been less painful for you to watch!" With a shout, he lunged recklessly, one leg far outstretched. It was the opening for which André had been waiting: a quick jerk of his wrist, a flash of steel, and Gravillac's sword was caught on his point and sent flying. The momentum of Gravillac's thrust had carried him forward, his balance precarious from the lengthy stride; now he slipped to one knee— and found the point of André's rapier at his throat.

Gravillac's eyes, black and full of hatred, still showed

no fear as he waited for the final blow—there were worse ways to die than in an honorable duel, even if Crillon had tricked him into carelessness. For his part, André would have thrust the point of his blade into the man's throat, and exulted as the lifeblood poured out of him, but something made him stop and look toward Marielle. He knew suddenly that their happiness together depended on the staying of his hand, and he waited for her decision. She came quickly to his side, her eyes searching his, and then looked scornfully down at Gravillac, still kneeling in the dust. She felt nothing but disgust and contempt; her lip curled with loathing, she spat full upon his face. She turned then to André with an air of weary finality; he sheathed his sword and led her away, nestling her in his comforting embrace.

Gravillac went mad then, the rage exploding behind his eyes. His face glistening with sweat and spittle, he scrambled to his feet. Snatching up his sword from where it had fallen, he flew at André's retreating back, the rapier clutched tightly in both his hands and upraised like a huge dagger. The innkeeper shouted to André, who whirled, pushing Marielle swiftly behind him; Barrault and Tapié leapt at Gravillac, grasping his arms so violently that the sword clattered to the ground.

"*Nom de Dieu*, Renard!" cried Barrault. "It was a fair fight! Have you forgotten we are gentlemen? He spared your life! He had that right! Would you repay him with treachery? Come, come," he cajoled, as Gravillac took a great gasping breath and fought to regain his self-control. "She is his wife, and only a woman, after all. Think of the beauties in Spain! Come away!" He motioned for Tapié and Molbert and the rest to mount their horses, then indicated the black stallion, nervously pawing the ground. "See? Your horse awaits. Spain awaits. We have no further business here. Come away!"

Gravillac hesitated, struggling to recover his pride; he wiped his face and even managed to swagger a little as he made for his horse. A shrill cry stopped him, a voice that froze him in his tracks.

"Perrot!"

Perrot. It was the name he had used many times in the past to keep his father from learning of his escapades. Perrot. He turned slowly.

"Mon Dieu! Perrot, is it you?" Clothilde stood in the stable doorway, her eyes wild, her voice sharp with hysteria. He could not even remember her name—just some woman he had known. He looked at her with contempt: the flying hair, hay-covered, her face red and blotchy, the veins distended in her neck. She was disgusting. For a second, regret clutching at his vitals, he allowed himself a glance at Marielle, serene and beautiful in the warm shelter of André's love, then turned back to Clothilde with a sneering laugh.

"What? *Petite mouche?* Little fly, would you buzz around my ears? Did I not show you the world, merchant's daughter? Was I not generous enough?" He felt suddenly weary, deflated, defeated. With a tired sigh, he turned away. "Molbert, give the wench a few *sous* and let us be on our way." He sheathed his sword and reached for the stallion's reins.

With a demonic shriek, Clothilde leapt toward his turned back, seeming almost to fly through the air;

hands upraised, she plunged the pointed shears between his shoulder blades. He turned slightly, his face mirroring his shock and astonishment, like a disappointed, wondering child. He staggered. "But . . . *mouche—*" he gurgled, his voice low and choked. Stumbling, he clutched at his horse, reaching desperately for the reins; instead, his clawing fingers found and held the poor animal's ear. The black stallion snorted in terror as Gravillac's other hand pulled savagely at the bit, tearing the animal's mouth. With a half-turn toward Marielle, standing in shock and awe, Renard de Gravillac smiled, coughed and fell lifeless against his horse, his fist still clasping the bit, his body tangled in the reins.

Clothilde, distraught and remorseful, began to scream wildly then, her voice high and shrill. "Ah no! *Mon amour!* Ah, *Dieu!*" and ran frantically toward Gravillac. The highstrung horse, already terrified, was now beside himself; her sudden movement and screams unnerved him completely. As she rushed over, the stallion reared up—Gravillac still caught in the harness—and struck out fiercely with his forelegs. The lethal hooves flashed once, twice, and Clothilde lay dead upon the ground, blood pouring from a gaping wound in her skull.

"André, keep still! *Nom de Dieu!* What shall I do with you?" Marielle perched on her knees on the big bed at Vilmorin, André seated by her side. Frowning in concentration, she fumbled with fresh bandages while a shirtless André fidgeted and twisted, more concerned with planting kisses on Marielle's soft neck than in having his wound tended.

"It is healing well, my love. I see not why you must continue to tend it. 'Twas a trifling wound to begin with!" André laughed wickedly, surveying his bare chest and arms. "But then the healing arts give a maid a nice excuse to strip a man mother-naked! Was your father teaching you to be a doctor—or to snare a husband?"

"Wicked knave!" she cried, and gently cuffed the side of his head. Her green eyes narrowed, a tantalizing smile upon her red lips. "Besides, you above all should know a woman has other wiles to catch a man—I scarce needed Gravillac's swordpoint to lure you to my bed in midday!" She laughed gaily, her voice a silver bell, and planted a kiss firmly on André's shoulder. "No. I think rather that you enjoy being nursed—you shall never convince me that you did not allow him to strike you!"

André looked thoughtful as Marielle finished binding his arm and sat back on her heels. "Perhaps," he said pensively. "They say the sight of blood will enrage a bull—it seemed a fitting trap for a viper." They were both silent for a moment.

"Poor Clothilde," said Marielle suddenly.

André looked at her in surprise. "You can pity her? She meant you naught but harm, from the moment I brought you to Vilmorin—though I was too much the fool to see it."

"Poor André!" laughed Marielle. "To have been deceived so easily!"

He shook his head ruefully. "It disquiets a man to the very core. If marriage had not cured my wandering, Clothilde surely would have. Such deceit! And still you pity her?"

"She brought me heartache, but she had her own secret griefs. God grant her tormented soul peace at last. I am glad you gave the gold to the innkeeper."

He frowned. "I could not have taken it back . . . tainted coins. . . ." He fell silent, filled with remorse. "She took advantage of my grief, true enough . . . but I was a willing party to her schemes." He sighed deeply.

Marielle smiled gently in sympathy. "Think you that the King can trust Tapié and Barrault, now that you have persuaded them to return to their estates?"

"I shall speak in their behalf, certainly. If France goes to war, Louis will need every sword and loyal noble in the kingdom. It was Gravillac's poison that was sending them in desperation to Spain. Without him, they will, I trust, make their peace with the King. But enough! I would hardly have left Grisaille and the wine to sit here and talk to you of politics and war!" His eyes glowed clear and blue and warm; one strong hand went about her waist, the other deftly pulled the pins from her coiled hair, releasing the luxuriant masses. The blue eyes clouded suddenly, as though remembering a nagging thought. "Tell me," he asked suddenly, "why did you risk your life at the inn? When you knocked the pistol from Gravillac's hand?"

"But . . . I thought you wanted . . . you gave me such an odd look. . . ."

"I meant for you only to get out of the way!"

Marielle looked surprised, then dimpled prettily. "Can I not sometimes rescue *you* from evil men?"

He drew her toward him, his fingers caressing her downy cheek and tracing the line of her chin. She trembled at his touch. "I need only your love, *ma chère,*" he said softly, "for you have reached a place in my heart I thought barren and empty." He tipped up her chin and kissed her gently, while his hands moved insistently upon her shoulders and back and heaving breasts, and she shivered in anticipation.

With an effort, she pulled her lips from his. "And will you take me to Paris again?" she asked, half playful and half in earnest. "Or will your doubts yet torment you?"

He pondered a moment, and then laughed softly. "But there will be no more ballets, I think. By my faith, Madame, I was minded to beat you well for that disgraceful costume you wore!"

She smiled nervously. "Then it is well for me that you did not see the gown I refused to wear."

"No matter. You were fetching in it, and I hated every man who looked at you!"

"Oh my love!" she cried, and threw her arms about his neck. "Were there a thousand men in the room, I would see only your eyes upon me!"

He pressed her down upon the soft bed, his hot lips finding her mouth and neck and tremulous bosom; her arms, twined about his strong shoulders, caressed the glistening flesh that rippled under her hands. The sunny room, the sounds from without, faded away in the passion that roared in their ears, ignited by the spark that seemed to pass between their two bodies, pressed one upon the other. There was a soft knock at the door, and Louise called softly for Madame. André raised his head impatiently.

"Go away!" he said fiercely. "Madame is occupied!"

Marielle giggled. "And besieged and under attack," she whispered. She might have said more, but his hungry lips closed possessively over hers in a fierce and conquering kiss.

Although, in truth, it would have been hard to say who was the victor—and who the vanquished.

ENA HALLIDAY lives in New York City with her husband and four children. *Marielle* is her first novel.

Enjoy your own special time with Silhouette Romances

Take 4 books FREE!

Silhouette Romances take you into a special world of thrilling drama, tender passion, and romantic love. These are enthralling stories from your favorite romance authors—tales of fascinating men and women, set in exotic locations.

We think you'll want to receive Silhouette Romances regularly. We'll send you six new romances every month to look over for 15 days. If not delighted, return only five and owe nothing. **One book is always yours free.** There's never a charge for postage or handling, and no obligation to buy anything at any time. **Start with your free books. Mail the coupon today.**